Kingsman
THE GOLDEN CIRCLE

THE
Official Movie
NOVELIZATION

Kingsman

THE GOLDEN CIRCLE

THE
Official Movie
NOVELIZATION

By Tim Waggoner
Based on the screenplay written by
Jane Goldman & Matthew Vaughn
Based on the comic book *The Secret Service* by
Mark Millar and Dave Gibbons
Directed by
Matthew Vaughn

TITAN BOOKS

Kingsman: The Golden Circle – The Official Movie Novelization
Print edition ISBN: 9781785657320
E-book edition ISBN: 9781785657337

Published by Titan Books
A division of Titan Publishing Group Ltd
144 Southwark St, London SE1 0UP

First edition: September 2017
1 3 5 7 9 10 8 6 4 2

A CIP catalogue record for this title is available from the British Library.

Printed and bound in the United States.

Did you enjoy this book?
We love to hear from our readers. Please email us at
readerfeedback@titanmail.com or write to us at
Reader Feedback at the above address.

To receive advance information, news, competitions, and exclusive
offers online, please sign up for the Titan newsletter on our website
www.titanbooks.com

This one's for Sean Connery, Patrick Macnee, Diana Rigg, Dean Martin, James Coburn, Don Adams, Barbara Feldon, Robert Vaughn, David McCallum, Patrick McGoohan, and Roger Moore—the spies of my youth.

Chapter One

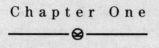

Savile Row, London. Night

Eggsy Unwin, looking dapper in a navy double-breasted pinstripe suit, woven-silk tie, and black leather Oxford shoes, exited the Kingsman tailor shop. The establishment was exactly what it appeared to be from the outside: a sophisticated clothing boutique where well-to-do customers were able to obtain the finest bespoke suits money could buy. But that's not *all* it was, of course. Nor was Eggsy a mere tailor.

A black sedan was parked in front of the shop, the driver waiting patiently for him. Eggsy had already turned off all the lights inside the building and activated one of the deadliest security systems on the planet. Now all he had to do was lock up, and he'd be off—and glad of it, too. Working as an operative for an elite intelligence organization could be a real kick, but sometimes it was as interesting as watching paint that had only just started to *think* about getting round to drying.

Today had been one of those days. He'd just gotten back from a mission in Australia, where he'd been investigating a group that called itself rEvolution. They presented themselves to the world as a Scientology-like religion, but in truth they were an organization of renegade scientists who conducted all manner of bizarre—not to mention highly illegal—experiments on unwitting church members. Eggsy had managed to infiltrate one of their facilities located in Perth and "take it off the board," which was Kingsman-speak for "blow it the fuck up"—*after* rescuing the scientists' human guinea pigs, of course. All quite satisfying. But as with any mission, it was the subsequent debriefing session, along with the attendant reports he had to write, which came near to driving him as mad as one of rEvolution's scientists. He'd spent most of the day tending to these tedious duties, dragging his heels so badly that it had taken him forever to finish. In fact, he was the last one out of the shop tonight. But after this, he was due for a few days off, and he was looking forward to going home and getting out of this suit and into something more comfortable.

Grinning, he put a key into the front door's lock, turned it, and was rewarded with a soft *click*, along with a nearly inaudible hum that told him the security system was online and functioning properly. The shop served as Kingsman's London headquarters, but it was also an access point for the underground shuttle system that led to the organization's country house training facility, and it wouldn't do to have someone break in and stumble across secrets that had *remained* secret since World War One. Kingsman was an independent international intelligence organization, with ties to no government. The world was utterly unaware Kingsman existed, and that's just the way its agents liked it. And they hadn't kept their secrets all these years by not being thorough.

Eggsy reached up and touched the side of his square-framed eyeglasses. Like all Kingsman equipment, these glasses had several hi-tech modifications, chief among them being augmented-reality displays on the inside lenses. A simple touch activated the glasses, and Eggsy directed his gaze first at the door and then at the shop's front window. His lenses revealed red lines of crisscrossing energy covering both, and once he'd confirmed the security system was doing its job, he touched the glasses again to deactivate the sensor readout. Now that all was right with the world, Eggsy turned, descended the steps to the sidewalk, and headed for the Kingsman taxi that awaited him.

On my way, babe, he thought.

He was about to pull open one of the taxi's rear doors and slide inside when he heard someone behind him say, "Eggy."

The word took him by surprise for two reasons. One, it was spoken in the cold tones of an electronic speech-generating device, and two, there was only one person on Earth who had ever called him *Eggy*, and that sonofabitch was dead.

Eggsy spun around, but before he could do anything, he felt the hard metal of a gun muzzle press against his chest. A pistol, he guessed, 9mm most likely. But having a weapon jammed against his body didn't bother him all that much. Occupational hazard, really. No, what disturbed him was *who* was doing the jamming. He found himself looking at a man with a buzz cut, wearing a dark hoodie, jeans, and sneakers, someone who by all rights should've been a long-moldering corpse by now, and a headless one at that.

"Mind if I share your cab?" Charlie Hesketh said in his synthesized voice.

Even after everything Eggsy had experienced since joining Kingsman—and he'd come across some astoundingly weird shit in his brief tenure as a spy—he couldn't believe what he was seeing. Charlie had been recruited to try out for Kingsman the same time as Eggsy, but when Charlie had failed to make the grade, primarily due to his being a self-centered coward and a complete bastard, he'd thrown in his lot with Richmond Valentine as one of the chosen few the megalomaniacal billionaire had selected to survive his self-engineered apocalypse. When Eggsy, Merlin, and Roxy preempted Valentine's doomsday, those "chosen ones" had quite literally lost their heads when the small electronic devices Valentine had implanted in their necks—designed to protect them from the tech he used to initiate the end of the world—had been used against them, resulting in a series of impressive, not to mention extremely messy, explosions.

But here was Charlie, head and all. Although it seemed he hadn't gotten away entirely unscathed, if his voice was any indication.

Charlie looked him up and down.

"Ironic, isn't it? You look like a gentleman, and I look like a pleb. My parents and mentor would be turning in their graves—which you put them in."

Charlie's lips formed a cruel, smug smile. He wasn't a bad-looking guy, Eggsy supposed, but when he smiled like that, he looked like a mean little kid who couldn't wait to catch and torture the first small, defenseless animal unlucky enough to cross his path.

Seeing Charlie risen from the dead had knocked Eggsy off balance, but his training kicked in, and he quickly recovered.

"What's with the voice? You gonna shoot me or tell me your new theory on black holes?"

"Very funny. Just open the door… Unless you want a black hole in your gut."

Charlie nodded toward a trio of gold-colored SUVs approaching fast from the far end of the street. His message was clear: *I'm not working alone, escape isn't possible, and you have no choice but to do as I command.*

Who was Eggsy to argue with logic like that?

He gripped the door handle, the built-in biometric reader scanned his prints, and the door opened. But instead of trying to get away from Charlie, Eggsy grabbed hold of the fucker and shoved him into the taxi. Charlie was so surprised that he didn't resist, and Eggsy climbed in after him and yanked the door closed. Before Charlie could recover his wits, Eggsy grabbed hold of his former rival's gun hand by the wrist and pressed it down against the brown leather seat. He saw Charlie was indeed holding a 9mm—a Glock to be specific—and he didn't intend to give him a chance to use it.

The front and rear seats of the taxi were separated by a glass partition, and through it Eggsy caught the driver's gaze in the rearview mirror. The man looked worried, but he was a Kingsman driver, trained to remain calm in the most stressful situations, and he wouldn't react until given an order by a superior. So Eggsy gave one.

"Drive! Lose them!"

Without hesitation, the man hit the ignition and the sedan's engine roared to life. He stomped on the gas pedal and the vehicle shot away from the curb, tires squealing in protest. Eggsy glanced out the back window and saw the three SUVs had caught up to them and were following close behind.

Charlie wasn't about to simply lie there, though. With his free hand, he punched Eggsy in the ribs, driving the breath out of his lungs. Eggsy returned the favor by head-butting Charlie, who followed up by kneeing Eggsy in the stomach. Eggsy used *his* free hand to give Charlie three quick blows to the jaw. But all this was really just a warm-up, and soon the two men began fighting in earnest, hurling rapid punches and throwing each other around the taxi's back seat. As they fought, one of them struck the stereo controls, and Prince's "Let's Go Crazy" blasted from the sound system, providing a soundtrack to accompany their battle. At one point, Charlie's Glock fired and the shot ricocheted around the taxi's interior for a few heart-stopping seconds before striking the glass partition and shattering it. The driver flinched, but he didn't slow down. If anything, he increased their speed.

Pete, Eggsy suddenly thought. The man's name was Pete... something. Gallagher! That was it! And he'd been driving for Kingsman for seventeen, no, *eighteen* years. The better part of Eggsy's life. He was an experienced driver, one of the agency's best, and Eggsy knew he could count on him.

Eggsy kicked Charlie in the chest, knocking him back against the passenger door. The impact caused the door to open, and Charlie fell out, but he caught hold of the door frame with one hand before he could tumble to the pavement. His free hand hit the road and created a shower of sparks as it was dragged along.

What the fuck? Eggsy thought.

In the confusion, he hadn't gotten a good look at Charlie's hand up to this point, but he did now, and he saw that the man's flesh-and-blood arm had been replaced by a robotic one.

Eggsy pressed a control on top of the back seat, and a panel opened to reveal a Kingsman pistol. He grabbed hold of it and spun toward Charlie, intending to empty the clip into the bastard. But before Eggsy could fire, Charlie pulled himself back into the cab, grabbed hold of Eggsy's gun hand with his robotic appendage and twisted. Charlie's fingers were cold and hard, and they squeezed Eggsy's hand like a vice. He grimaced in pain and fought to get a shot off, but Charlie had angled the gun away from him, and Eggsy knew that even if he managed to pull the trigger, the round would miss.

Charlie increased the pressure until Eggsy was forced

to let go of the gun, and it fell to the floor of the cab. The cab door was still open, and Charlie pressed his metal hand against Eggsy's face and pushed him. Eggsy grabbed hold of the door frame to prevent Charlie from shoving him out of the cab, but Charlie continued pressing Eggsy downward until his face was mere inches from the pavement rushing by. Eggsy saw a car approaching fast in the other lane, and he knew he had to do something fast if he wanted to avoid being decapitated. He drew back his leg and kicked Charlie hard in the chest. The blow knocked Charlie backward, and once his hand was removed from Eggsy's face, Eggsy swiftly pulled himself up, caught hold of the door frame, and hauled himself onto the roof just as the approaching vehicle roared past. He flattened himself against the roof, arms spread wide, fingers gripping the roof's edges in a desperate attempt to hold on. There was a loud *whump* and Eggsy felt the roof shudder beneath him. A fist-sized section of metal bulged upward only a few inches from his head, and Eggsy realized Charlie was striking the inside of the roof with his robotic hand. Eggsy rolled to one side and then the other as Charlie repeatedly punched the roof, trying to hit Eggsy and dislodge him. He knew it would only be a matter of time until Charlie succeeded, so he slid toward the edge of the roof, and swung in upside down, holding onto the open door to steady himself. He grabbed a decanter of scotch from the back seat's mini-bar and smashed it against the side of Charlie's head. But before he could swing all the way inside and attack Charlie anew, the door gave way and Eggsy fell to the street.

He managed to land on top of the door, and he stood up in a half-crouch, gripping the door frame with his right hand and riding the metal panel like it was a makeshift surfboard, sparks trailing behind.

He was done mucking about. He abandoned the detached door and pulled himself back into the cab. Charlie immediately came at him, but before the fucker could lay a hand on him, Eggsy jammed his signet ring against the side of Charlie's neck and released an electric charge into the man's body.

Charlie grinned, unaffected.

"That shit won't work this time," he said. "I had a circuit breaker fitted."

Eggsy threw a wild haymaker at Charlie, putting all the strength he had behind the punch with the intent to put the asshole down for the count. Once the sonofabitch was unconscious, Eggsy could concentrate on escaping the pursuing SUVs, and then he could get to work figuring out just how the hell Charlie had managed to keep his head when the rest of Valentine's friends had lost theirs.

But Charlie managed to move before the punch could land, and he took the blow on his shoulder. The impact didn't come close to knocking him out, but it jolted him enough so that Eggsy could snatch the Kingsman pistol from the floor. He pointed it at Charlie and fired, emptying the clip. But Charlie's robotic hand moved lightning-quick and blocked the rounds.

As fast as Charlie had moved his robot arm, Eggsy

knew that he had been toying with him up to this point. The fucker wanted revenge, sure, but he intended to take his time and enjoy it.

"Another upgrade I owe to you," Charlie said. "Dunno if I should thank you or kill you." He paused. "Actually, I do."

Eggsy dropped the useless pistol.

"Pity they didn't upgrade your tiny balls," he said.

He grabbed hold of Charlie's crotch and squeezed as hard as he could. He might not have a tricked-out robot arm, but he didn't need the aid of biomechanical technology to accomplish this job. Charlie screamed and pushed his robotic hand forward. The impact sent Eggsy tumbling out of the speeding cab. As he fell he reached out and managed to grab hold of the door frame, and he held on for dear life. His feet slid across asphalt, and while the special material of the Kingsman shoes provided some protection from the friction, the heat still hurt like hell.

Seeing Eggsy helpless, Charlie lunged forward, but Eggsy wasn't about to give up that easily. He released his grip on the door frame and, keeping his hand pressed against the side of the cab to steady himself, slipped backward until he was holding onto the vehicle's back bumper and foot-surfing asphalt. The SUVs were still close behind, and one of the drivers gunned his engine and surged forward, clearly intending to smash Eggsy between the two vehicles.

He quickly raised his watch to his mouth, pressed one of the controls against his teeth, and sent an electronic signal that opened the boot, climbing in a split second before the SUVs smashed into the rear of the cab. Shaken but unharmed, he clicked his heels together and a poison-coated blade jutted from his right shoe. He used the blade to slice an opening in the back seat, and as he climbed through, he saw that Charlie had leaned his head out the open doorway, no doubt looking to see what had happened to Eggsy.

Once he was all the way inside, Eggsy lashed out with his foot, intending to slash Charlie and allow the fast-acting poison to take the fucker out once and for all. But Charlie managed to bring up his robotic arm in time to block the strike. The blade broke and flew toward the back of Pete's head. It buried itself at the base of his skull, and the poison did its work. The man died instantly, but his hands continued gripping the sedan's steering wheel, and when his body started to slump to the side, the wheel was yanked to the right, sending the sedan off course and careening toward a post box on the street corner.

Charlie saw what was coming, and he let go of Eggsy and grabbed hold of the window pillar with his robotic hand to brace himself, his mechanical fingers digging into the metal. Lacking such technological enhancement, Eggsy opted for a simpler tactic: he ducked behind the driver's seat, and hoped for the best.

The cab slammed into the post box with the sound of shrieking metal, and Eggsy, Charlie, and the newly deceased Pete were all thrown forward. The back of the driver's seat cushioned Eggsy from the impact, but

Charlie and Pete had no such protection—not that it would've made any difference to the latter at this point. Pete's body flew forward and smashed through the windscreen in a shower of glass. Charlie followed, sailing through the now open space where the partition had been and taking out the remainder of the windscreen as he passed through. Unfortunately, his robotic hand's grip on the window pillar had been too strong, and the arm remained behind while its owner made a hasty and not particularly dignified exit from the vehicle.

Hope the fucker lands on his head, Eggsy thought. He sat up, hoping to see that Charlie had joined Pete on his journey to the great beyond, but then he heard the sound of engines approaching, and instead he saw the three SUVs pull up, surrounding the taxi.

Shit.

He climbed into the front seat, grabbed hold of the steering wheel and hit the ignition. The vehicle had stalled out when it struck the post box, and he was relieved when the engine returned to life. He then flicked a switch on the dashboard. He hoped the sedan's systems were still online, because if they weren't, he was well and truly fucked. Nothing happened for several long seconds, but then he felt the vehicle shift subtly beneath him, and he knew the battered cab still had some life in it. He shouldn't have been surprised. Everything Kingsman made, from cufflinks to customized weapons, was always top of the line. He threw the sedan into reverse and pulled away from the post box, and when he had enough clearance, he put the vehicle into drive and floored the accelerator. The switch he'd thrown had caused the cab's hubcaps to blow off and the tires to widen, transforming them into racing slicks. He spun the vehicle on a dime, and executing a spectacular—if he did think so himself—drifting maneuver, he looped around the SUVs and sped away.

A quick glance in the rearview showed him Charlie, one-armed and disheveled but far from dead, rising to his feet. He touched the side of his neck, and his electronic voice boomed out at deafening volume.

"STOP FUCKING AROUND AND GET HIM!"

Air blew in through the opening where the windscreen had been, buffeting Eggsy. Good thing he had his eyeglasses on, otherwise he'd have had a hell of a time seeing. He checked the rearview and saw the SUVs were in pursuit and close on his tail. And as if that wasn't bad enough, hatches on the roofs opened and Gatling guns began to emerge. The weapons rose up, locked into place, and an instant later three men stood up to operate them. The men were dressed in black and wore military-style VR goggles and head mics. No amateurs these.

Fuck me.

Eggsy touched his eyeglasses, activating the device's comms system.

"Merlin, we have a code purple. My driver's down."

He wasn't worried overmuch about the guns. Kingsman taxis were built to withstand gunfire, and even Gatling guns... His thoughts were interrupted by a message that came up on the cab's dashboard monitor.

19

ARMOR-PIERCING ROUNDS DETECTED.

Well, isn't that just lovely?

"Permission to use anti-weapons?"

A transparent image of Merlin, Kingsman's tech wizard and chief of ops, appeared on the inside of Eggsy's glasses, the middle-aged Scotsman's narrow face displaying a stern expression. He was bald, wore a pair of regular eyeglasses, and was dressed in his usual wool military sweater over a white shirt and black tie.

"Denied!" Merlin said. "Cannot be contained. Head south. I'm clearing the route."

Right. The whole innocent bystanders thing.

Eggsy weaved through traffic and around parked cars. He was coming up fast on an intersection, and the light was red. He'd have to run it and hope—

The light turned green, as did the light at the next intersection, and the one after that. Eggsy grinned. Merlin was working his magic.

Eggsy roared through each intersection, weaving back and forth to make it more difficult for the SUVs' weapons systems to get a lock on the cab. The Gatling guns roared as the gunmen started firing. Bright bursts of light issued from their muzzles, sending a hailstorm of bullets streaming toward the sedan. Most of the rounds zipped past harmlessly, but a number struck the cab, tearing through the vehicle's reinforced metal as if it were papier-mâché. Eggsy executed a drifting turn around Hyde Park Corner, hoping to evade the rounds, but despite his efforts, a bullet struck one of the sedan's rear tires. The tire blew, and Eggsy found himself fighting to retain control of the cab.

"Shit!"

A glance at the sideview mirror showed sparks shooting off the tire rim as it ground asphalt. No way in hell was he going to outrun the SUVs now, not with only three good tires. It was a matter of moments until the armor-piercing rounds shredded the cab—and him—into confetti, and without the ability to fight back, there was nothing he could do about it. But then he saw Hyde Park ahead of him, the gates shut, and beyond them darkness.

That'll do.

"Merlin! Going into a dark zone!"

Eggsy smashed through the gates and entered the unlit park, the SUVs still close on his tail and firing at him.

"Dark mode confirmed," Merlin said. "Permission to fire."

"Thank fuck for that." Eggsy flipped a switch on the dashboard, and a compartment slid open on the back of the taxi. A single missile *whooooshed* straight upward, the fire from its propulsion system illuminating the night. When the missile reached the zenith of its flight, it paused, almost as if it were temporarily frozen in space, before separating into three smaller missiles. Propulsion systems activated, targeting systems engaged; and each of the three mini-missiles screamed toward an SUV with uncanny precision. Neither the drivers nor the men manning the Gatling guns had time to react, and each of the vehicles disappeared in flame and thunder.

Eggsy grinned. *Easy-peasy.* But before he could congratulate himself on escaping certain death (which was, after all, a Kingsman specialty), Merlin appeared in front of his eyes once more.

"No time to relax; the police are behind you. You have thirty seconds before they reach your position. Go directly to rendezvous Swan."

Of course the bloody police were coming. A car chase, gunfire, explosions… He wasn't exactly keeping a low profile tonight. And it wasn't as if he could simply explain what had happened. Strictly speaking, none of what Kingsman did was legal. That was part and parcel of the *independent* part of *independent intelligence agency.* So he needed to get out of here before London's finest caught up with him. But, rendezvous Swan?

"You *do* realize I haven't got a windscreen right now?" he said.

Merlin gave Eggsy a wry smile. "I seem to recall from your training that you were rather good at holding your breath."

Eggsy had continued driving during their conversation, and now he approached The Serpentine. The curving body of water separated Hyde Park from Kensington Gardens, and it was a popular destination for Londoners and tourists alike. Of course, that's not *all* it was, and since it seemed like he didn't have much choice, Eggsy took several deep breaths and drove straight into the lake's black water. Within seconds, the cab was fully submerged, and when a few moments later the police arrived, all they saw was the calm, undisturbed surface of the lake.

Eggsy steered the sedan through cold, dark water, the vehicle's headlights doing their best to cut through the inky blackness. The windscreen might be history, but the cab's underwater mode functioned just fine, and the vehicle glided easily across the lakebed. The ride would've been pleasant enough if he'd been dry and could take a sip of oxygen now and again. As it was, his lungs were soon burning with the need for air, and when he saw the trapdoor open on the lakebed in a cloud of mud and silt, it came as a huge relief. He guided the cab through the opening and into a room that was scarcely larger than the vehicle itself. Overhead lights came on as the sedan settled onto the floor. The trapdoor shut, the airlock sealed, and water began to flow into the floor drains. But Eggsy couldn't wait any longer. He swam through the open windscreen and up to the top of the room. Enough water had drained to create a pocket of air, and as soon as he broke the surface he began taking great gulps of the life-giving stuff. He trod water while the room continued to drain, and by the time he was standing on the floor next to the cab—absolutely drenched—his breathing had returned to normal.

Cut it a little close there, bruv, he thought.

Merlin appeared once more on Eggsy's eyeglass lenses. He was seated in his office at Kingsman headquarters, and although his face showed little expression—the man preferred to maintain a strict veneer of professionalism when he was working—Eggsy could tell by the slight softening around his eyes that he was glad his young friend was all right.

"That wasn't a revenge mission," Merlin said. "Charlie could have just killed you immediately. No boasting, but I trained him well enough that even *he* wouldn't make such a mess of it."

Especially not with the help of that arm, Eggsy thought. "What did he want? And more to the point, how the fuck is he alive?"

"Good questions. We'll have time to ponder them while we wait for the police to clear the park."

Eggsy felt a flare of panic at the thought of any further delay. "No can do, mate. I've got a dinner tonight. If I miss it… let's just say Charlie might as well have killed me."

Merlin hesitated before speaking again. "Well… there *is* one other way out. Three o'clock."

Eggsy turned in the direction Merlin indicated and saw a hatch set into the floor. A wave of relief washed over him, one even more powerful than he'd felt when he'd gotten his head above water again.

"You're the guv'nor, Merlin."

Merlin didn't respond verbally, but his knowing smirk made Eggsy suspicious.

He frowned. "What's so funny?"

When Merlin didn't answer, Eggsy walked over to the hatch and opened it. He immediately recoiled at the stench that wafted forth, and he felt his gorge rise. Fighting to keep from vomiting, he leaned over and peered into the hatch. He saw a ladder that led down into London's Victorian sewerage system, and beyond that he saw—and more to the point, smelled—a winding river of human shit.

"How important *is* that dinner?" Merlin said, sounding amused.

"Let me show you."

Ignoring the ladder, Eggsy dropped down the hole and disappeared into the brown morass with a sludgy splash.

After Eggsy's hasty—and more than a little disgusting— departure, the chamber was quiet for a time. The cab's systems had powered down automatically once the vehicle was settled and secure, and now it sat, battered and waterlogged, but still essentially intact. A few days in Kingsman's motor pool, a week, tops, and the agency's mechanical engineers would have it ready for action again. But the cab wasn't the only thing Eggsy had left behind in the chamber. Charlie's robotic arm still clung to the window pillar, hanging lifelessly, fingers embedded in the vehicle's metal with a death grip. Until, with a sudden motion, the fingers disengaged from the metal, and the arm dropped to the cab's floor. It began crawling up the back seat, fingers moving with inhuman precision, as if the hand were some sort of mechanical insect. The arm crawled through the broken partition and flopped into the front seat. The elbow flexed, and the hand was lifted toward the dashboard control system. Despite the interior of the vehicle having been flooded with lake water, the system remained operational, and it took only a quick manipulation of the controls to activate it and bring it online. Once this was accomplished, a small compartment opened on the tip of the index finger and a USB drive emerged. The hand inserted the drive into a port on the dashboard, and within seconds, the arm's internal computer had not only accessed the cab's system, it had linked to Kingsman's mainframe through that system.

If Eggsy had been present, he would've noticed a logo on the back of the robot hand: a circle wrought in gold metal. But he wasn't there, and so the arm went about its work unimpeded.

Somewhere deep in the jungles of Cambodia

———————— ✆ ————————

A beautiful redheaded woman in her fifties wearing pearls and a puppy-patterned apron over a vermilion dress stood at the counter of what appeared to be a 1950s-style American diner. The tiled floor was laid out in a black-and-white checkerboard pattern, the tables were chrome with a slight art deco feel to them, and the chairs were upholstered in sparkle-flecked ruby red. There was a long counter with stools in front of it, along with booths against the walls. Old-fashioned salt and pepper shakers and metal napkin dispensers sat atop the tables, and the entire place was brightly lit by fluorescent lights on the ceiling. The overall effect was kitschy while at the same time warmly nostalgic. At least, that's what Poppy liked to think. She had to admit that without a crowd of customers—families with young children, teenagers on first dates, older couples who came here to remember what it was like to be young—the diner had an empty, almost depressing feeling. She supposed the sight of jungle foliage through the diner's windows fought against the atmosphere she was trying to create. Maybe she could see about having some kind of holographic projection system installed in the windows to create the illusion of a 1950s small-town street outside. That might help. Then again, it might look too… what was the word she was searching for? Too *staged*. Ah, well. Money couldn't buy everything. And that, really, was the entire point of her current project, wasn't it?

The diner might be mostly empty, but Poppy wasn't alone. Two men sat in front of her, one wearing a beige jacket and peach shirt, the other a light blue jacket and dark blue shirt. Both of them looked dangerous, as if they'd be just as happy slicing their grandmother's throat as they would kissing her cheek. But Poppy wasn't intimidated. After all, she could be rather dangerous herself when she wished. Charles and Angel might be of the same rough type—cold-eyed and cold-blooded—but Charles was clean-shaven while Angel sported a neatly trimmed black beard.

Angel was a new recruit, and he kept glancing around the diner, as if he couldn't quite believe what he was seeing. Poppy couldn't blame him, really. She supposed it was something of a shock to walk in here after trudging through the jungle. But if the man was having trouble dealing with *this*, she wondered what he thought about the rest of her compound. It wasn't exactly a stereotypical jungle camp.

Laid out on the counter in front of Poppy were immaculately prepped ingredients: lettuce, tomatoes, onions, and pickle slices. Behind her was a huge industrial-sized meat mincer, which looked quite out of place in the diner, and—truth be told—that *did* bother her. But sometimes aesthetics had to give way to practicality. This really was the best place in the compound for the mincer. The tiled floor made it much easier to clean up after the device had been used.

"I never enjoyed drugs myself, but here I am, running the biggest drug cartel in the world," Poppy said. "The only downside is living in the middle of nowhere. These ruins are actually undiscovered, and I made a few changes to make them more homey. I grew up in the fifties, and I loved TV shows like *Andy Griffith* and *Happy Days*. It reminds me of home. Nostalgia, y'know?"

As she addressed the two men, she did her best to sound both friendly and professional. In her experience, employees responded best to a boss who was firm and direct, but who also demonstrated she had a human side. To help create this effect, she strived for a Martha Stewart meets Margaret Thatcher vibe in both her manner and dress. An odd combination, perhaps, but one she thought suited her nicely.

Poppy went on. "But I digress. As I said, I have a global monopoly on the drug trade. And for that, I owe a debt to Richmond Valentine. Do you know how many drug barons around the world died on V-Day? People may have only gone nuts for a few minutes, but if you were in a room full of bodyguards with guns… Good night, sweetheart."

Poppy had not been invited to attend Valentine's apocalyptic shindig, a fact that privately galled her. Evidently drug lords hadn't rated high on the insane entrepreneur's personal social registry, no matter how wealthy they were. And Poppy was among the wealthiest on the planet, if not *the* wealthiest. But considering what had happened to those he *had* invited, she wasn't too upset over being left out. She'd much rather be snubbed than have her head explode. And as for the sim cards Valentine had given away for free—cards that, once inserted into a cellphone or other device, broadcast a signal that turned everyone in the vicinity into a homicidal maniac—neither Poppy nor any of her guards had gotten one, so they'd been in the clear when the madness of V-Day struck. It seemed there were some advantages, however few they might be, to having one's compound located deep in a secluded Cambodian jungle.

"I used to run the Golden *Triangle*," she continued. "But so many of my rivals died that day—turning the Triangle into a *Hexagon* was easy!" A pause. "The important thing to understand is the hard work and ingenuity that went into turning that Hexagon into a *Circle*... Taking over the *whole* industry, worldwide. Not to toot my own horn! I just think it's *so* important for new recruits to fully understand the history of the Golden Circle."

Both Charles and Angel nodded enthusiastically. Poppy looked from Charles, to Angel, and then back to Charles.

"So the two of you are lifelong friends, huh?"

They nodded.

"And you... It's Charles, right? You think your buddy here is worthy of joining us?"

Beads of nervous sweat clung to Charles's brow, but his voice was steady as he answered in an English accent. "I would not have brought him all this way to see you, if I did not, Ms Poppy."

"Hmm. Okay, gentlemen. I have questions. Do you understand that in the Golden Circle, my authority is never to be questioned?"

They nodded again.

"And do you understand the importance of following orders?"

Again, they nodded.

"And... the value of loyalty? Is that something you understand too?"

One last pair of nods.

She looked at the men for a long moment, then said, "Easy to nod, isn't it?"

Charles and Angel exchanged uncertain looks. Then, evidently unable to decide on a different reply, they simply nodded one more time. Poppy considered herself an extremely patient person, but the needle on her patience tank was beginning to dip dangerously close to E, and when she next spoke, her voice had a hint of steel in it.

"Unfortunately, I don't like easy. I like proof."

She turned away from the men and flipped the switch that turned on the mincer. The machine came to life instantly, blades whirring loudly. She turned back around in time to see Charles and Angel exchange concerned glances, but neither man spoke.

Poppy looked at Charles's friend. "You. What's your name?"

"Angel, ma'am."

"Okay, Angel. Listen carefully: your old pal Charles here has screwed up. That's all I'm gonna say, because that's all you need to know." She paused, then added, her voice cold as ice, "Put him in the mincer, please."

Charles hadn't really screwed up—not as far as Poppy knew, anyway. Although given how hard it was to find good help, the possibility was always there. But as someone who enjoyed cooking, she knew that sometimes you had to crack a few eggs—or hurl them to the ground and stomp on them repeatedly—if you wanted to make an omelet.

For an instant, neither man reacted, both too stunned by Poppy's command. But then Poppy laughed, and Charles and Angel followed suit, although their laughter held a nervous edge. But when the laughter died away Poppy fixed Charles with a cold, level gaze. Charles realized he was in deep shit, and he jumped up from his seat and ran like hell for the diner's entrance. Poppy sighed, then put two fingers in her mouth and blew a loud, high-pitched whistle. In a hidden corner of the diner, two kennels sprang open, and a pair of large dogs—or at least, what at first glance *looked* like dogs—ran toward Charles at amazing speed. The creatures bounded over tables and knocked down chairs in their rush to reach him, and Charles shrieked in terror and froze, knowing he couldn't possibly hope to outrun these things. They were robots, constructs of metal, plastic, and programming, and while outwardly they possessed the basic shape of dogs—like oversized Dobermans—they were faster, stronger, and deadlier than any flesh-and-blood canine could be. Poppy loved her doggies, and she was especially fond of their wickedly curved steel claws and their razor-sharp steel teeth. She liked the way the light glinted off the metal as they tore someone to shreds.

The dogs made no move to attack Charles, though. The whistle Poppy had used to summon them had also been a specific command: *herd*, not *kill*. The two robots stopped in front of Charles, and then began closing in on him slowly, optical scanners glowing an eerie red, speech synthesizers producing tinny barking sounds, metallic claws clicking on the tiled floor. As they approached, Charles backed up until he was standing next to Angel once more. Charles, trembling and covered with sweat, didn't take his gaze off the robot dogs. Now that Charles was back where Poppy wanted him, the dogs stopped advancing, but they continued keeping watch on the man, optical scanners fixed on him in case he tried to bolt again.

Poppy ignored Charles and spoke to Angel. "So, you want to join the Circle? Or follow your friend into the mincer?"

Angel didn't hesitate. He stood, and punched Charles twice in rapid succession. Charles went limp, but he didn't fully lose consciousness. Angel caught him before he could fall to the floor, and tossed him over his shoulder. He carried Charles behind the counter, lifted him up, and without so much as an instant of hesitation, fed him head-first into the whirring mincer.

"Oh my God!" Charles said, and then shrieked again as the mincer went to work. The machine was huge and powerful, and it reduced Charles to tiny pieces of meat quickly and efficiently. Poppy watched Angel's face throughout the process to gauge the man's reaction, but his expression remained stony the entire time. She nodded with approval.

When Angel was finished and Charles—with the exception of his legs protruding from the mincer—had been transformed into a substantial pile of fresh meat sitting on the mincer's large metal tray, she placed her hand on Angel's back, just for a few seconds. She knew that, strictly speaking, she shouldn't touch him. The last thing she wanted to do was create a sexually threatening atmosphere in the workplace, but she believed that a literal pat on the back could go a long way to making an employee feel appreciated. And since she had no human resources department to get on her ass about it, she figured: what the hell?

"Good job!" she said, then pointed toward one of the windows. "See my salon across the way?"

Angel nodded.

"Head over there."

Angel left, and Poppy stepped over to the robo-dogs and patted them on the head, first one, then the other. Their names were Bennie and Jet. She actually couldn't tell them apart, but that was okay. They never seemed to mind. Maybe she could paint the first letter of their names on their sides or something. That would help, but the letters would mar their sleek futuristic design. No, she decided. They were fine the way they were, interchangeable names or not.

She went behind the counter, picked up a handful of minced Charles, and began cheerfully shaping it into a patty.

Chapter Two

———— ✖ ————

Despite the mask of indifference Angel had worn for Poppy, he was shaken by killing Charles. Charles had overstated the case when he said the two of them were friends. More like casual acquaintances who'd worked for some of the same drug lords in the past. The work paid well, it was easy enough, and it was far less hazardous than most people would've believed, especially when you were one among a cadre of henchmen and guards. Most of the time, all you had to do was stand around holding a gun and scowling, and that—plus the presence of so many others who were doing the same—was enough to deter most people from trying to start trouble. And on those occasions when trouble did come, a few well-placed bullets usually took care of the situation.

But just as Poppy had said, during V-Day most of the drug lords and their employees had slaughtered each other, not just in Cambodia, but all around the world. Angel had been lucky. When Valentine triggered his aggression-causing signal, Angel had been nursing a truly epic hangover from the night before, and he'd remained in bed, head pounding, room spinning, blissfully unaware of the chaos taking place across the Earth. When he recovered, he learned the man he worked for was dead, which meant he no longer had a job. He looked for another, but *all* the drug lords were dead— all, that is, except for Poppy Adams. At first Angel had considered trying another line of work, but he knew he was kidding himself. Working as hired muscle was all he knew, and he was good at it. He didn't want another job. And so when he'd learned that his good "buddy" Charles was working for Poppy, he managed to convince him to introduce Angel to his employer.

That didn't work out so good for you. Did it, amigo?

So now he had a job. That was good. But it appeared his new employer was a crazy woman who didn't mind sacrificing one of her workers during the course of a job interview. That wasn't so good. He'd worked for sociopaths, psychopaths, narcissists, sadists—people who were, not to put too fine a point on it, bad to the fucking bone. But Poppy was unpredictable. Volatile. And, from what he had seen so far, absolutely ruthless and merciless. But the job came with decent benefits— both health *and* dental—so Angel figured he could put up with the rest of it.

One thing that was going to take him some time to get used to was Poppy's compound. That it was located so far away from even the merest hint of civilization was no surprise. You could hardly conduct her sort of business in a corner shop somewhere. But her architectural tastes were… well, *eclectic* was a kind way to put it. *Batshit crazy* was more accurate. She had constructed it using ancient ruins as a base, but the main gate was a large metal wall with the word POPPYLAND emblazoned at the top in cursive neon letters. And behind that gate was a bizarre collection of buildings that were miniaturized versions of the world's most famous structures and tourist attractions: the Eiffel Tower, the Empire State Building, the Great Wall of China, Mount Rushmore, the Great Pyramid of Giza, the Golden Gate Bridge, the Taj Mahal, the Sydney Opera House, Big Ben, the Statue of Liberty, the Leaning Tower of Pisa, Seattle's Space Needle, the Shanghai Tower, Disney World's Cinderella Castle, and more. Angel had never been to Las Vegas, but he had seen pictures and video, and he knew that the casinos were lavish, overdone replicas of real-world places built on a smaller scale. That's what Poppyland reminded him of: the Vegas Strip somehow stolen from its home in America and plonked down here in the middle of the jungle.

But that wasn't all. Poppyland was filled with amusements, too. Miniature golf courses, ice cream parlors, ferris wheels, theaters showing the latest films in IMAX 3-D, water parks with wave pools and twisting-turning slippery slides… And as if all that wasn't strange enough, aside from Poppy's guards—none of whom partook in the amusements around them—Poppyland was absolutely empty. There were no people at all. It was as if Poppy had built all of this for herself, as if—stuck here in the jungle—she had tried to bring the world, or at least some of the most fun parts of it, to her. It was kind of sad, really, when you thought about it. Poppyland was, in a way, a reflection of a highly unstable mind. But the woman must have a shit-ton of money to have been able to construct such an elaborate patchwork kingdom, and as long as she paid regularly, Angel didn't care how sane she was.

He had no idea why Poppy wanted him to go to the salon. Maybe new employees got a standard haircut or something, and maybe that was where he would be issued a uniform and weaponry as well. "Salon" might simply be a nickname that Poppy had given to her armory. Then again, it might not. Whichever the case, he was about to find out.

It certainly looked like a salon from the outside, a modern one, all chrome and glass. The sort of place rich women went when they wanted to spend far too much money trying to enhance what nature gave them, conceal it, or both. He pushed the door open and stepped inside.

What confronted him was as much hi-tech lab as beauty salon. There were chairs for sitting in while your hair was being worked on, but they looked more like the seats you might find on a spaceship, made of golden plastic, with coils of wires protruding from the back and a series of buttons and dials on the arms. There were sinks for having your hair washed, made from highly polished chrome with black hoses attached to tanks that looked like they'd been designed to dispense rocket fuel instead of soap and water. The massage tables—at least, that's what Angel assumed they were—looked like cryosleep chambers: clear plastic lids covering white tables on top of rectangular consoles with computer screens on the sides. Mirrored walls lined the interior of the salon, and large glowing globes hung from the ceiling on thin white rods, providing the finishing touches to the salon's futuristic ambiance.

But odd as all this was, there were two things odder still. The first was a robot designed to resemble a human female standing next to one of the salon chairs. Her pink-and-white metal body had been cast in an exaggerated parody of an old-fashioned feminine ideal—golden hair, large breasts, wasp-thin waist, curving hips. But what was most disturbing about this, this... *beautybot* was her face. Her features were immobile, white as bone, and her eyes were an inhuman silver. But as weird as the robot was, the large machine on the other side of the salon chair was even stranger. One of the bosses Angel had worked for previously had been hopelessly addicted to chocolate. He never touched the drugs he produced and sold, but he couldn't keep his hands off any kind of chocolate. Cheap mass-produced bars sold in grocery stores or luxurious hand-made chocolates—a dozen of which cost more than most cars—he didn't care. If it was chocolate, he devoured it and wanted more. This man had a giant chocolate fountain installed in his home: a metal tower and basin from which liquid chocolate perpetually flowed. The damn thing was so large that the man could actually take a bath in it if he wanted, and Angel had seen him do so on more than one occasion. The machine he was now looking at resembled that fountain in many ways, only instead of chocolate, molten *gold* flowed through it.

The sight of so much gold stunned Angel, and it caused him to reconsider his estimate of Poppy's wealth. She wasn't just rich; she was Rich. As. Fuck. Hell, she was probably worth more than most countries, and if he'd had any doubts about working for the woman, they vanished when he saw that gold. There was money to be made in this place, that was for damn sure, and he intended to get his share of it.

The beautybot had been silent up to this point, but now her head swiveled toward him, and a woman's voice—high-pitched, chipper, and full of energy—issued from a small round speaker embedded in the base of her throat.

"Appointment confirmed. Welcome. Please take shirt off."

Angel did so, folded it, and placed it on the counter behind Beautybot. The robot gestured to the chair, her metal hand moving with a graceful precision that only a highly sophisticated machine could achieve. Angel didn't know what he was supposed to do here exactly, but the message was clear: *sit down and let's get to work*. He walked to the chair and sat, unable to take his gaze off the flowing gold. Once he was in the chair, a headrest rose up to meet the back of his head, and a footrest deployed beneath his feet. Now the chair looked less like something that belonged in a salon and more like something that should've been in a doctor's surgery. As this realization hit him, metal bands snapped into place around his wrists and ankles, trapping him in place. Out of reflex, he struggled against the bands, but they were too strong and didn't give so much as a millimeter.

"My apologies," Beautybot said in her too-happy voice. "Everything will go much more smoothly if you remain still."

And then, before Angel could ask what was going to happen to him, she went to work. Moving with blinding speed, she inserted a metal brace into his mouth to force his jaws apart, and then the tips of her fingers retracted and were replaced with ten metal files.

Angel shook his head and tried to shout "No!" but it came out as "O! O!"

Beautybot jammed her fingers into his mouth and began filing his teeth down—without anesthetic. Angel cried out in pain, but the robot moved so fast that the procedure was over almost as soon as it began. The finger files retracted, and her regular fingertips returned, except for her right index finger. A thin plastic tube now protruded from it. Beautybot removed the metal brace from his mouth with her left hand, then stuck the tube finger between his lips.

"Rinse," she ordered, and water flowed from her finger tube into Angel's mouth.

Angel did as she said. Every one of his teeth throbbed like hell, and it almost felt as if she'd extracted them. He ran his tongue across his teeth as he rinsed to reassure himself they were still there. They were, but they had all been flattened.

Now I can't be identified from dental records, he thought.

She retracted the water tube, and it disappeared into her finger. She then cupped her hands and held them in front of his mouth.

"Spit," she said, and he did so. Pinprick-sized holes opened in her metal palms, and the water was quickly drained into them.

Angel hoped he was finished, but the metal bands holding him to the chair didn't release. Beautybot turned to the counter behind her, picked up a small bowl of liquid, moved over to where his left hand was bound against the chair arm, and slipped the tips of his fingers into the liquid. He screamed as flesh began to dissolve, and when he caught a whiff of the liquid's acrid tang, he understood what was happening. *It's acid. She's removing my fingerprints.*

The process didn't take long, only several moments, although it seemed like hours to Angel. When Beautybot removed his fingers from the acid, he let out a shuddering gasp of relief. But then she moved to the other side of the chair and repeated the process with his right hand, and he screamed once more.

Later, he would think that he must've blacked out for a few seconds at that point, because he had no memory of Beautybot taking his right-hand fingers from the acid. The next thing he was aware of was Beautybot looking down at him. Her facial features were incapable of expression, but when she spoke her tone was apologetic.

"I am told that this hurts. I am sorry."

Angel almost laughed. Like everything she'd done to him since he'd walked into this place had been painless? But then she reached toward the fountain of gold and removed a pen-like object hanging from a clip on its side. A metal tube stretched from the end of the pen to the machine, and it reminded Angel of something, but he couldn't quite… and then it came to him: a tattoo needle.

"Please," he said. "Don't—"

Beautybot touched the needle to his chest and began tattooing a circle of molten gold there. Angel had thought he'd screamed before, but when he heard the throat-shredding sound that burst forth from his mouth then, he realized that he hadn't known shit.

Angel returned to the diner, unsteady on his feet and lightheaded, but determined not to appear weak in front of Poppy. He had a feeling that displaying weakness before this woman would be a seriously bad career move, and the sight of Charles's legs jutting upward from the mincer only reinforced that feeling.

While he'd been in the salon, Poppy had been busy working at the fry table behind the counter, and the air was filled with the greasy smell of cooked meat. She turned around to greet him with a broad smile as he approached, and she set a plate holding a freshly made and perfectly garnished burger down on the counter.

"What do you think?" she asked. "Beautiful, right?"

Angel looked down at the golden tattoo on his chest,

and he reached up to touch it. The metal was still warm. It had hurt like a motherfucker while Beautybot applied it, but he had to admit, it looked damn awesome.

"Not that," Poppy said, irritated. "*This.*" She pointed to the burger and then smiled at Angel. "*Bon appétit!*"

His gaze darted to the giant mincer, then back to the burger, and his stomach cramped with sudden nausea.

Evidently, his disgust showed on his face, for Poppy frowned.

"Now, Angel… you're not going to insult my cooking, are you?"

For a fraction of a second, Angel considered running, but he remembered the robot dogs. He didn't see them, figured they had probably returned to their kennels, but he knew Poppy could summon them easily. All she had to do was whistle, after all.

He stepped forward, reached out to pick up the burger—*the Charles Special*, he thought—and brought it to his lips with trembling hands, Poppy's gaze fastened on him the entire time. He closed his eyes, opened his mouth, and took a bite. He chewed slowly, trying not to taste the gummy mass, fighting to keep from throwing up.

"It's… delicious," he managed.

Poppy smiled in satisfaction. "Welcome to the Golden Circle."

Eggsy emerged from a manhole near the lovely mews home formerly owned by his mentor Harry Hart, the best agent Kingsman ever had. But as he trudged toward the house, leaving a trail of dripping shit behind him and earning horrified stares from those pedestrians out for an evening stroll, he wondered what Harry would think if he could see him now. Harry had worked hard to teach Eggsy how to be a gentleman, and Eggsy was fairly certain that swimming through sewage wasn't the sort of thing discussed in *Etiquette for Gentleman Spies*.

After Eggsy, Merlin, and Roxy had stopped V-Day, Kingsman had been in turmoil for a bit. Arthur—real name Chester King—had thrown in his lot with Valentine. He'd died when he'd attempted to poison Eggsy and Eggsy managed to switch their drinks without Arthur noticing. Several Kingsman agents had sided with Arthur, and they'd died when the chips implanted inside their necks exploded. The good thing was that all the traitors in the agency were dead. Unfortunately, Kingsman needed some rebuilding. It had taken several weeks, but a new Arthur was installed and new agents were recruited, and now the agency was humming along smoothly.

Eggsy had moved into Harry's house during this transition period out of sheer practicality. Merlin and the other staff were too busy restoring the agency to full strength to worry about locating a different house for him just then. At first being in Harry's house made Eggsy feel like he was trespassing in another man's life. And all around him were reminders of Harry, which made him grieve his mentor's loss all the more. But after a while, he began to grow used to being there. It helped that he was away on missions so often that he was hardly in London, let alone at home, for any length of time. Lately, though, he'd found himself looking forward to returning to the house after a mission. In a way, Harry was still very much alive in the house—or at least his memory was—and Eggsy found his mentor's intangible presence comforting. So much so that he had changed very little since moving in. He was certain a psychologist would have a field day with his keeping the house as a shrine to Harry, but he didn't give a damn. Eggsy knew that when he was ready, he would put most of Harry's things in storage, keeping only a select few as reminders of the man who'd made such a huge difference in his life. He simply wasn't ready yet.

Mum and Daisy had joined him when he'd first moved into the house, but they hadn't stayed long. No matter how many times Eggsy tried to reassure his mum, she thought she was getting in his way. *How're you supposed to have any fun with your old mum hanging about?* she would say. Truth was, he thought, she couldn't take Eggsy not being able to tell her what he *really* did for a living. His dad never told her he was trying out for Kingsman, and she'd never learned the details of how he died. In the end, she couldn't get used to her son keeping secrets from her too.

Eggsy jogged toward the house. Thank god Merlin had guided him through the sewers or else he never would've found his way home. When he reached the front door, he removed his filth-slicked shoes and sodden socks. He didn't want to track shit all over the place. If he did, Harry's ghost would likely return from the afterworld to have a few choice words with him about that. He considered taking off the rest of his clothes before entering the house, but decided he'd scandalized the neighbors enough for one evening with his manhole entrance, so he opened the door and stepped inside.

"Babe, I'm home!" he called out.

He made his way through the hall and into the kitchen, where he found Tilde waiting for him, wearing a dark blue sweater over a light blue blouse. His pug JB—named after the TV character Jack Bauer—sat on the floor nearby. Tilde took one look at him and her eyes widened with shock. Then she got a whiff of him, and her face wrinkled with disgust.

"For fuck's sake," she said. "What the hell happened?"

"It's a long story that deserves a kiss," Eggsy said. He leaned his face toward her.

She drew back.

"If you really love me," he said, "you'll give me just one little kiss."

Looking more than a little reluctant, she stepped forward to kiss him. Eggsy pulled back before their lips touched.

"You were really gonna do it," he said.

Tilde shrugged. "Yeah."

He grinned. "Now *that* is true love right there. Amazing."

Tilde was a beautiful blond woman, and she spoke with what Eggsy thought was the most adorable Swedish accent. Which was only proper, seeing as how she *was* Swedish. More than that, she was an honest-to-Christ *princess*. Her parents were the king and queen of Sweden, and Tilde had been abducted by Valentine when she'd refused to go along with his plan to "cull" the human race in order to save the planet. Valentine had imprisoned her in a cell within his stronghold in the Swiss Alps—along with all the others who refused to cooperate with him but whom he considered worth saving. Eggsy had met Tilde when he and Merlin made their assault on Valentine's stronghold. After Eggsy had stopped Valentine— by stabbing him with one of his assistant's deadly prostheses—he'd visited Tilde in her cell to collect on a reward she'd promised him if he saved the world. It was an impulsive act for both of them, brought on by the stress of their circumstances and the exhilaration of victory. But, surprisingly, it became the beginning of something much more, and they'd been together ever since. They made an odd couple, no doubt, but they were happy with each other, and that's all that mattered to Eggsy.

"Give me five minutes to shower," he said.

Tilde fanned her face in a vain attempt to keep Eggsy's shit-stench at bay.

"Might need longer," she said wryly. The pug whined then, and Tilde laughed. "I think JB agrees!"

"This Brutalist architecture is beautiful," Tilde said, with no hint of sarcasm in her voice.

He grinned. "Brutal, more like."

The council estate where Eggsy had grown up—and where his friends Brandon, Jamal, and Liam shared a flat—had been constructed in the 1970s, and its age showed. Its once white concrete was gray and weathered, and with five hundred and twenty interchangeable flats, it looked more like a prison than a place people lived. Once, he would've been ashamed to bring someone like Tilde here. She was royalty, used to the finest things life had to offer. But he'd done a lot of growing up since that day he'd called Kingsman from the police station—the day he'd first met Harry Hart. Eggsy's father had been a Kingsman too, or near enough, and he'd died saving his fellow agents from an explosive device hidden on the body of a suspect they were interrogating. Harry had been one of those agents, but more than that, he'd sponsored Eggsy's dad for membership in Kingsman. When Eggsy had contacted Kingsman, hoping for nothing more than to escape going to jail, Harry had taken him under his wing, sponsored him for membership in the agency, and served as a mentor to him, in part to pay Eggsy's father back for saving his life. Eggsy was a baby when his dad died, and he had no memories of the man. Harry had been a strong male presence in his life, something Eggsy hadn't known he'd been missing, and although Harry had died only a short time after Eggsy had met him— shot in the head by Valentine after the billionaire's test of his aggression-causing tech at the South Glade Mission Church—Harry's impact on his life, on the man Eggsy had become, couldn't be overstated.

He remembered something that Harry had told him once. *There is nothing noble in being superior to your fellow man; true nobility is being superior to your former self.*

Words to live by, Harry, he thought.

As soon as Eggsy had gotten out of the shower, he'd opened the medicine cabinet and removed a pill bottle with the Kingsman logo on it: a circle enclosing the letter K turned on its side to resemble a pair of eyeglasses. The bottle contained a powerful single-dose antibiotic especially created for agents. Eggsy took one, thought for a moment, and then took a second. Considering the legions of lethal bacteria he'd exposed himself to in the sewer, his system would need all the help it could get if he hoped to remain healthy. He'd gotten rid of his ruined suit—literally, he'd tossed it in the bin out back—and he now wore a black cap, blue jacket, white shirt, jeans, and sneakers. As much as he'd grown accustomed to wearing a Kingsman suit when he was working, it felt good to be back in civvies again. Especially when said civvies weren't slathered in shit. Tilde wore a white hoodie and jeans, but even dressed down she looked like royalty to him. He supposed she always would.

As they walked up the steps toward his friends' flat—Eggsy carrying a bottle of liquor, Tilde carrying a plastic container holding a cake—he thought they might stop by his mum's for a bit after the party. Mum loved Tilde, although it had come as something of a shock to her to learn that Tilde was a literal princess, and Tilde loved her right back. The two of them got along so famously that when they got to talking, it was like he ceased to exist. He didn't mind, though. He loved seeing the two most important women in his life—well, two of three, counting Daisy—enjoying each other's company so much.

Soon, Eggsy and Tilde were sitting on the floor next to a cluttered coffee table, Brandon, Jamal, and Liam crowded together on a small, threadbare sofa. The cake Tilde had brought sat in the middle of the table, thin white candles burning. They sang "Happy Birthday" to Brandon, and when they finished, Brandon blew out the candles.

"Tilde made that cake for you herself, bruv," Eggsy said.

Jamal grinned. "What happened? The royal baker not available?"

Everyone laughed, and Tilde gave Jamal a playful frown.

"Shut up, especially if you want some of this."

She cut pieces of cake for all of them, and as she put the slices on paper plates, Jamal distributed it, along with plastic forks. Eggsy raised the bottle of liquor he'd brought, and Brandon eyed it suspiciously.

"Is that that Swedish stuff? Last time you brought it, I was *wrecked*."

They laughed again. Eggsy opened the bottle and poured generous portions into plastic cups. He didn't, however, pour a drink for himself.

"What's wrong?" Liam asked. "Now that you work for a fancy tailor's, you too good to drink with us?" He smiled to show he was joking.

"I'm gonna meet Tilde's parents for the first time tomorrow night," Eggsy said. "I want to make a good impression."

"So no hangover!" Tilde said, and they laughed.

Liam pointed to a clear plastic bag filled with marijuana resting amid the junk on the coffee table.

"I guess that's out then," he said.

"'Fraid so, mate," Eggsy said.

Jamal sipped his drink then shook his head. "Meetin' a proper king and queen… I can't imagine how nervous you must be, bruv."

Eggsy *was* nervous, even more so than when he was risking his life on a mission. In fact, he'd rather be fighting a horde of enemy agents armed with energy blasters than meet Tilde's parents—not to mention have dinner with them at the royal fucking palace. But Tilde had met his family and friends and had gotten along well with all of them. She might've been a princess, but she didn't put on airs and she treated everyone the same, highborn or not. It was his turn to meet her people, and however nervous he might be, he was determined to go through with it. For her.

It hadn't been easy explaining to his friends how he'd come to be dating an actual *princess*. He hated lying to them, but he couldn't tell them how they'd really met. They knew nothing about his work with Kingsman, and it had to stay that way, not only as a security precaution but also for their own protection. Eventually, Eggsy had come up with a story about Tilde shopping at Kingsman Tailors during a visit to London. She'd been looking for a new tailor for her father, and Eggsy had been the lucky bastard who'd gotten to assist her. Sparks flew, one thing led to another, and soon afterward, they were a couple. A crap story maybe, but his friends bought it, and that was all that mattered.

The five of them talked and laughed for a time, enjoying one another's company. After a while, Eggsy said, "Hey, can one of you dog-sit JB tomorrow night?"

"Sorry, bruv," Jamal said. "I got to look after my gran tomorrow."

"Not me," Liam said. "I'm allergic." He paused, then added with a laugh, "To dog shit, actually."

Everyone looked at Brandon. He sighed, then smiled. "Okay, on one condition. Have a drink with us, Eggsy."

Eggsy grinned. "I think I can manage one."

Poppy's compound was large—*huge*, even—but she spent the majority of her working hours in the diner. She liked its ambiance, sure, but the truth was that she found the rest of Poppyland more than a little depressing. As hard as she'd worked to recreate the outside world here in her private jungle kingdom, she knew none of it was *real*, and every time she walked through Poppyland, its faux buildings and cheesy attractions mocked her. So she mostly stayed in the diner. It was the least fake of all the fake stuff she'd created. She'd installed a small office area on one side of the diner, and she sat at a desk, wearing a pair of VR glasses and looking at a holographic projection of Charlie, who appeared to be seated across from her. He wore a similar pair of glasses, and she thought they made him look kind of nerdy. She hoped they didn't look as bad on her.

"Charlie, congratulations on a successful mission."

Beads of sweat dotted his brow, and he spoke quickly, as if he were nervous. *No*, she realized. *He's* scared.

"I'm so sorry. I tried, I swear. I—"

"Relax, Charlie. Come on. Where does Napoleon keep his armies? Up his sleevies!" She waited for him to laugh, and when he didn't, she frowned and went on. "And what are *you* keeping up *your* sleevie? Or should I say, *not* keeping there right now."

He paled. "You… know that I lost my arm?"

She was beginning to find his fear tiresome. Yes, it was useful when your underlings were afraid of you. But it became a drag when you had to constantly reassure them that you weren't going to execute them for every little thing that didn't go exactly according to plan.

"Charlie, I *gave* you that arm when I employed you. Not only do I know that you lost it, but I can also remotely control it. Your mission is complete." She decided not to tell him that it hadn't mattered to her whether or not he survived his encounter with his former rival. All she'd cared about was getting the arm where she'd needed it to go.

Some of the color returned to Charlie's face, but he still looked doubtful. "You got what we needed?"

She'd received the data transmission from the arm a while ago, and she was already making preparations to use the knowledge she'd acquired.

"Uh-huh. You can come back to HQ now. Everything's in place."

There was a bounce in Eggsy's step the next morning as he descended the stairs, dressed in a fresh Kingsman suit and ready for another day of protecting the world. But when he entered the dining room, he saw Tilde had made a full English breakfast of scrambled eggs, bacon, sausage, fried bread, black pudding, beans, and tea. And as if that wasn't enough, she'd set the table formally, using Harry's best china and silverware. She was dressed in a dark blue sweater and white blouse—and looked quite fetching in them—and she rose from the table as he approached to give him a kiss. JB danced around their feet, barking to get Eggsy's attention, so Eggsy knelt and gave the little beast a quick scratch behind the ears. The smell of all that food was probably driving JB mad, Eggsy thought.

"Oh. Shit," he said. "I was gonna grab breakfast at work, babe."

She'd been smiling, obviously in a good mood, but now her smile faded. "I just thought maybe we could... practice? For tonight?"

Eggsy frowned. Something was going on here, but he wasn't sure what. "Practice... eating?"

She gave him an impatient look. "You *said* you'd never eaten at a palace before. And... Pappa *is* sort of picky about table manners."

Tonight, it would be Tilde's turn to introduce him to her

parents: the king and queen of bloody Sweden. Admittedly, he was nervous. Until recently, he'd barely known which end of a fork was which. But he didn't want to *seem* nervous, because if Tilde started worrying about him, then *she'd* get nervous, and he didn't want that to happen.

So he gave her what he hoped looked like a confident grin and said, "As it happens, darling, I got this shit on lock."

Harry gestured for Eggsy to take a seat at the dining table. He'd done the whole bit: laid out china, silverware, and a napkin, just like Eggsy had seen serving staff do in the movies. There was only one place set, and Eggsy took it.

Harry Hart was a handsome man in his fifties, and he wore the Kingsman suit as if it were a second skin. He moved with precision and economy of motion, and he spoke the same way. His tone was emotionally balanced, even detached at times, but there were notes of warmth and good humor there, if you knew how to recognize them. His normal expression was one of benign politeness, but his eyes told a different story. They radiated a focused intensity that indicated a man of keen intellect who was deeply aware of his surroundings, and who always had a plan to kill everyone in the room if necessary.

There were a number of different types of glassware on the table, and Harry identified them as he pointed to each in turn.

"White wine, wedding wine, pudding wine, pop, and whatever tipple takes your fancy."

Eggsy nodded to show he got it.

"Time to learn how to eat like a gentleman," Harry said. "First thing you do is unfold your napkin and place it on your lap."

Eggsy did so. He'd never used a fancy cloth napkin before, and he was surprised at how heavy it felt. He draped it across his lap. Evidently he did it right because Harry said nothing to correct him.

Harry then stepped over to Eggsy and picked up one of the knives at his place setting.

"This is a butter knife," he said. "The only one to remember. The rest of the cutlery is easy: start on the outside, work your way in with each course. And *never* let anyone describe you as 'H.K.L.P.'" He returned the knife to its proper place on the table.

Eggsy frowned. "What's that?"

"'Holds knife like pen.' A habit erroneously believed to be upper-class dining etiquette. It is *quite* the opposite."

There was a tureen in the middle of the table, and now Harry ladled some soup into a bowl and placed it in front of Eggsy.

"Do I wait 'til everyone's been served to start eating?" Eggsy asked.

"Only if the dish being served is cold, or if the queen is present. Otherwise, tuck in."

Eggsy picked up a spoon, dipped it into the soup, brought it to his lips and quietly sipped. Even he knew better than to slurp. The soup—which Harry would later tell him was a Moroccan soup called harira—contained lamb, tomato, chickpeas, lentils, and was flavored with harissa hot sauce. It was absolutely delicious.

"Other way. Always push the spoon *away* from you."

Eggsy decided to have a little fun with his mentor. He put down the spoon, picked up the bowl, and brought it to his lips as if he planned to drink directly from it.

"This is okay, though, right?"

Harry smiled. "Actually, if you're in Japan, it's absolutely the done thing."

Eggsy grinned and took a big slurp from the bowl.

Eggsy smiled wistfully at the memory.

"Gotta be honest," he said, "I never thought the royalty bit would be relevant. Harry would've been chuffed."

"I wish I could've met him," Tilde said.

I wish that too, Eggsy thought. *So much.*

Harry's dog Mr Pickle, or rather his taxidermied remains, sat on a shelf in the dining room. Kingsman gave recruits a dog to train and care for during the selection process. What recruits didn't know was the final exam was a killer. Literally. The candidates who made it to the end of training were handed a gun and told to shoot their dog. If they refused, they were sent home. Harry had shot Mr Pickle, only to discover that the gun had been loaded with blanks.

A Kingsman only condones the risking of a life to save another, Harry had explained.

Mr Pickle lived out his natural lifespan, and when the dog died, Harry had had him stuffed—which Eggsy had found more than a little odd, but hey, who was he to judge? He loved little JB so much he might not be able to give him up either after he died. Harry had kept Mr Pickle in the downstairs bathroom, along with framed displays of butterflies he had collected over the years. Eggsy couldn't get used to staring into Mr Pickle's glass eyes every time he took a slash, so he moved the poor little fellow into the dining room. It was more than a little weird, he supposed, but having Harry's dog here made him feel more like part of the family.

"You miss him too, Mr Pickle, don't you?" He paused a moment, then turned to Tilde. "Mr Pickle says yeah."

He was hoping to lighten the mood, maybe even make her laugh, but all he got from her was a sad, understanding smile.

Chapter Three

Eggsy entered the Kingsman dining room, which was located on the second floor of the tailor shop, accessible by a set of stairs in the back. The room served as the primary meeting space for agents, and seated at the grand dining table were Merlin, Roxy, and the new Arthur. The room practically reeked of age and tradition, and nothing communicated this more than the paintings hanging on the walls and the busts on pedestals in the corners. They depicted men in old-fashioned suits, tuxedos, or uniforms, their poses formal, their faces serious as death. These were the founders of Kingsman, upper-class men who'd lost their sons in World War One and who had decided to use the money those sons hadn't lived to inherit to create an independent intelligence agency, one that would prevent the kind of evil their sons had died fighting.

"Galahad. You're late," Arthur said. "We were wondering if you'd had a second encounter with Charlie."

This Arthur—a man in his sixties named Augustin Edmonds—had until recently been an agent like the rest of them. He'd taken over the mantle of leadership when the agency rebuilt itself after the events of V-Day. Eggsy liked him well enough. He was firm but fair, and although he could be a bit of a prig at times, all in all he was a good boss to work for. Eggsy had certainly worked for worse in his time.

Merlin and Roxy suppressed smiles, and Eggsy knew what they were thinking: *Like mentor, like protégé.* Harry had been infamous for being late to meetings. He'd considered them a chore at best and a waste of time at worst. Eggsy agreed.

"I wish," he said, slipping into the seat next to Roxy. "I'm looking forward to finishing him off."

Eggsy donned his eyeglasses, and now he could see that the remaining chairs at the table were filled with the ghostly holographic images of those agents who were on assignment and could only attend the meeting in virtual form. He acknowledged them with a nod, which they returned in kind.

"'Bout time," Roxy whispered, teasing. Eggsy kicked her gently beneath the table as a way of getting her back, and she grinned. They'd met when they were both recruited to join Kingsman, and they'd become friends right off. They'd each had the other's back throughout the training period, and they'd learned that not only did their personalities complement each other, but they worked together so effectively it was as if they'd been partners for years. They'd been the last two recruits standing at the end of the training process, and ultimately they'd both become agents. Eggsy admired her enormously. He thought of her as a model agent, the absolute best that Kingsman had to offer, and he was proud to be her friend.

She was an attractive brunette with long straight hair, and she wore a woman's version of a Kingsman suit: a slim tailored dark-gray blazer over a light gray blouse, with gray trousers and black shoes. While her outfit might look different to those of the men in the room, it possessed the same qualities: it moved so that it didn't constrain physical activity, no matter how extreme, and best of all, it was bulletproof—the latter an absolute must for the modern, well-dressed spy.

"Well, no further business," Arthur said to the assembled agents. "Galahad and Lancelot, please remain for Merlin's debrief. Everyone else—reconvene at nineteen hundred hours. Dismissed."

The other agents nodded their goodbyes and their images winked out.

Arthur gave Merlin a nod. "Merlin, please begin."

Merlin stood and tapped a command on his computer tablet, and the mirror above the fireplace behind him revealed itself to be a hi-tech video display.

"This is CCTV footage from our encounter with Charlie—rejected Kingsman applicant turned bad—back at Richmond Valentine's HQ," Merlin said. "We've never had reason to go back over this before."

Eggsy watched himself join the traitorous Swedish prime minister at his booth table. The man was surfing the Net on a laptop, and Merlin needed Eggsy to find him a Wi-Fi connection to Valentine's mainframe so he could hack into the man's system. Eggsy tranquilized the prime minister by shooting a small fast-acting sleep dart from his watch into the man's neck. The prime minister slumped over, Eggsy inserted the USB drive Merlin had given him into the computer, and *voilà*! Connection established.

That's when Charlie came up behind Eggsy and pressed a wickedly long knife to his neck. There was no sound with the video, but Eggsy remembered what they'd said to each other.

Nice and slow, Charlie said.

The fuck are you doing here? Eggsy asked.

Charlie made a face as if it was the stupidest question he'd ever heard. *My family were invited, obviously. Get the fuck up—slowly.*

Eggsy raised his hands and rose from the booth, Charlie holding the blade to his throat the entire time. The booth was located on a mezzanine in Valentine's control center-slash-night club, and Charlie steered Eggsy over to the railing.

Valentine! Charlie shouted. *I caught a fucking spy!*

In a single swift motion, Eggsy had pressed his Kingsman sovereign ring to Charlie's right temple, hitting the bastard with a 50,000 volt electric charge. Charlie's body began convulsing instantly. He lowered the knife and took a step back, and he might have fallen on his own, but Eggsy—pissed—punched the asshole in the jaw and laid him out.

Eggsy then jumped over the railing, landed on the

main floor, and—thinking his work was done—ran like hell to get out of there.

"Can we see that again?" Eggsy asked.

Merlin gave him a look, but he tapped his tablet, and everyone watched the scene play out once more.

When the footage was finished, Merlin spoke again. "Now, like everyone else there, Charlie had a security implant in his neck. A weakness we had no choice but to exploit."

Merlin tapped his tablet and a different video came up on the screen. The assembled agents watched as the heads of all the revelers in Valentine's self-proclaimed "ark" exploded in a series of sickening, yet somehow strangely beautiful, explosions.

"Still 'fucking spectacular,' eh, Merlin?" Eggsy said, doing a passable imitation of Merlin's Scottish accent. When no one reacted to his impression, Eggsy scowled. "Bloody hell, loosen up, guys. We saved the world!"

"You also saved Charlie," Merlin said.

He brought up new video. This footage showed Charlie regaining consciousness and rising painfully to his feet. He gazed upon the room full of headless bodies with wide-eyed horror. He then ran off, unsteady on his feet, grimacing as he rubbed the area where his security chip had been implanted with one hand, while his other arm dangled limply at his side.

"You shorted out his implant," Merlin said. "He survived but lost his arm and vocal cords."

Eggsy understood what had happened. "So me giving

him a few volts saved him. Fucker should be *thanking* me."

"And now he's back for revenge?" Arthur asked.

"We don't think so, sir," Merlin said. "We believe he's been recruited by an unknown organization. Lancelot?"

Roxy stood. "Got the police autopsy reports for Charlie's colleagues in the SUVs. They're not just goons-for-hire."

One of the reports appeared on the screen, along with an image of a dead man, naked, with a gold circle tattooed on his chest.

Roxy continued. "Fingerprints removed. Teeth filed smooth. And I ran photo recognition—nothing."

Arthur pointed to the gold circle on the man's chest. "And this thing?"

"A cosmetic tattoo," Roxy said, "made of twenty-four carat gold. They all had them. I suspect we're looking at some kind of underworld organization."

Eggsy didn't care all that much about who was employing Charlie. He just wanted to get his hands on the fucker and this time make sure that when he put him down, he *stayed* down.

"While Roxy's figuring that out, I'll track Charlie," Eggsy said.

"Good," Arthur said. "Bring him in." He paused and gave Eggsy a hard look. "*Alive*. Dismissed."

Eggsy wasn't happy about it, but he nodded. Of course, sometimes out in the field accidents *did* happen…

* * *

Eggsy was loading a steamer trunk—a quite heavy one, actually—into the back of a Kingsman taxi outside his house, while Tilde stood nearby, holding JB on a leash. Both of them were dressed casually: Eggsy in jeans, T-shirt, hoodie, and ball cap, Tilde in a peasant blouse (ironic since she was royalty, Eggsy thought) and black leggings. As Eggsy finished stowing the trunk, his friend Brandon came running up the mews to join them, out of breath. He was dressed much the same as Eggsy, but without the cap.

"About fucking time!" Eggsy said. "We're late!" He instantly regretted snapping at Brandon, but despite the façade he'd been putting on for Tilde, he was quite nervous about having dinner with her parents. It was hard enough to meet your girlfriend's folks, but when they were actual royalty, it added a whole other layer of tension to the event. And it didn't help that he was on edge about Charlie. He had no way of knowing when the bastard might try to attack him again, and he was on high alert, not wanting Tilde to get caught in the crossfire if Charlie had another go at him.

Tilde frowned at Eggsy. "Stop that!"

"Sorry!" Brandon said. "Tube strike. Some of us still have to use public transport, bruv." He patted the taxi's hood, smiling to show that he meant nothing by the comment.

Eggsy's life had changed drastically over the last few months, and he couldn't tell Brandon the full truth about Kingsman, but none of that had hurt their friendship. They were still mates, and Eggsy hoped they always would be.

"Don't worry, Brandon," Tilde said. "It's very nice of you to dog-sit." She gave Eggsy a pointed look. "Isn't it?"

Eggsy let out a long breath and forced himself to calm down. "Yeah. Cheers. We owe you one." He fished the door keys out of his pocket and handed them to Brandon. "Make yourself at home. But don't go in my office. And no friends, yeah?"

Eggsy didn't want Brandon to think he didn't trust him, but there were things inside the house that no civilian should see—and some of those things could be dangerous.

If Brandon took any offense at Eggsy's words, he showed no sign. He slipped the keys into his trouser pocket, took JB's leash from Tilde, and gave Eggsy a grin. "What about if ma bitch wants a booty call?"

"JB's a boy. And he ain't interested in your booty." Eggsy knelt down and gave JB a kiss on the top of his head. "Are you, mate? No."

JB barked and wagged his tail, and the three of them laughed.

Drottningholm Palace was located on the island of Lovön, only a half-hour drive from Stockholm's city center, but to Eggsy, being here was like traveling back in time. It was a *proper* palace, built in the late sixteenth century, and it was absolutely *huge*, of course. The damn thing even had its own theater where the Royal Swedish Opera performed. The castle was surrounded by beautiful parks and gardens that were popular tourist attractions, and they enhanced the palace's fairy-tale appearance. When Eggsy first laid eyes on the palace, he tried to imagine what it had been like for Tilde growing up here, but he couldn't. This wasn't just a different place to where he'd grown up in London—it was like a whole other fucking planet!

After they'd arrived and gotten settled, they dressed for dinner. Tilde wore a black dress designed to leave the left shoulder bare. Eggsy thought the dress looked classy and informal at the same time—an outfit that perfectly reflected Tilde's personality, he thought. Eggsy wore a red velvet smoking jacket with a black bow tie, black trousers and—naturally—his Oxfords. He felt silly in the outfit, but Tilde had chosen it for him and, once he'd donned it, she'd assured him he looked quite handsome. He had added one touch of his own, though: his Kingsman eyeglasses.

Tilde held onto Eggsy's arm as they made their way to the palace anteroom. Liveried footmen dressed in blue uniforms with white trim and silver epaulets bowed as they passed, and Eggsy acknowledged them with a serene smile, as if he were used to such treatment. But inside he felt like a complete poseur.

"Fuck me," he said under his breath.

"Oh, I will," Tilde said softly. "Later. Maybe in the throne room."

They both giggled, and continued down a long corridor until they reached a large pair of double doors, flanked by more footmen. The men bowed, then opened the doors for Eggsy and Tilde to pass through. Eggsy told himself not to be nervous. Whatever the king and queen were like, he knew they were good people. After all, they'd refused to throw in their lot with Valentine, unlike so many other world leaders, wealthy businesspeople, and famous entertainers. A butler was waiting for Eggsy and Tilde just inside the room—a man in his sixties, wearing a black suit and a blank, slightly bored expression, as if he'd seen just about everything in his time and nothing impressed him anymore. He formally announced them.

"Prinsessa Tilde, *och Herr…*" He paused, as if having to force himself to say Eggsy's name, but he soldiered on. "Gary 'Eggsy' Unwin."

The king and queen stood stiffly nearby. Tilde's mother and father were both in their sixties, having had their daughter later in life. The king was bald with a fringe of silver hair around the sides and back. The queen's hair was blond—probably a dye job, Eggsy figured, but it looked natural enough. However, the way they were dressed came as a complete shock to him. Tilde had told him that her parents normally dressed professionally but simply: her father in suit and tie, her mother in dresses, accessorized with pearls and earrings. Nothing too fancy. But tonight they were dressed as if for an official royal dinner. The king wore a tuxedo with a light blue sash across his chest. The left side of his jacket was covered with medals of various shapes and sizes. Eggsy had no idea what they were for, but they looked impressive as hell. The queen wore a long-sleeved white lace dress—also with a blue sash across the chest—and diamond earrings and a diamond necklace. She wore jeweled bracelets and—he couldn't believe it—a fucking silver crown.

Tilde gave her parents a look that said she was surprised by their formal dress as well, but she said nothing. She gave them a quick curtsey before stepping forward to air-kiss them, first her mother, then her father.

Eggsy bowed to the queen, then to the king, and addressed them in Swedish.

"It's an honor."

The king gave him an amused, condescending look.

"I think we should do you the favor of conversing in English, yes?" he said.

Eggsy smiled, but inwardly he groaned. It was going to be a long night.

Tilde had told Eggsy they would eat in one of the palace's smaller dining rooms since it was just the four of them, but the king and queen led them to a large banqueting hall with a long table capable of seating at least fifty people, maybe more. There was a series of chandeliers hanging from a curved ceiling upon which scenes from Sweden's history had been painted. Eggsy felt as if he were standing in a museum instead of a place where people ate. A gigantic white tablecloth covered the table, and the plates and cutlery were made from silver so well-polished they practically glowed. The glassware was made from the finest crystal, and a gold candelabra sat atop the table close to where their places had been set. Four uniformed servants—one for each of the diners, Eggsy realized—stood against the walls, silent and immobile, as if they were part of the architecture. But when the king and queen entered, they sprang to life, pulling red leather chairs away from the table so everyone could sit. The queen was seated first, then the king, Tilde, and last, Eggsy.

And then came the food: roasted Bresse pigeon with Jerusalem artichoke, roasted onion, pickled elderflower capers and creamy green peppercorn sauce. And for dessert: lemon cheesecake with sabayon, meringues, and sour cream ice cream. There was also wine, and plenty of it, which Eggsy was profoundly grateful for.

They ate in silence for a time, but Eggsy knew it wasn't good manners for a guest to remain quiet throughout an entire meal.

He turned toward the queen and said, "This is delicious, your Highness."

The king cut in before his wife could respond. "You may address my *daughter* as 'your Highness.' Please address the queen as 'your Majesty.'"

"Pappa!" Tilde said. "This is a family dinner, not some state function."

The king smiled at Tilde, but otherwise didn't acknowledge her words.

Eggsy understood what was going on here. He'd met a few girls' dads before, and it didn't matter if they poured drinks at the local pub or were bloody royalty. A dad was a dad. The king was suspicious of his daughter's boyfriend, and this wasn't merely a get-to-know-you meal. This was intended to be an interrogation, and the king decided to get on with it.

"So, *Eggsy*," he said, "what do you make of the current situation in the Indian financial markets?"

Tilde gave Eggsy a worried glance and then turned to scowl at her father. She knew exactly what he was doing, and she didn't like it.

"*Pappa…*" she said in a warning tone.

The king ignored her and stared at Eggsy, waiting for a response.

"I… I don't think we can underestimate the impact of the ECB's quantitative easing measures. And of course, the liquidity wave from the US Federal Reserve rate-hike getting pushed back."

The king, the queen, and even Tilde looked surprised. Eggsy speared a caper with his fork, popped it in his mouth, and smiled. And from that point on, the battle was joined.

"Frida Kahlo?" the king asked.

"Besides the 1939 acquisition by the Louvre, she wasn't acknowledged until the Neo-Mexicanismo art movement of the late seventies."

He frowned. "The Battle of Stalingrad?"

"The Germans lost more soldiers taking Pavlov's house than they did taking Paris," Eggsy said.

The king leaned toward Eggsy, eyes narrowing. "Moorish Revival."

Eggsy sat back, perfectly relaxed. "The Palazzo Sammezzano in Tuscany."

"Bluetooth technology," the king said through gritted teeth.

"Which of course got its name from the legendary Danish king Harald Blåtand—which translates to 'Bluetooth' in English," Eggsy said, sounding a trifle bored.

The king's brow was furrowed, his cheeks red with annoyance. But Tilde grinned from ear to ear, and the queen smiled approvingly.

Eggsy heard Roxy's voice in his ear:

"And the Bluetooth logo is his initials, in Norse runic symbols."

"And I'm sure you're aware the Bluetooth symbol is his initials," Eggsy said.

Eggsy imagined Roxy sitting at her desk in her London apartment, a dozen windows open on her laptop as she furiously researched whatever topic the king brought up next and relayed the information to Eggsy via the tiny receiver in his ear.

"Oh my god, Eggsy. Why isn't he eating his fucking pudding? I need to research this gold tattoo. I've found records of other people with the same body modification. All of them have high-level involvement with crime and international drug trafficking. And there's rumors of something called the Golden Circle."

Using the AR display on his eyeglasses, Eggsy sent her a quick text using eye movements to "type" the message on a virtual keyboard.

UR DA BEST ROXY

"Best agent or best friend?"

Eggsy could hear the smile in her voice. He sent another text.

BOTH. X

The king finally stopped asking Eggsy questions and, grimacing as if suffering from indigestion, took a bite of his cheesecake.

Brandon was happy to dog-sit for Eggsy. He loved dogs—not counting the creepy stuffed one Eggsy kept around for some strange reason—and since he didn't have any pets of his own, he was glad of the opportunity to borrow the pug for a bit. And of course it was nice to have a whole house to himself. It made a welcome change from the cramped apartment he shared with Jamal and Liam. But the main reason he liked dog-sitting for Eggsy was that he got to get a taste of what it was like to *be* his friend. Not that he was jealous of Eggsy's good fortune. He was genuinely happy that Eggsy had done so well for himself. Great job, new place, *fantastic* girlfriend... And he had changed so much! These days Eggsy had a newfound confidence, a strength that Brandon knew had always been inside him, but which had needed some coaxing to be brought out. And unlike some people who went through a time of major growth and change in their lives, Eggsy hadn't lost sight of the person he used to be. He was still the same Eggsy at heart, and he hadn't forgotten his old mates.

JB had been a bit out of sorts since Eggsy and Tilde left, moping about the place and whining softly. So

Brandon had decided that a quick game of fetch might lift the little dog's spirits. He found a ball and led JB to the upstairs hallway. It was the longest open space in the house, and since they could hardly go outside and play in the dark, it would have to do. He stood by the stairs, JB sitting at his feet, and threw the ball.

JB looked up at him as if to say, *Are you serious?* But the pug got up and trotted after the ball. It hit the far wall and bounced back, and JB intercepted it before it could roll past him. He snatched it up in his mouth, but instead of taking it back to Brandon, he looked at a door nearby. A second later, he dropped the ball, ran toward the door, and began scratching at it.

Brandon walked over to JB and looked down at him.

"Come on, JB. Give it a rest, mate. Eggsy ain't here. Stop scratching at the door. I'm gonna get the blame!"

But JB continued scratching, almost frantic now. Brandon sighed. Maybe one of JB's favorite toys was in there, and if he could get it, he'd settle down. He tried the knob and found it locked. He was about to give up and try the ball again, when he decided to see if one of the keys Eggsy had left him would unlock the door. He pulled the key out of his pocket and found the right one on the second try. The door unlocked, he pushed it open, and JB rushed inside. Brandon turned on the light just in time to see JB curl up in a dog basket in the corner. It was then that he realized this was Eggsy's study—the one room he'd asked Brandon not to go into.

JB lowered his head to his paws and closed his eyes.

Brandon understood what was going on. Since this was Eggsy's study, it probably smelled like him. Being here made JB feel close to Eggsy, and because of that, the little dog didn't want to leave. Brandon considered letting JB stay here with the door open so the pug could leave whenever he wished. He'd go back downstairs, get a beer from the fridge, maybe watch a little telly... But a trio of framed pictures on the wall caught his attention. No, not pictures. They were the front pages of tabloid newspapers. *Why the fuck would Eggsy have those?* Curious, he stepped into the room.

As a study, there wasn't much to it, really. A wooden desk, a closed laptop resting on the surface, a couple of pens, a clamp-on desk lamp, two framed photos: one of Eggsy and Tilde laughing on a beach, and one of an older guy in a suit whom Brandon didn't recognize. There was also a martini bar in the room, which—cool as it was— seemed out of place. And that was all. But then again, Eggsy worked in a tailor's. It wasn't like he needed a fully equipped home office. Brandon walked over to the tabloid pages and examined them. The headline on the first read BURGER OUT OF ORDER! It was dated the same day as V-Day, but the paper had come out before the world lost its mind, so it hadn't covered the story yet. The headline on the second was WELL HUNG! And the headline on the third and most recent asked WHERE IS ELTON?

Unable to make sense of why Eggsy would frame such nonsensical shit and hang it in his study, Brandon decided to check out the martini bar. It seemed too old-fashioned for someone Eggsy's age, but maybe he was on some kind of nostalgia kick. On top were several bottles of vodka—different brands—a decanter of amber liquid, martini glasses, and tumblers. He picked up the decanter, removed the stopper and took a sniff. Scotch. And from the smell of it, damn fine stuff! He poured himself a couple fingers in one of the tumblers, but before he could drink it, he noticed what looked like a small button on the edge of the bar. Frowning, he touched his index finger to it, pushed, and felt it click.

In response, the wall on the far side of the room slid upward to reveal what appeared to be a weapons cache of some sort, with items hanging from hooks or resting on shelves. There were a couple of handguns with what looked like sawed-off shotgun barrels attached to the underside. There were several regular guns: rifles and submachine guns, two apiece. There were also several wardrobe items and accessories: watches, sovereign rings, fountain pens, lighters, an umbrella, and a pair of fancy men's dress shoes. There was also a pair of eyeglasses like the kind Eggsy sometimes wore.

Brandon couldn't believe what he was seeing. "You a gangster now or something, Eggsy?" And the weirdest thing of all? JB hadn't so much as stirred in his basket, as if the wall sliding upward was a perfectly normal thing to him. Brandon was beginning to get the idea that his good mate Eggsy might not really be a tailor after all.

Brandon picked up one of the strange pistols and examined it. Then he put it back and picked up the

glasses. What was so special about these that Eggsy
would keep them locked and hidden in his study? They
were just fucking glasses. He decided to see for himself,
so he put them on.

The ordeal that had been dinner with Tilde's parents
was over at last, and everyone was finally drinking coffee.
Eggsy was beginning to think he was going to make it
to the finish line without any major mishaps, and for the
first time all evening, he began to relax a little.

"I must say, you're really not as I expected," the king
said in a tone of grudging acceptance.

Eggsy tried not to sound too pleased with himself
when he responded. "Thank you, your Majesty."

He then heard a voice in his ear—one that didn't
belong to Roxy:

"Eggsy? That you? What the hell are these glasses?
Fuck me, is that Tilde's mum and dad's house?"

Brandon appeared as a holographic image in Eggsy's
eyeglasses display, overlapping where the king was sitting.

Eggsy knew at once what had happened. Brandon
had gone into his study and stumbled on the switch
that revealed Eggsy's miniature home armory. The
AR display on Eggsy's glasses activated, and he saw
Brandon's hands reaching for one of the lighters in the
weapons cache: lighters that were actually grenades
in disguise. Horrified at the thought of his friend
accidentally activating the grenade, Eggsy pointed at

Brandon—which meant he also pointed at the king.

"Put that down!" he shouted.

The king—who'd been about to take another sip of coffee—looked at Eggsy, startled, but he put his cup down on the table.

"Why?" he asked, frowning in puzzlement.

But Eggsy didn't hear him. He was too busy watching Brandon flip open the lighter's lid. Now activated, the grenade began to beep, signaling its countdown had begun.

"Shut it!" Eggsy said, practically screaming the words. "Fucking shut it, *now*!"

Tilde and her parents were staring at Eggsy aghast. He was dimly aware of their reaction to his words, but he was too focused on keeping Brandon from blowing himself to bits to care right now.

"I beg your pardon?" the queen said.

"Eggsy!" Tilde shouted.

"All right. Chill yer boots." Brandon snapped the lighter closed and the beeping stopped.

Eggsy breathed a deep sigh of relief. Disaster averted.

"What's that sound?" Brandon said. He walked toward the study's window.

While Eggsy could see what Brandon saw via the connection between their eyeglasses, he didn't hear anything. At first he was afraid the lighter's countdown had somehow started up again, but that didn't make sense. Obviously, whatever Brandon heard was coming from outside. And then Eggsy heard it too: a whooshing sound that grew louder with each second. He then heard something else: JB whine with fear.

Eggsy went cold when he realized what was making that sound. It was a missile, and it was heading straight for the house.

"What the fuck is—" Brandon's voice was drowned out by a loud explosion, and Eggsy saw a bright burst of flame in his AR display. Then the link between the two pairs of eyeglasses was severed, and both the audio and visual feed from Brandon's glasses cut out.

Eggsy cried out in shock, and then he heard Roxy's voice in his ear. She must've kept the link between their glasses live in case he needed more of her help.

"Eggsy? What's wrong? What—"

The visual feed from Roxy's glasses activated in time for him to see the room around her disappear in fire and thunder.

Arthur sat in the Kingsman dining room, chairing an evening meeting. All agents—with the exception of Eggsy, Roxy, and Merlin—were present in holographic form.

"So," Arthur said, "for our next order of business. Agent Percival—you've looked over the Drummond files?"

Percival opened his mouth to speak, but then his holographic image shuddered and vanished.

Arthur frowned. "Percival?"

A second agent vanished, and then a third.

"Seem to be having a spot of bother with my glasses," Arthur said. He reached up and fiddled with the frames, but agents continued disappearing, one after the other, until Arthur was alone.

He then saw a message flashing on the wall screen. WARNING: INCOMING MISSILE.

"Oh fuck," Arthur said.

For a split second Arthur was engulfed in noise and flame, and then he was gone.

Eggsy stumbled into the hallway and tore the glasses from his face. He had no memory of getting up from the dining table, crossing the room, and pushing open the door. He couldn't think, couldn't speak, couldn't breathe... But then he thought of his friends. He put the glasses back on and found his voice.

"Brandon? Can you hear me? Roxy? Roxy, are you there?" Deep down, he knew it was useless, that they were no longer alive, but he didn't know what else to do.

Tilde rushed out into the hall to join him.

"Eggsy, what the fuck is *wrong* with you? It was all going so well!"

He tapped the controls on the side of his glasses.

"Merlin? Merlin?" No response. "Shit! Comms have gone dark." He turned to Tilde. "Sorry, but something terrible's—" He didn't want to say anything further, as if by doing so, he'd make it real. "Stay here, it's *safe*. Babe, I have to go."

Her expression softened, and she put her arms around him. At first he tried to pull away, but then he hugged her back tightly.

Chapter Four

———— ◉ ————

Poppy—her hair in a ponytail and wearing a short-sleeved yellow bowling shirt and black trousers—lifted her ball, eyed the pins at the end of the lane, and started her approach. She took several smooth steps forward, curved her body to the side, and threw the ball. It rolled down the lane fast and true, and with a sound that she thought was not unlike a missile explosion, knocked all the pins down. Strike! She wasn't all that thrilled with her achievement, though. She was used to throwing strikes. She'd gotten damn good at it given all the time she had to practice.

She turned around to see Charlie, who stood close by, applaud her strike by pounding his hand against his chest. She smiled in acknowledgement, and then turned to look at the large-screen TV in the corner, which was silently playing a news channel. The on-screen ticker read: SUSPECTED TERRORIST ATTACK IN LONDON.

She grinned. "Kingsman is crumpets! Like toast? But British. Get it?"

"That's actually quite a good joke."

Charlie chuckled, but Poppy could tell he did so only to be polite. She decided not to make an issue of it. That joke *had* been kind of lame now that she thought about it. As the pinsetter got a new batch of pins ready, Charlie walked over to the ball return and lifted his ball one-handed. He'd actually been doing fairly well with just the one arm. His balance was a bit off, and of course he was nowhere near as skilled a bowler as she was, but overall she was impressed.

Poppy moved back to give Charlie room, and he stepped up to the lane.

"Just wish I'd had a second chance at killing Eggy myself," he said.

"Aw c'mon, Charlie. Look on the sunny side. He's dead along with the rest of them. And *you* dodged any chance of failing again and becoming part of my next recipe."

Charlie had begun his approach as Poppy spoke, but upon hearing her say *recipe*, he stumbled and threw a gutter ball.

Poppy laughed. "You're such a nervous Nellie! You really think I'd go to the trouble of finding you, recruiting you as my intelligence consultant, and then *cooking you* before my project's even *started*?"

Charlie walked back to join her. "Can I be honest? Yes. Maybe? I mean, you mainly seemed interested in mining my knowledge about where Valentine went wrong. And now that Kingsman is out of the way…"

Poppy made a pouty face to show Charlie that she was disappointed in how little faith he had in her. She walked over to the benches, reached beneath one, and pulled out a large golden box. Charlie gave a little squeal and flinched, as if he thought the box was some sort of weapon that Poppy intended to use on him. Poppy walked back to him, and although he cringed a bit as she approached, he didn't move away.

"Then how about asking yourself: if I didn't plan to keep you on, why would I have got you… *this*!"

Poppy removed the box's lid in a grand gesture and hurled it away. Inside, packed in molded foam rubber, was a new robotic arm. But this was a huge upgrade from his last one. It was larger, sturdier, and equipped with all kinds of deadly-looking accessories. Poppy almost wished she was missing an arm too so she could use it. Charlie's eyes widened as he took in the prosthesis, and he slowly smiled.

"You like?" Poppy asked. "My guys made it just for you. Bigger, better, and badder. I call it… ARMageddon!"

Poppy laughed at her joke—one of her best, she thought—and Charlie chuckled again, this time sounding more genuine. He removed the arm from the box and affixed it to his stump with a *click*. The arm whirred to life, and Charlie flexed it and wiggled the fingers.

"Let's see if your game improves," Poppy said.

Charlie's ball emerged from the ball return. He walked over to retrieve it, lifting it with his new arm as if it weighed nothing. Then he stepped up to the lane without making an approach, pulled his arm back, and hurled the ball toward the pins. The ball flew through the air as if shot out of a cannon, shattered the pins to pieces and smashed through the back wall, making a hole large enough to see the jungle foliage outside.

Charlie turned to Poppy and grinned.

Eggsy—his steamer trunk sitting on the ground next to him—stood in the street outside where the tailor shop had been since 1849, long before Kingsman established headquarters there. The entire building had been reduced to rubble, and he could see through to the street on the other side. It was raining, and he stood beneath his open umbrella. He still wore the red velvet smoking jacket Tilde had picked out for him, and he knew the rain would likely ruin the fabric, but right then he didn't care. It was a two-and-a-half hour flight from Stockholm to London, but for Eggsy the trip seemed to take an eternity. He'd thought about his friends and colleagues, prayed they were okay, feared they weren't. He'd thought of Tilde and the massive cock-up he'd made of dinner with her parents and vowed to make it up to her when he could. Once he was back in town, he'd caught a cab—a regular one—and gone straight to the house to find it in a similar state of destruction. He'd taken the cab to Roxy's apartment building and saw it too was destroyed, along with *all* the residents, not just her, and then he'd come here. He'd paid the driver and sent him on his way after that. He had nowhere else to go.

On the parallel street, a silhouette of a man came into view, open umbrella in one hand, a canvas bag in the other. He stopped when he saw Eggsy and looked at him a moment before speaking in a familiar Scottish accent.

"Galahad?"

Eggsy lowered his umbrella and thumbed the switch on the handle to activate weapons mode. The bulletproof umbrella flared open and the inner AR display came online. Eggsy pointed the umbrella, which was capable of stunning or killing an opponent depending on the holder's wishes, at Merlin. Eggsy had the device set to kill.

He spoke loudly so Merlin could hear him over the rain:

"Someone decided to wipe out every Kingsman property, every agent, even the trainees... And *you* conveniently weren't home."

Merlin paused a moment before answering. "I could say the same thing to you."

Fury gripped Eggsy. "You think I'd kill Roxy? And my mate Brandon? And my fucking *dog*?"

"No," Merlin said calmly. "Do you think *I* would?"

The two men stared at each other for several moments. Finally, Eggsy deactivated weapons mode, and his umbrella became a device solely for keeping rain off one's person. He raised it over his head—not that it mattered much now, given how soaked he was—and picked his way through the rubble to join Merlin.

When Eggsy had reached him, Merlin reached into the canvas bag and removed the robotic arm that Charlie had left behind in the cab when he'd tried to kill Eggsy.

"This fucking thing hacked us," Merlin said. "Never seen technology like it. Clearly it can be remote controlled. I'm only alive because my address isn't on the same database as the agents'. Apparently whoever Charlie's working with doesn't consider mere 'staff' missile-worthy."

Merlin's joke struck Eggsy as wildly inappropriate given the circumstances.

"That ain't funny. Everyone's gone. Dead. Do you even care?"

Merlin bristled for a moment, but then a deep calm settled over him. "Pull yourself together. Remember your training. There's no time for emotion in this scenario. Now that all surviving agents are present, we follow the doomsday protocol. When that's done *then* you may shed a tear in private."

Eggsy nodded. Merlin, as usual, was right. They had a job to do, and they'd best get to it. It was what their fallen comrades would've wanted.

"Okay. What's the doomsday protocol?"

"We go shopping."

Eggsy and Merlin entered a quaint old shop called Berry Bros. and Rudd: Wine Merchants. Bottles of wine were arranged on shelves, displayed atop barrels, and the shop was lit with soft light intended to suggest candlelight. The place smelled of ancient, musty wood, and Eggsy wouldn't have been surprised if it was even older than the tailor shop had been.

A man in a suit was arranging bottles on one of

the shelves, turning them so their labels were perfectly aligned. *OCD much?* Eggsy thought. Merlin headed straight toward the man.

"We're from Kingsman," he said. "Here to use the tasting room, please."

The man turned to look at them, glancing at a grandfather clock in one corner.

"This early in the morning?"

Merlin and Eggsy had been up all night inventorying the assets that remained to Kingsman. Unfortunately, there weren't many. A couple offsite weapons caches that hadn't been used for years and were in desperate need of restocking, and several vehicles—none technologically enhanced—stowed in various garages throughout the city. And that was about the sum of it.

"Or late in the evening," Eggsy said.

At first the man seemed at a loss for words, but then he composed himself.

"Follow me, gentlemen."

The tasting room was located in the cellar. It was long and narrow, with stone walls, brick floor, mahogany wine racks filled with bottles, and a large table with numerous chairs beneath a metal chandelier. Normally the man would've remained to pour for them, but he said Kingsman had a standing account with their shop—a very lucrative one—that came with the stipulation that anyone affiliated with their organization could conduct their own tasting in private whenever they wished. It was an unusual request, but one with which they were happy to comply.

He smiled, then left, closing the door behind him. Merlin lost no time. He began searching the cellar, running his hands over bottles, shelves, the wall...

"None of my predecessors has ever found himself in this situation," Merlin said as he continued searching and Eggsy watched, perplexed. Then Merlin stopped, as though he had found what he was looking for.

Embedded in the stone near one of the racks, so small that it was barely noticeable, was the Kingsman logo. Merlin pried it loose and held it out for Eggsy to inspect.

"Remember this?"

It was a Kingsman pin, just like the one Harry had left with Eggsy's mother after his father died.

"How can I forget?" Eggsy said.

Merlin returned the pin to its place in the wall and pressed hard, at the same time giving it a turn. A rectangular panel of stone slid upward, revealing a black iron safe with a combination lock.

"Whatever's in this safe is meant to be the answer to all our problems," Merlin said.

Merlin began working the combination. No biometrics here. A few seconds later, the lock disengaged and Merlin pulled the door open to reveal an old bottle of liquor. Whiskey, to be precise, with a label that read "Statesman". It was a brand Eggsy had never heard of. There was nothing else in the safe.

Merlin stood looking at the whiskey for a long moment before speaking. "I suppose that's… upper-class humor. I never really did get it." He sounded disappointed and lost. Eggsy knew exactly how he felt.

"Me neither, mate. What the fuck are we supposed to do now?"

Merlin didn't answer at first, but when he did, his voice was strong and determined.

"We toast to our fallen comrades."

Merlin removed the bottle, carried it to the table, and opened it. There was a small side table containing glasses of various kinds, and Eggsy selected two tumblers and brought them over for Merlin to fill. They stood and lifted their glasses.

Eggsy made the first toast. "To Roxy."

They drained their glasses, and Merlin refilled them.

"To Arthur," Merlin said, and they drank again.

"For Brandon," Eggsy said after another refill. They drank, and then he added, "Should we do one for JB?"

"I think we should," Merlin said.

Merlin refilled their glasses, and they toasted again. And again. And again, until—sooner than Eggsy expected—the bottle was nearly empty. By this point, Merlin was hunched over the table crying, his sweater and glasses off, tie loosened. Eggsy—jacket off and tie loosened as well—patted him on the back, attempting to comfort him.

"I should have seen it. Charlie… the taxi… the arm… This is all my fault."

Eggsy's thoughts were clouded by an alcoholic haze, but he knew Merlin was being too hard on himself.

"Bullshit, Merlin. It ain't. You're the *best*, bruv. If you weren't here, I'd have lost it."

Cheered a bit, Merlin said, "I think we should drink to Scotland."

"Fried chicken?" Eggsy suggested. "I love fried chicken."

"No," Merlin said. "Country music. I fucking *love* country music." He began singing John Denver's "Take Me Home, Country Roads" and reached for the bottle, but Eggsy moved it away before he could get hold of it.

"I think you've had enough," Eggsy said. He glanced down at the bottle, debating whether he should finish off the dregs so Merlin couldn't. As he considered, he noticed the label on the back of the bottle: "Distilled in Kentucky." He looked away, but a sudden realization hit him, and he did a double-take. The K in "Kentucky" had a circle around it, just like the Kingsman logo.

Eggsy grinned. He'd been in the spy business long enough to recognize a coded message when he saw one.

"Merlin, I think we're going to Kentucky."

Kentucky, USA

———— ✖ ————

Eggsy had never been to a distillery before, but as he and Merlin pulled up in a rented car—Merlin at the wheel because Eggsy had no experience driving on the wrong side of the road—it was impossible not to know they were in the right place. For looming over all the other buildings was one constructed in the shape of a gigantic Statesman whiskey bottle, resembling the one from the tasting room at Berry Bros. and Rudd. The other buildings were nothing special—box-like utilitarian structures—but the grounds were beautifully landscaped with elm and birch trees, and the entire facility lay on the banks of the Kentucky River. It was quite a lovely place for what essentially was a factory that made a product people used to get shit-faced.

The lot in front of the main building was nearly full, and they had trouble finding a space. According to the distillery's website, tours ran daily, and evidently they were quite popular. They parked, went inside, and paid a fee to join the next tour. Eggsy had considered wearing civvies for this visit, but since they had no idea what they were heading into, he'd donned his Kingsman suit and eyeglasses, and he carried an agent's preferred sidearm: a modified Tokarev TT30 pistol. He imagined Harry voicing approval. *A good agent is prepared for anything at all times.* Merlin wore his usual outfit—military sweater and slacks—but he also wore a pair of Kingsman eyeglasses.

As the tour commenced, several tourists snuck curious glances at Eggsy. He supposed he *was* dressed a bit formally for the occasion, but they soon forgot about him as their guide led them through the Statesman facilities, keeping up a lively spiel as they went. The woman wore a blue polo shirt with the Statesman logo on it, and she spoke with a silky southern drawl that Eggsy found charming.

"Now, some believe 'bourbon' refers to Bourbon County, or the Bourbon dynasty of old-time France. But truth be told, folks just liked the name because it sounded classy."

Several of the group chuckled. Eggsy and Merlin hung back at the rear of the crowd, pretending to pay close attention to what their guide was saying, but in reality they were looking for any indication that this place was more than it appeared to be on the surface. She took them to Grain Receiving, the Mash House, the Dry House, and the Main Bottling Hall. As they continued toward what for many of the tourists was their *real* destination—the gift shop—they passed an extremely, almost absurdly, hi-tech security door.

"Through here is where we leave the casks to age," she said. "Unfortunately, we can't go in, as it's a temperature-controlled environment."

She smiled apologetically and continued down the hall, the group following her obediently. All except Eggsy and Merlin, who hung back to check out the door. It was the first thing they'd seen that didn't appear to belong with the rest of the distillery, and it was worth a closer look. There was a security panel next to the door, and Eggsy recognized some of the equipment.

"Biometric retina scanner just to protect some old barrels of whiskey?" he said. "Pull the other one, love."

Merlin had brought his computer tablet with him. He opened a program, entered several commands, and a second later there was a loud *clunk* as the door's locking mechanism disengaged. The door opened, and Eggsy and Merlin hurried inside—

—only to find a cavernous hall filled with barrels, just as the tour guide had said.

Merlin looked around the room, using his eyeglasses' sensors to scan the area. When he looked down, he said, "Hang on. There's a huge underground structure beneath us."

Merlin looked around some more. His gaze fastened on a particular barrel, next to which a large cooper's mallet was propped against the wall.

"I think this is the way in." He stepped over to the mallet, picked it up, positioned himself in front of the barrel, and swung at it with all his strength. The wood split, and a stream of whiskey jetted out.

"Fucking hell," Merlin muttered. He dropped the hammer and pressed his hand against the leak, sealing it temporarily, like the Little Dutch Boy. *Little Scotch Boy, more like*, Eggsy thought.

"Shame it's not scotch," Merlin said.

Eggsy was debating how they could seal the leak for good—or at least long enough for them to get out of here—when a voice came from nearby.

"My momma always told me the British gave us southerners our good manners."

Eggsy and Merlin turned to see a man in his thirties dressed like a true all-American male: camel-colored cowboy hat, denim jacket, denim jeans, crisp white shirt, cowboy boots, and the crowning touch: a silver flask belt buckle. But the man's outfit didn't concern Eggsy as much as the shotgun he was aiming at them.

He had a mouthful of chewing tobacco, and he turned his head and spit some excess saliva onto the floor. He looked at the pool of spilled whiskey and then turned to face them again.

"Ain't that a pity," he said. "You didn't keep any for yourselves."

"Actually, we had an invitation," Eggsy said. "In the shape of a bottle. We're from the Kingsman tailor shop in London. Maybe you've heard of us?"

"Kingsman, huh? Y'all look damn sharp. Did they make that fine suit and those fancy eyeglasses?"

"Yeah," Eggsy said.

"And do you think it's normal for a tailor to hack through an advanced biometric security system? That dog don't hunt." He spun the shotgun around to cock it. "Get on your knees—and tell me who you *really* work for."

"He just did," Merlin said. "Look, why don't you lower the gun and we can talk."

"Cut the crap and do as I say."

Merlin shrugged, removed his hand from the broken barrel, and a stream of whiskey jetted out at the cowboy. He pulled his head back, then thrust it forward, spitting a large wad of tobacco as if he were a cobra spitting venom. The tobacco splattered onto the hole in the cask, instantly sealing it.

"That's 1963 Statesman reserve," the cowboy said. "You just made it personal."

Eggsy and Merlin moved in to attack. The cowboy wielded his shotgun like a staff, blocking their blows. He rammed the shotgun's butt into Merlin's stomach, and then he grabbed hold of the Scotsman's arm and threw him toward one of the casks. Merlin's head smacked against wood, and he staggered back several steps before falling to the floor, unconscious. Eggsy leveled his gun at the cowboy, but the man swung his shotgun and knocked the pistol out of Eggsy's hand. As the weapon hit the floor and skidded away, the cowboy slammed his gun butt into Eggsy's side.

Eggsy stepped back and raised the arm on which he wore his Kingsman watch. The cowboy looked amused.

"You think you're gonna stop me with nothing but a little bitty watch on?"

The cowboy spun behind Eggsy and slammed the gun butt into his back, driving him toward one of the casks. The man ran up behind him and shoved him hard against the wood. He held his shotgun in one hand while he grabbed Eggsy's wrist with the other. Before Eggsy could react, the man pressed a button, and the watch—which was aimed at Eggsy's neck—fired a tranquilizer dart. And then everything went black.

Eggsy woke, and the first thing he did before he was fully conscious was try to raise his gun and fire. But not only was he not holding a gun, he couldn't move, and an instant later he realized why. He was tied to a chair, bound so tightly he could barely breathe, let alone move.

He glanced to the side and saw Merlin, also tied to a chair, begin to come around.

The cowboy stood several feet away, arms crossed. He no longer carried his shotgun, but he wore a sidearm on his belt. Eggsy saw that they were in a stark interrogation chamber: concrete walls and floor, harsh lighting, and an opaque window on the other side of the room. Eggsy assumed it was an observation window, and someone was on the other side, watching. Behind the cowboy was a wooden table atop of which rested a bottle of Statesman whiskey.

The cowboy asked Eggsy to explain how he and Merlin had ended up at Statesman distillery, and Eggsy began to groggily explain.

When Eggsy finished, the cowboy said, "A bottle. In a secret vault. You expect me to take that seriously?" He considered. "Know what I think? I think your story is a load of horseshit to cover up your failed rescue mission. I think you boys are here for the lepidopterist."

Eggsy and Merlin were both fully awake now, and they exchanged confused looks. They had no idea what this crazy American was going on about.

The cowboy went to the table, picked up the bottle of whiskey, and walked over to Eggsy and Merlin. He held the whiskey closer so they could inspect it.

"Your mystery bottle look like this?" he asked.

Eggsy nodded. "Same brand. But much older."

The cowboy smiled. He removed the cap from the bottle and tucked it in his pocket. He then stepped forward and poured half the bottle's contents over Eggsy.

Eggsy closed his eyes to keep the alcohol out of them, and he sputtered as liquor ran into his mouth.

"Do you know why the measurement of alcohol content is called 'proof?'" the cowboy asked. He stepped over to Merlin and emptied the rest of the bottle onto him, continuing to talk the entire time. "It goes back to the old days when pirates wanted to test the strength of their rum. They used to pour it on gunpowder."

There was one last swallow left in the bottle, and the cowboy drank it. He sighed in satisfaction. "That'll make you slap yo momma. So. If the gunpowder still burnt when it was set alight, they considered it 'proof' that the rum was good 'n' strong. I don't have me any gunpowder." He removed a butane lighter from his pocket. "But I'm sure you boys will make a loud sound when I set your balls on fire. Or... you can tell me who you *really* are and how the hell you found us."

Merlin's face darkened with anger. "For the last time: we have nothing left to protect but our honor. So you can take your cheap horse piss that you call whiskey— which, by the way, is spelled *without* the 'e' and is nothing compared to a single malt Scotch—and go fuck yourself."

The cowboy looked at Merlin for a moment. He then turned to Eggsy and flipped open his lighter.

"How about you?" he asked.

Eggsy didn't particularly relish the idea of being set on fire, but after losing Roxy, Brandon, JB, and the rest of the Kingsman agents, he was in no mood to put up with the cowboy's shit any longer.

"Nah. I love a Jack and Coke, mate. But I do agree with the part where you go fuck yourself."

The cowboy looked at them both for a moment, his expression unreadable. Then he clicked his lighter shut.

"Nothing to protect but your honor, huh?" he said. "Let's see what happens if we change that up."

He slipped the lighter back in his pocket, walked over to the desk and put the empty bottle down, before continuing to the window. He flipped a switch on a panel next to the window, and the glass became clear, revealing not someone observing them, as Eggsy had expected, but a middle-aged man wearing a gray tracksuit and an eyepatch. It was a small room with a cot, toilet, mirror, and sink. The man stood at the sink, looking into the mirror as he shaved. The walls of the room were decorated with hand-drawn pictures of colorful butterflies, hundreds of them, all different types.

The man was Harry Hart.

Eggsy and Merlin reacted at the same time. "What the *fuck*?" they said in unison.

The cowboy drew his gun and aimed it at Harry through the glass. "Look at him. Smiling like a dead pig in the sunshine. You have three seconds to tell me the truth," he said. "One…"

"Harry!" Eggsy shouted.

"He can't hear you," the cowboy said. "But *I* can. So talk. Two…"

Eggsy was about to shout Harry's name again, when a woman's voice called out, "Stop!"

The three men turned to see that the door to the interrogation chamber was open, and a beautiful African-American woman in her forties had stepped inside. She wore a black vest over a white blouse, black slacks, and a bolo tie made from a thin black ribbon. She wore glasses and her hair was styled in a shaggy bob cut. What's more, she was holding an umbrella. She threw the umbrella to the cowboy who caught it easily with his free hand.

"Little late for this, Ginger," he said. "They're already wetter than a duck's pussy."

"Their story checks out," she said. "I just opened *our* doomsday scenario locker. This umbrella was in it. Kingsman brand. And it has *our* logo on it."

Eggsy could just make out a letter S inside a square stamped on the umbrella's handle.

The cowboy examined it for a moment, then he holstered his gun, and put the umbrella on the table. He walked over to Eggsy and began to untie him, while Ginger did the same for Merlin.

"Apologies, boys," the cowboy said. "No hard feelings, I hope. Just doing my job. Welcome to Statesman. Independent intelligence agency. Just like you, I guess. Only our founders went into the booze business, thank the sweet lord above. This is Ginger Ale, our strategy executive. And I'm Agent Tequila."

The cowboy extended his hand for Eggsy to shake, which he did, but he couldn't take his eyes off Harry.

"Now we know why we never found his body," Merlin said, sounding as dumbfounded as Eggsy felt.

Eggsy continued shaking Tequila's hand without being aware he was doing so.

"How is he alive? Why didn't you let him contact us?"

"Your momma never tell you it's polite to look someone in the eye when you shake hands, boy?"

Eggsy released Tequila's hand. Ginger gestured for Eggsy and Merlin to follow her. She led them out of the interrogation room into the hallway beyond, Tequila bringing up the rear. She stopped at a door with a biometric lock and pressed her palm to the panel. An instant later, the door unlocked and she opened it to reveal Harry, still shaving at the sink in his cell.

Eggsy and Merlin rushed inside. Ginger and Tequila remained in the doorway, watching.

"Harry!" Eggsy shouted, confused but overjoyed to see his mentor alive.

Harry turned toward Eggsy and smiled. Eggsy ran over to give him a hug, but Harry recoiled and stiffly stuck out his hand.

"How do you do?" he said, then added, frowning, "Have we met before?"

For a second Eggsy was taken aback, but then he understood what was happening. Harry, ever the professional, was pretending not to know him and Merlin so he wouldn't blow their cover.

"Harry," Eggsy said, "they know we know you."

Harry lowered his hand. He looked at Merlin, then at Ginger and Tequila, and then back to Eggsy, an expression of confusion on his face.

"I think there must be some mistake," he said.

Eggsy turned to Merlin and gave him a questioning look. Merlin stepped forward to join the two of them, and he began speaking slowly and softly.

"Harry—it's been a long time and my brogues need to be resoled."

Eggsy understood what Merlin was doing, and he joined in. "Yeah, my Oxfords are done in too."

Harry looked at them both as if they were insane. "Why are you... telling me about your shoes? I'm a lepidopterist."

Eggsy frowned. "A what now?"

Harry smiled. "I study butterflies."

A cold chill rippled up and down Eggsy's spine. "You... wanted to when you were a child. Harry, look at me..."

Harry did, and Eggsy saw no recognition in his eyes whatsoever. Harry wasn't acting. He genuinely had no idea who they were.

Eggsy and Merlin said goodbye and stepped back into the hallway. Ginger left the door to Harry's cell open, and they spoke softly so he couldn't overhear. Harry seemed completely uninterested in them, though. He returned to shaving, humming to himself as he worked.

"What's wrong with him?" Eggsy asked, the question coming out more as an accusation.

"I think you mean, 'Thanks for saving my buddy's life,'" Tequila said, irritated.

"He has retrograde amnesia," Ginger explained, her

voice kind. "We knew from his eyeglasses that he worked for an intelligence agency. We just didn't know whose. I hope you understand why we had to keep him."

Eggsy felt as if he were on the verge of exploding. Harry, his friend and mentor, was alive! Just when he and Merlin needed him most—but he had fucking *amnesia*? Eggsy's emotional distress must've been evident, for Merlin put a hand on his shoulder to calm him.

"How did he get here?" Merlin asked.

and Ginger rode the elevator platform up, and rushed outside to where a helicopter was fueled and waiting for them. They got in, and Ginger—computer tablet in hand—navigated for the pilot. While the aircraft looked no different to any standard commercial helicopter, it was outfitted with a number of concealed hi-tech augmentations, and the miles literally and figuratively flew past as the two agents tracked the ELFs.

Eventually, Ginger pointed and said, "Down there!"

They were approaching a white building with a steeple, and Ginger recognized it as the South Glade Mission Church. She groaned inwardly. *Not these guys*, she thought. Having to deal with bigoted assholes like these could ruin a woman's whole day. Still, whatever was going on here, they had to check it out. The pilot landed the helicopter as close to the church as he could, and Ginger and Tequila disembarked. The moment their feet were on the ground, the pilot lifted off. He'd return to pick them up when they called for him.

The first thing Ginger noticed was how quiet and still it was. The helicopter had made a lot of noise, but even though there were a number of cars in the parking lot—enough to indicate the church should be full—no one had come out to see what was happening. The second thing she noticed was a well-dressed man lying on the ground in front of the church's entrance. As they drew closer to the man, they began to run. His left eye was gone, in its place a crimson ruin, and a pair of broken eyeglasses lay in the dirt nearby. The left lens was shattered, and Ginger understood what had happened. The man had been shot, the bullet having passed through the left lens of his glasses, and whoever had done the deed had walked away, leaving him for dead. But was he?

Ginger rushed over, knelt by the man's side, and placed her fingers to his neck.

With no time to lose, Tequila removed his hat and handed it to Ginger.

"Use my alpha gel," he said.

Ginger nodded, reached into the hat, and removed a concealed gel pad. As she applied the gel to the man's head—making sure to put a good amount into his ravaged eye socket—Tequila ran back to the copter to get a stabilizer unit. Ginger watched the nanites in the gel activate and start to move about as they prepared to begin their work. Tequila returned with the stabilizer unit, an electronic device roughly the size of a portable defibrillator, and put it on the ground next to the injured man. She removed a pair of probes that were attached to the device by thin black wires and inserted them into the gel. Nanites swarmed around the base of the probes to keep them steady, and Ginger activated the stabilizer. The nanite-infused gel swelled up to cover the man's head, leaving his nose and mouth free so he could breathe.

Tequila looked on grimly and then nodded silently to himself. He drew his sidearm and stepped into the church.

Eggsy and Merlin didn't need to guess what Tequila found inside.

Eggsy had seen it through Harry's glasses. It was an absolute massacre. Harry was responsible for most of it. Valentine had been testing his aggression signal on those in the church, while Harry was there, investigating. Everyone had turned into a homicidal maniac and started trying to kill each other. Eggsy didn't want to think of how Harry was that day: a merciless, highly efficient, almost inhuman killing machine. Those god-bothering bastards had never stood a chance. When the test was over, Harry came back to his senses, but Valentine shot him.

"We developed the alpha gel technology for our own agents, in the event of a headshot," Ginger said. "It's... miraculous. But it has to be applied almost immediately."

"I'm impressed," Merlin said, taking a step closer to Ginger. "I experimented with alpha wave technology but found it was too volatile. And—" he glanced through the doorway at Harry, who had finished shaving and was applying aftershave with gentle pats of his hands— "potentially damaging to the brain." He looked at Ginger again and smiled. "Still, you have our deep gratitude. Do you have his medical records? I'd like to take a look."

A clipboard hung on a hook by the door. Ginger removed it and handed it to Merlin, who immediately began examining the pages.

"You must be my opposite number," she said.

"Indeed." He flipped back and forth through the pages, becoming more excited. "Low velocity round. Clean exit. No damage to the ventricles, brainstem, or thalamus."

"Yup! Just the neural pathways, and we have the

capability to rebuild those. We just need a map. Someone who knew him. So now you're here, in theory, we could do it." She paused and then added, almost shyly, "You could be my GPS."

She smiled, as did Merlin, and Eggsy could've sworn he saw his friend blush a bit.

"Sorry to bust your tech-nerd love bubble here," Tequila said, "but, Ginger—you don't have time to waste fixing up vegetables for fun. You'd need Champ to authorize it."

Eggsy bristled at Tequila's use of the word "vegetable" to describe Harry.

"Who's Champ? Your boss? I wanna talk to him."

Tequila locked eyes with Eggsy and held his gaze a moment before replying.

"Well, ain't you luckier than a puppy with two peters?" he drawled. "He wants to talk to you too."

Poppy, hair down and wearing a long-sleeved flower-print dress, sat in the fifth row of her Vegas-style concert hall, facing the stage. Her chair—large, golden, and *very* plush—was one of only two VIP chairs in the place. The hall was a huge arena-style auditorium, with a gigantic crystal chandelier hanging from the ceiling and a pair of video screens one hundred feet tall on either side of the stage. The gaudy orange curtains were closed, and Poppy was waiting impatiently for the show to begin. As far as she was concerned, the fifth row was the perfect place to watch a performance. Any farther back, and you couldn't see the performers' faces; any closer, and you risked having their sweat flung onto you.

She heard an awkward shuffling coming down the aisle toward her, and she turned to see Charlie approaching. He wore a heavy suit of green body armor and carried a helmet with a transparent face guard beneath his new arm.

"You're late," she said. She glanced at his outfit. "And why on earth are you still wearing *that*?"

Charlie sat in the VIP chair next to hers and tucked his helmet under his seat.

"Until you get rid of the perimeter landmines, I'll keep wearing the suit, thank you very much."

"Ooh, thank you! Reminds me, I forgot to move them this morning. I'd hate for anybody to get too comfortable about visiting."

She removed a tablet computer from her purse. On the screen was a map of her compound. Numerous dots around the perimeter showed the position of landmines. She tapped a button labeled RANDOM RESET and watched as the dots began to move. She imagined the hi-tech mines burrowing beneath the surface like mechanical moles as they traveled to their new positions and settled.

Satisfied, Poppy put the tablet away. The lights in the hall turned off. The show was about to start—finally!

The curtains pulled back to reveal a grand piano resting atop a white dais, and sitting at the keyboard was a grumpy-looking blond-haired man in his late sixties, wearing a gaudy red-feathered shirt and a pair of literally rose-colored glasses.

"'Crocodile Rock,' please!" Charlie called out.

"Fuck you," said Elton John.

Elton's legs were held to the piano bench—the *metal* bench—by padlocked leather straps. Poppy reached into the purse sitting on the seat next to her and pulled out a small remote control device. She pointed it at the stage and pressed a button. Elton's teeth slammed together and his body convulsed as the bench sent an electric charge surging through him. Poppy kept the electricity going for several seconds before she pushed the button again and turned it off. Elton slumped forward, breathing harshly, but still conscious.

"Now, now," Poppy chided. "Language, Sir Elton. Anyway, fabulous as your catalogue is, *I* feel like a bit of Gershwin right now."

He looked toward her, and when he didn't respond right away, Poppy pointed the remote at him once more. He sighed deeply, turned to the piano, and began to play "Rhapsody in Blue."

"I still can't believe you got away with kidnapping Elton John!" Charlie said.

"I know! But with Valentine abducting all those celebrities, it seemed silly not to take advantage of the confusion."

The two settled back and enjoyed the music. After a while, Charlie frowned and leaned his head closer to Poppy's.

"Is Elton… okay?" he asked. "What's that rash?"

Poppy squinted, but she couldn't see what Charlie was talking about. She removed her glasses from her purse and put them on. Once she did, her vision sharpened and she saw tiny blue dots speckling Elton's neck and the backs of his hands.

"Lights!" she called out. The auditorium's automated systems—programmed to obey only her voice—did as she commanded, and the lights came up. As soon as they did, Elton stopped playing.

"Elton! Did you get out of your cell again?"

He shook his head.

"You're lying," she said. "You took something. Look at your hands."

Elton looked at his palms, and when he didn't see anything wrong, he turned his hands over to examine the backs. His eyes widened with fear when he saw the blue spots there.

"What is it?" he said.

"Proof that my plan is going to work," Poppy said. "And also the first sign of a slow, horrible death."

Elton went pale, and Poppy hurried to continue. "But don't worry. I can take care of it. On two conditions. First: you tell me who you partied with."

Elton sighed. "It was the guy who brought my food. I wouldn't usually but... I was depressed," he added defensively, and then pursed his lips. "Unsurprisingly."

"Huh," Poppy said. "Not very angelic. Gonna have to clip his wings. And as for the second condition..."

She stood, moved past Charlie, and walked down the aisle. Elton groaned as she used a small set of side steps to ascend to the stage and went over to join him on the dais.

"Really?" he asked.

Poppy grinned. "Uh-huh. And this time, honey, you're gonna do it like you *mean* it."

Elton placed his fingers on the keyboard and grudgingly began to play.

Poppy sang. "Don't go breakin' my heart…"

Looking as if he were hoping the Angel of Death would take him right then and there, Elton joined in.

Tequila showed Eggsy to quarters where he could shower, and he had his clothes cleaned, pressed, and returned within short order. Merlin stayed to consult with Ginger, and Tequila took Eggsy to see Statesman's leader, whose office it seemed was inside the whiskey bottle-shaped building. Tequila led him through a secret compartment in one of the barrels and down a short hallway until they came to an elevator. They rode it upward, got out, and walked toward a door at the end of another short hallway. Tequila knocked, and a gruff but not unkind voice called for them to come in.

They entered a large office where a man in his late sixties with silver hair and a hard-bitten face that made him look as if he'd just been magically transported from the Old West sat behind an antique desk. Like Tequila, he was dressed in western chic, but, unlike the agent, on him it looked natural. He wore a cowboy hat, a brown suit jacket, a gray vest, a white shirt with the collar open, and a kerchief around his neck in place of a tie. Jeans and brown cowboy boots completed his look, and for good measure he wore a gold S pin on his jacket lapel. Eggsy wouldn't have been surprised if the man had been wearing a pair of six-guns on his belt.

There was a laptop computer on the desk and a digital stock ticker display on the wall behind it, but they were the only tech visible. There was an antique lamp on the desk and an equally antique mirror hanging on the wall, and several wooden chairs were placed in front of the desk. The room was decorated with framed paintings of serious-looking men wearing nineteenth-century suits. Statesman's founders, Eggsy assumed. Shelves lined the walls, and on them bottles of whiskey and numerous trophies were displayed. Eggsy wasn't sure what the trophies were for. Liquor competitions of some sort?

And the crowning touch: a bottle of whiskey and several tumblers sitting on a silver tray on the desk in front of him, and next to them a wooden cigar box.

Now that's class, Eggsy thought.

The office's most impressive feature was a large boardroom table surrounded by leather chairs. An intricate carving had been worked into the center of the table—a miniature version of the distillery enclosed with the Statesman logo. It was more... *ostentatious* than the dining table in Kingsman's meeting room, but Eggsy had to admit it didn't lack for style.

The older man looked at Tequila and spoke in a gruff voice. "At what point are you gonna start behaving like a Statesman? You wanna go back to being a rodeo clown?"

"No sir. I apologize, sir."

The older man stood, removed his hat, and tossed it toward a large liquor bottle. The hat landed on the bottle's neck, spun once, and came to rest. He offered his hand, and Eggsy shook it. He had a firm, friendly grip, and an easy smile.

"I'm Champagne, but anyone who knows what's good for 'em calls me Champ." He let go of Eggsy's hand and gestured for him to take one of the chairs. He did, and Tequila took the other.

"Agent Galahad," Eggsy said.

"I know," Champ said. "I've been listening in. And I'm sorry for your troubles. As your American cousins, I'm placing all of Statesman's *considerably larger* resources—" he indicated the screen behind him, upon which a series of numbers and letters incomprehensible to Eggsy scrolled by—"at your disposal." He looked at Tequila. "Hey, Tequila, can you imagine *us* in the clothing business?"

"Sends a shiver down my spine, sir," Tequila deadpanned.

Champ poured the three of them whiskey from the bottle on his table, and then turned his attention to Eggsy. "That said, you boys mentioned it was *you* who saved the world from Valentine. Impressive. We dropped the ball there." He shot Tequila a glance. "And it happened here on our home turf, right under our noses, so maybe we shouldn't poke fun. Kingsman's clearly worth saving. I've given Ginger the go-ahead to rehabilitate your comrade. Now, how else can I help you?"

Eggsy was relieved by Champ's words. Given how his and Merlin's visit to Statesman had started out, he hadn't expected the American spies to end up being so helpful. He took a moment to consider Champ's question.

"Well, Agent Galahad always said—"

Champ frowned. "Wait, I thought *you* were Galahad."

"He means butterfly guy," Tequila said. "Used to be his handle."

Champ nodded his understanding, and Eggsy continued.

"He always said, look at the big picture. Someone wanted Kingsman out of the way. We gotta ask *why* as well as *who*. Chances are, they're planning something major."

"So what do you know?" Champ asked.

"They're a drug cartel, we think," Eggsy said. "The name 'Golden Circle' came up."

"We'll look into them," Champ said. "What else?"

"One of our ex-trainees is working with them," Eggsy said. "Charlie Hesketh. Total prick."

"Got any leads on him?" Champ asked.

Eggsy took his phone out of his pocket, called up a picture of a scruffy, pretty woman, and showed it to Champ.

"His ex-fiancée, Countess Clara Von Glucksberg. Hippy aristocrat. Been tracking her through social media. I believe they're still in contact. And I know where we can find her: she's gonna be at the Glastonbury music festival."

Champ gave a decisive nod. "Good. Agent Tequila: grab your dancing shoes and get to the jet."

Eggsy and Champ turned to look at Tequila and saw his skin was now dotted with a bluish rash.

"Damn," Champ said. "Tequila, you feeling okay?"

He looked puzzled. "Maybe a little tired, sir, but fine. Thanks for asking." He downed his whiskey and placed the tumbler on the desk before turning to Eggsy. "Ready, Galahad?"

"Tequila—your face." Champ sounded worried. "You got a…" He trailed off, at a loss for words.

The agent raised his empty tumbler and examined his reflection in the glass. He gasped when he saw the patches of raised blue skin on his face.

"Go to the sick bay and have Ginger check you out, okay?" Champ said. "And give Eggsy your glasses before you go."

Tequila gave a hasty nod. He removed a pair of wireframe glasses from his shirt pocket and handed them to Eggsy before practically fleeing the room. Whatever was wrong with Tequila, Eggsy hoped Ginger would be able to make him well. "Put 'em on," Champ said, and Eggsy did so. Champ removed a pair of glasses from his desk and donned them as well.

"Your lucky day, kid," Champ said. "You get our finest senior agent joining you instead."

Champ gestured to an empty chair. But with Tequila's glasses, Eggsy saw the holographic image sitting there—a mustached man in his forties dressed all in black: black cowboy hat, black jacket, black tie, black pants, and black boots.

"This is Agent Whiskey," Champ said. "Right now he's in our New York office."

"You can call me Jack," the man said. "As in Jack Daniels." He gave Eggsy a smile. "Looks like we're hooking up with a chick at a rock concert. My favorite kind of mission. I'm sending my jet to pick you up."

"Boys?" Champ said. "You make sure that the only Golden Circle vexing me is the one my glass leaves behind on the table."

In the beauty parlor, Poppy and Charlie sat in sumptuous recliners. Beautybot was giving Poppy a manicure, and they both had their bare feet in glass tanks filled with water. Little *Garra rufa* fish swam around, nibbling away at their dead skin. *Absolute bliss*, Poppy thought. She held a computer tablet, and she was scrolling Twitter, reading tweets aloud.

"'Doc said maybe allergy to laundry detergent, but two of my coworkers have it too! Hashtag blue rash.' 'Wanna bet it's something in the water supply? Another governmental disgrace. Hashtag blue rash.'"

"We have a hashtag now?" Charlie asked.

Poppy smiled as she continued scrolling through tweets. "We're *trending*, Charlie."

Charlie grinned. "It's so refreshing to be working with someone who doesn't think capitalism is a dirty word. Not like that tree-hugger Valentine. We're getting so close now, I can almost *smell* my new fortune."

Poppy stopped scrolling, glanced up from her computer screen, and gave Charlie a dangerous look. "Working *for*, Charlie. Not *with*."

Charlie looked properly chastened, but before he could begin groveling, Angel walked in, flanked by Bennie and Jet.

Poppy beamed at her newest employee. "Ah, Angel. Glad you could join us."

Charlie lifted his feet out of the tank one at a time, then stood and gestured for Angel to take his place. Angel looked at the tank, shrugged, then removed his boots, sat in the recliner, and tentatively slipped his feet into the water. The *Garra rufa* went to work immediately. He stiffened at first, as if he found the sensation of the tiny fish eating his dead skin disquieting.

One of Beautybot's fingers became an airbrush, and she began applying color to Poppy's nails.

"Just wanted to have a catch-up," Poppy said. "See how you're settling in."

Angel squirmed a bit in his chair, but he didn't remove his feet from the tank.

"They tickle, don't they?" Poppy said. "Anyway, I'm hoping that by now you've had a chance to see first-hand how much work goes into running the Golden Circle."

"*Si*, Señora Poppy," Angel smiled at her and some of the tension left his body. The effect the *Garra rufa* had on people was truly remarkable, Poppy thought.

"Great, great. Because I think that will make it easier for you to understand why it's so frustrating for me when someone breaks the rules. It can feel a *li'l bit* like a lack of respect for everything I do. Y'know?"

Beautybot stopped working on Poppy's nails. Her

airbrush attachment slid back into her finger, and she quickly stepped behind Angel, her arms extending until her hands clamped his wrists to the chair. A panel slid open in the bottom of the tank, and from a tube hidden beneath the floor, half a dozen piranhas swam upward, and the predatory fish immediately began devouring the *Garra rufa*.

Poppy leaned closer to Angel. "Did you give Elton John a little something from the cookie jar?"

Sweat broke out on Angel's brow as he struggled to free his arms, but Beautybot was too strong. The piranhas polished off the last of the *Garra rufa*, the tiny fish little more than appetizers for them, and then they started on the main course.

"No, Señora Poppy, I—" Angel screamed in pain as the piranhas took their first bites. He tried to yank his legs out of the tank, but Charlie placed his powerful robotic arm on the man's legs, forcing him to keep his feet in the water.

"It's cute that you felt sorry for him," Poppy said. "But lying… in my book, that's a big, big no-no."

The piranhas went into a feeding frenzy then, the bloody water churning as if it were boiling. Angel screamed again, louder this time.

"Okay! I confess! I confess! I did it! I'm sorry! I'm *sorry*!"

Poppy continued talking calmly. "You can't just go giving people treats, Angel. Especially when you don't know what's in 'em."

Angel shrieked his next words, making them barely intelligible. "Let me go! I beg you! Forgive me!"

Poppy smiled as she reached out and patted one of Angel's knees.

"Of course I forgive you."

She nodded to Charlie, and he lifted his arm off Angel's knees. But before the man could pull his half-eaten feet out of the tank, Charlie's robot hand—moving faster than any human eye could track—took hold of Angel's neck and gave it a swift, savage twist. There was the sound of snapping bone, and Angel's body shuddered and went limp. Charlie released his grip on the dead man's neck, and Beautybot removed her hands from his wrists. Angel's feet remained in the tank, and the piranhas continued to feast. The fish had done good work, and Poppy thought they deserved to eat their fill.

She admired her manicure, which Beautybot had managed to finish before she'd needed to attend to Angel. The manicure was only the finishing touch, however. Poppy had been in the parlor for hours while Beautybot worked her magic on her hair, skin, and eyelashes. She rose from her chair and turned to Charlie.

"How do I look?" she asked.

"Gorgeous," he said, and for once he sounded as if he meant it.

Poppy smiled with satisfaction. "Then go get my director, and tell him I'm ready for my close-up."

Merlin and Ginger were in her lab, running tests on Harry. He was dressed in a hospital gown and lying on a gurney inside an Alpha Wave Stimulator, a contraption that looked something like an MRI machine, only this device was far more sophisticated—and twice as noisy, Merlin thought. Sensor wires were attached by pads to Harry's temples, and Ginger and Merlin watched the incoming data flow across a console screen. But the machine wasn't merely collecting information about Harry's condition; it was actually transmitting signals into his brain in an attempt to repair his damaged neural pathways. The machine was only one of the many amazing pieces of scientific equipment Statesman possessed. Ginger's lab, which resembled a combination medical bay and engineering facility—with a bit of junkyard thrown in—contained tech *way* beyond cutting edge, and while Merlin was impressed, he couldn't help being a wee bit jealous. The things he could accomplish with these toys!

"Harry's like a computer that needs to be rebooted," Ginger said. "We just need to find the right start-up protocol."

"You ever had success with this?" Merlin asked.

"Yes, but… never so long after the injury." Her voice softened. "I just want to be straight with you."

Merlin nodded. No one on earth could've gotten to Harry faster than Ginger and Tequila—and no one else would've had the technology to save him. He knew that, and he was grateful for what they'd done. A miracle had happened today: he'd found out that his old friend was alive! But then he'd learned that only part of Harry had come back, and there was a strong possibility that the remainder was lost forever.

"How's Agent Tequila?" He asked this as much to take his mind off Harry as out of concern for the Statesman agent.

"Blue," Ginger said, "but otherwise fine. Weird thing is, this doesn't seem to be an isolated case of this skin condition. I'm finding reports online from all over."

Merlin didn't like the sound of that. Whatever the blue rash was, it sounded like it was spreading at a phenomenal rate. "We should try and contact other sufferers. If we can find a correlation—"

"It might lead to a cause," Ginger said. "Exactly. Already fired off a bunch of emails. But thanks, Merlin."

He felt embarrassed. Ginger was one of the most brilliant people he'd ever met. Of *course* she'd thought of that. He was trying to come up with a graceful way to apologize when the Alpha Wave Stimulator finished its work and went silent. Merlin and Ginger hurried over to the device and pulled Harry's gurney out of it. Ginger detached the wires, and Harry sat up and rubbed his head.

"Harry?" Merlin said. "Do you remember me?"

Harry looked at Merlin for a moment, his one eye narrowing. Merlin allowed himself a moment of hope, but then Harry dashed it.

"Very sorry, old chap," he said. "I don't think we've met." He grimaced and rubbed his head again. "And I've got the most *wretched* headache. Can I go now?"

Ginger put her hand on Merlin's arm and spoke to him in low, comforting tones. "It's a process. The alpha waves are just part of it. Triggering access to his old memories is the key now."

Merlin nodded and turned back to Harry.

"Harry, I'm Merlin. We were colleagues. *Friends.* You had a brain injury."

Harry smiled vacantly. "Well, that explains my headache. But otherwise, I'm quite fine, I assure you. As Mother always said, nothing should be perfect or one won't appreciate it." He paused, then tilted his head to the side, curious. "Are you a lepidopterist?"

Merlin tried not to let the disappointment he felt show in his voice. "No. I'm sorry."

"Oh. You said we worked together. I assumed you were going to take me away from this awful place." He gave Ginger a scowl, as if he blamed her personally for keeping him here.

"Soon, Harry," Merlin said. "We'll bring you back soon. I promise."

Merlin prayed it was a promise he'd be capable of fulfilling.

40,000 feet above the Atlantic Ocean

Eggsy lined up the shot and tapped the cue ball. It rolled into the eight ball and sank it in one of the corner pockets.

He grinned at Jack. "Six in a row, bro."

They were aboard Statesman's private jet, well on their way to England. The main cabin had plush leather seats, a full bar, and a pool table, upon which Eggsy had been absolutely decimating the American spy.

"You've been spending way too much time in bars, kid."

"Bollocks, I never go to bars." Eggsy paused, then added. "*Pubs*, yes. And we play snooker, not pool. Much harder game. Much bigger table." He glanced around the cabin. "Probably still fit in here, though." He changed the subject. "Tell me something, Jack: why do you think the founders of Kingsman and Statesman never told their agents that there were *two* organizations? Obviously, they knew about each other. So why keep us apart? We could've been working together ever since World War One. Think of all the good we could've accomplished."

"I've been asking myself the same question, Eggsy, and you can bet Champ has been too. Best I can figure it, since both our agencies are independent, we've got no oversight. The good thing about that is no politicians looking over our shoulders or trying to use us to help them get re-elected. The bad thing is there's no one to keep an eye on us and make sure we don't cross the line. The way I see it, our founders intended us to be each *other's* oversight. If one agency went rogue, the other would eventually learn about it and take the necessary steps to shut them down. Kinda hard to do that if you're best buddies, y'know?"

"Makes sense," Eggsy said. "But the founders wanted to make sure we *could* help each other out if things got bad enough."

"Yep. And that's why they came up with the doomsday

scenarios, so we'd have a way to find each other when we had to."

Agent Whiskey—who liked to call himself Jack Daniels—had the same good-ole-boy attitude as Champ and Tequila combined with a no-nonsense professionalism. He exuded the calm confidence of a man who could handle himself in any situation, whether he was sweet-talking a woman or slicing an enemy's throat. He reminded Eggsy of an Old West gunfighter, and he had no doubt Jack was as deadly as any sheriff who'd ever stared down an outlaw in the middle of a dusty street at high noon.

The captain's voice came over the PA. "We'll be landing in sixty minutes, gentlemen."

"Let's get to work," Jack said. They returned their cues to the wall rack, and Jack pressed a button on the side of the table. In response, the tabletop rose upward and flipped over to reveal an impressive display of weapons and gadgets.

Very nice, Eggsy thought. *Nothing like one-stop shopping.*

"Now… gear for tomorrow," Jack said. "Take your pick of defense items, just in case."

"My turn," Eggsy said. "I brought us some clothes."

Jack raised his eyebrows. "Clothes? From *Kingsman*? I'm good, thanks. I don't figure I'm gonna need to dress like a limey stiff."

Eggsy gave him a look and walked over to his steamer trunk, which he'd brought along on the trip. He opened it to reveal an array of casual streetwear.

"We're going to a festival," he said. "We gotta blend in. And I've sorted our tickets too. My contact's staying at a hotel near the festival site, so we can grab 'em on the way."

He smiled. He couldn't wait to see his "contact."

Chapter Six

M erlin stood in Statesman's interrogation room, watching Harry through the two-way mirror. When Jack had questioned Eggsy and him in here, Merlin had assumed someone was on the other side of the mirror watching, but it turned out that all the watching was done from *this* side. Harry was sitting on his bed, quietly reading a book about—what else?—butterflies.

Ginger entered the room carrying a folder. She placed it on the table and opened it. Merlin joined her, and she spread pages out on the table's surface for him to examine as she spoke. Prominent among the material was a photo of a beautiful woman with long red hair and striking green eyes.

"Poppy Adams," Ginger said. "Background in the military. Business degree. Looks like she's our woman: head of the Golden Circle. But she's going to be hard to find—no record of her whereabouts in the last decade." When Merlin didn't respond, she added, "I'll pass this on to the agents."

Merlin remained silent, looking at the material Ginger had brought, none of it really registering with him.

"Merlin," Ginger said, concerned, "you okay?"

He turned to look at her. "No, that's... excellent. Useful. Very good find. Hats off to you." He returned to the window. After a moment Ginger joined him, and they watched Harry read for several minutes.

After a time, Merlin said, "Ginger, I'm not sure about this."

Harry looked so relaxed, so peaceful. He had no idea what was about to happen to him.

"You think we should try a test he's unfamiliar with instead?" she asked. "I mean, we have plenty that you guys don't."

"No. It's not that. It's—"

Ginger cut him off. "I thought we agreed. Not only do we engage the fight-or-flight synapse paths, but it could directly stir memories of his past. His training."

They *had* agreed. The logic was sound, if speculative, but that wasn't the problem. Merlin wasn't certain he could put Harry—*this* Harry, the mild-mannered lepidopterist—through what was coming. He wondered what his Harry would say about this test if Merlin could somehow ask him. Would he agree to it? There was no way to know, so in the end Merlin merely nodded and hoped he wasn't making the wrong decision.

Ginger pressed a button on the control panel next to the window, and it began.

Come on, Harry, Merlin thought. *I know you're in there somewhere.*

At first, Harry wasn't aware of the water coming into

the room. He continued reading as it swiftly covered the floor and began rising, and it wasn't until it flowed above his ankles and began to soak through his tracksuit that he realized something was horribly wrong. He looked around the room in shock as water rushed over his legs, the level continuing to rise past his stomach, up to his chest. He stood on the bed, attempting to keep his head above the water's surface, but the room was filling up so fast, he only delayed the inevitable by a few moments.

"Oh god!" he cried out. "What's happening? Help!"

And then the water rose all the way to the ceiling, completely engulfing Harry and cutting off his oxygen supply. He flailed in the water, panicking, bubbles gushing from his mouth as he continued shouting for help.

Merlin couldn't take this anymore. "Get him out. *Now*."

"Hold up," Ginger said. "His instincts could kick in at any moment…"

Merlin forced himself to watch for several more seconds, but as Harry's exertions began to lessen, Merlin knew that his friend was drowning. He reached past Ginger and slammed the abort button on the wall panel. The water began to quickly drain out of Harry's cell, leaving him lying on the floor, terrified and gasping for breath.

Merlin and Ginger rushed into the cell, and Merlin knelt next to Harry.

"Harry! Are you okay?" he said.

Harry coughed several times before he managed to speak. "What… happened?"

"You've forgotten who you are, Harry," Merlin said. "We hoped... we hoped that this might jog your memory."

"You've done this before," Ginger said, "when you were young. You escaped."

"You used a toilet snorkel," Merlin added.

"I used a *what*?" Harry said, incredulous.

Merlin continued. "To get air. You put the shower tube down the toilet to get air!"

"In our exercise, the subject is just supposed to break the two-way mirror," Ginger said.

Merlin took hold of Harry's arm and gently helped him onto his feet.

"Look, Harry, when you were younger, you had a choice: to either become a lepidopterist or join the army. You chose the army. And that led you to Kingsman. You became a Kingsman agent."

Harry pulled away from Merlin and glared at him indignantly. "I very much doubt that I'd work for anyone who *drowns* their employees. I want to go home. I want to see my butterfly collection."

Merlin exchanged looks with Ginger. This was going to be harder than either of them had thought.

Eggsy and Tilde lay in bed, enjoying a post-coital cuddle. The hotel was a beautiful country house, and the room was decorated in a rustic fashion, with brick walls, wooden floor, thick ceiling beams, and a soft brown duvet on a bed with an old-fashioned metal frame. The box springs were a bit squeaky, but considering the workout the couple had put them through, they'd held up well enough.

Tilde traced circles on Eggsy's chest with her index finger as she spoke. "So I told my parents you lost a friend in the London bombings and that's why you freaked out. I said you got a text. They were totally fine with it. They liked you a lot. *So* much, I thought maybe… we could go house-hunting."

Eggsy would miss living in Harry's house, but it was gone now, and he needed *somewhere* to live. He liked the idea of Tilde and him choosing a place together, having an opportunity to make a home that was truly theirs.

"*Jag alskar dig*," he said in Swedish. *I love you.*

Tilde pulled him close and they kissed.

When they parted, she said, "Oh my god, I missed you so much."

"Likewise," Eggsy smiled.

Tilde gave him a mischievous smile. "You want your present now?"

"I thought getting to see you *was* my present. There ain't anything I want more."

She gave him another quick kiss, climbed out of bed, and walked across the wooden floor to the bathroom. She opened the door and a tiny pug puppy ran out, toenails skittering on the floor.

"Oh my days!" Eggsy said. Delighted, he bent down, and the little dog leaped up to enthusiastically lick his face.

"I know he could never replace JB," Tilde said. "But I hoped he might make you happy." She smiled. "*And* give you another reason to come home soon."

The pug rolled over on his back and Eggsy scratched his tummy.

"I love him." He gave Tilde an adoring smile. "But trust me, darlin'—I never needed another reason."

Eggsy had left his phone on the nightstand, and it buzzed now, indicating he had a text. He stood and walked over to the nightstand to check it out. The text was from Jack—and he was not happy. Eggsy put the phone down and began to pick up his clothes from the floor. They'd been in such a hurry to get in bed that they'd disrobed as fast as possible, and their clothes lay wherever they'd fallen. He began to dress quickly.

"So sorry, babe. Left someone waiting and he's getting pissy."

Tilde sighed in disappointment, but she managed a smile. "Gotta go save the world?"

"Yup. But I'll come back tonight if I can."

Her smile turned seductive. "If you save the world… Well, you know what *that* means."

He did indeed.

Poppy was seated in a black leather chair on the concert hall stage, the lighting on her soft, but not *too* soft. She wore a yellow blouse, black skirt, and glasses. She hoped the combination would strike the balance she was looking for: serious, but with a hint of warmth. It was important to project the right image when making a sales presentation.

She had just finished her latest take, and the director yelled, "Cut!"

The director—a wild-haired bad boy who was as famous for his off-set antics as he was for his films—stood behind a film camera on a tripod, with Charlie sitting next to him in a director's chair.

Poppy looked at the director, nervous. Beside him, Charlie held his breath, seemingly just as anxious.

"I mean… if you agree, Poppy," the director said. "Or did you want to go again?"

"Think I need to?" she asked.

He thought for a moment. "No, no. That was pretty good."

She bristled. "*Pretty good?* Listen, I'm introducing myself to *the world* here. Pretty good won't work. So how about you do your job and *direct* me? Was I too informal? I feel I could be a bit more businesslike, you know? Like Michael Douglas in *Wall Street*? Or… what? You can be honest with me."

The director didn't respond right away. The man usually crackled with energy, but when he finally spoke, he was subdued, almost fearful. "Okay… Then I'd say actually let's try for one that's more… animated? Right now you're maybe a little… monotone?"

Poppy's smile was strained. "You bet. Let's go again." She paused. "You must be *exhausted* after all these takes! I insist that after we're done, you let Charlie here take you to my salon for a nice relaxing mani-pedi."

This time her smile was genuine.

* * *

Merlin, Ginger, and Harry were outside on the Statesman grounds. Above them the sun shone bright in a cloudless blue sky. It was a bit on the warm side, perhaps, but a gentle breeze was blowing. Quite a pleasant day, Merlin thought. Too pleasant to be doing what they were about to do.

Harry lay on the grass between two horses facing opposite directions. Ropes were tied to the pommels of their saddles, the other ends wrapped around Harry's wrists and ankles. Harry looked confused and miserable, and Merlin didn't blame him one bit. The horses remained absolutely still, looking more like statues than living animals, until Ginger shouted a command.

"Go!"

The horses charged forward, drawing the ropes taut and lifting Harry off the ground.

Harry cried out in pain. "Ooww! OWWW! STOP! PLEASE!"

Merlin looked at Ginger, horrified. "*This* is your interrogation test?"

"Yeah," she said, sounding far too calm for Merlin's liking. "It should give us that fight-or-flight state we need. Jump-start the primal brain."

The horses pummeled the ground with their hooves as they tried to move forward, pulling harder on Harry's limbs.

Harry turned to Merlin, a pleading look in his eye. "You said you were my friend! Why aren't you helping me?"

This was just another version of the flooded room scenario. But Harry wasn't a damn guinea pig, and this wasn't a lab test. This was torture.

"Enough." Merlin removed a large pocket-knife from his trousers and ran toward Harry's feet. He pulled out the blade—which he kept sharp at all times—and quickly sawed through the rope wrapped around Harry's ankles. The rope came apart easily, but now with nothing to stop them, the two horses galloped off in different directions. Unfortunately, since Harry's wrists were still bound to one of the horses, that meant he went with it, howling in pain as the animal dragged him behind.

Merlin watched as his friend was carried away. "Jesus wept," he said. Could this possibly get any worse?

"Merlin," Ginger said, her voice concerned. "What the hell is Tequila doing?"

At first he had no idea what she was talking about, but then he turned to look in the direction she was facing, and he saw Agent Tequila—wearing a cowboy hat and boots with his hospital gown, skin covered with the blue rash—dancing on the grass a dozen yards from where they stood. *Sort of dancing*, he thought. The moves he made, while graceful enough, were… odd. He contorted his body in ways that should've been painful, but he seemed unaffected, smiling blissfully the entire time. If he kept going like that, he could end up breaking his own bones.

What the fuck *was* that rash, and what had it done to poor Tequila?

* * *

After Merlin got Harry settled in his room and tended to his scrapes and cuts—of which there were many—he went to Ginger's lab. Tequila lay on a rolling hospital bed, eyes closed, and hooked up to various pieces of medical equipment. An IV was in his arm, and sensor leads were attached to his head and chest. Ginger stood before a monitor screen, peering intently at the information it displayed. John Denver's "Take Me Home, Country Roads" was playing over the lab's sound system, and Ginger was singing along.

Merlin watched her for a moment, charmed, and then quietly walked over to join her. He began singing as well, and she turned to him, surprised and a bit embarrassed. But the two of them continued to sing together, finishing the song with gusto. When it was over, they looked away, suddenly shy.

"I love that song," Merlin said.

"Really?" Ginger didn't sound convinced.

"I have two things to thank *The Muppets* for: Beaker, that got me into science, and John Denver, who was *always* on the show."

"I have Olivia Newton John to thank for 'Country Roads,' but I would gladly be your Dr Honeydew."

Merlin frowned. "Who?"

"Dr Bunsen Honeydew. Remember? The scientist who always blows Beaker up."

They smiled at each other, but the moment, lovely as it was, passed, and it was time to get back to being professionals.

"How is he?" Merlin asked.

"I gave him a sedative." Ginger sighed, sounding weary and defeated. "He was delirious. We need to run more tests."

"It's definitely related to the skin condition," Merlin said. "The news wire said there were reports coming in from all over. Whatever it is, it's spreading to the brain. Find any correlations with the other victims you contacted?"

"Only... recreational drug use," Ginger said. "I know. Not very Statesman-like. Tequila is our resident bad boy. But if drugs are the cause, we're not talking about a single bad batch. The victims used a wide range of substances, hard and soft."

Merlin thought for a moment. "Don't think this could be connected to the Golden Circle, do you?"

Ginger frowned. "A drug cartel poisoning their customers? Makes no sense."

Maybe not, but Merlin's instincts told him there *was* a connection; they just needed to find it.

Eggsy hurried outside to find Jack leaning against the hood of a Bronco, smoking a cigarette. The American agent wore brown sunglasses, a leather jacket, white T-shirt, jeans, and brown boots. He still wore his cowboy hat, though. He'd refused to part with it. Eggsy was dressed in equally casual style: red flannel shirt over a white T-shirt, with faded jeans, white sneakers, and a red ball cap.

As Eggsy approached the car, Jack tossed the cigarette

to the ground and extinguished it with his foot. "You always bang your contacts?" he asked.

"What are you on about?" Eggsy said.

Jack pointed at Eggsy's shirt. "It was tucked before you went in."

Eggsy looked down, saw Jack was right, and hastily tucked his shirt in.

"She's my girlfriend," he explained.

Jack gave him a disapproving look. "At Statesman, we have strict rules about relationships."

"Course. Same at Kingsman. But me and Tilde… that's a special case."

Jack's eyes narrowed. "Says who? You?"

"I rescued her from Valentine's HQ. She saw everything. She knows what I am. Apart from classified stuff, I can tell her anything."

There was a knock from the window above them, and the two men looked up to see Tilde, wrapped in a sheet, smiling and waving cheerily down at them.

Jack stepped close to Eggsy, leaned in toward him, and spoke in a low, threatening voice. "You ever compromise Statesman, kid, in any way, I will not hesitate to take action. I make myself clear?"

Eggsy stood his ground, refusing to be intimidated. "Crystal. Let's get on with the mission."

He hoped there wouldn't be any trouble between them, but if there was, he was ready for it. They got in the car.

"Look in the glovebox," Jack said.

Eggsy did so and found two small boxes. He removed

one, opened it, and saw what looked to him like the world's smallest condom.

"Fucking hell, bruv. I thought *everything* was supposed to be bigger in America. No wonder you overcompensate with them big cars."

Jack ignored the gibe. "Goes on your finger. There's a tracker in the tip. Apply light pressure for three seconds to release it."

Eggsy nodded. He put the box back, started the car, and they were on their way to Glastonbury.

Eggsy had never been to Glastonbury before. He'd known it was big, but he'd had no idea how *huge* it actually was. Every year in late June, over 175,000 people—most of them in their twenties—swarmed to the fields of Somerset to party hard for five days. From classic rockers like The Rolling Stones, The Who, Lou Reed, and Bob Dylan to more contemporary artists such as Gorillaz, Beyoncé, Kanye West, and Lady Gaga, the roster of musicians who had played at Glastonbury read like a who's who of pop culture. Other arts beside music were represented at the festival, too, such as dance, comedy, theater, circus, and cabaret. Glastonbury had developed out of the hippie and counterculture movements, and—thanks to the presence of a small megalith structure similar to Stonehenge—it was also a New Age site of interest. It was the perfect place for someone like Countess Clara, an aristocrat who fancied herself to be spiritually evolved and highly attuned to the rhythms of the universe, when in reality she was just a spoiled rich kid looking for a good time.

Eggsy and Jack pulled into one of the festival's parking areas in the late afternoon. They left the car and headed for the VIP camping site, wearing the entry wristbands that Tilde had procured for them. The site was like a mini-fortress, enclosed by anti-climb fences topped with razor wire. *Wouldn't want the wrong sort getting in now, would we?* Eggsy thought. Beyond the fence was a small city of camper vans, tipis, and tents. All of them the best that money could buy, of course. Eggsy checked his phone as he and Jack headed for the security gate.

"According to Countess Clara's Instagram, she's in here, at the VIP bar."

But when they attempted to enter the camping area, one of the security guards at the gate stopped them. He was a tall, muscular man in his early twenties with a shaved head and an I-Don't-Take-Shit attitude.

"Wrong wristbands, gents," he said in a thick Brummie accent.

Jack shot Eggsy a dark look, as if to say, *Your girlfriend didn't just screw you; she screwed us both.* He then turned back to the guard.

"How much are they to buy?"

When the guard didn't reply, Jack reached into his pocket and withdrew a rolled-up bundle of American money.

"Let's call it a thousand," he said, holding the money out for the man to take. The guard looked at the cash as if Jack were offering him a large dog turd.

"Let's call it 'Fuck off and don't come back,' old man," the guard said, practically growling.

Jack scowled. "I'm sorry, my hearing aid must be busted. How about you say that again a little bit louder. And maybe without the weird-ass accent."

Sneering, the guard leaned in close to Jack. "I said, 'Fuck o—'"

A little puff of gas jetted from an invisible hole in the rim of Jack's hat and clouded the guard's face. The man's eyes rolled white, and he fell to the ground, unconscious.

Jack looked around, feigning alarm. "Hey! Help! This guy just collapsed!"

Other security guards rushed over to see to their fallen comrade, and in the commotion, Jack strolled through the gate without anyone noticing. Eggsy followed, impressed despite himself. They were in.

Eggsy and Jack headed across the field to the VIP bar.

"I say we both make an approach, and whoever gets on best with Clara goes for it," Jack said.

"Well, it doesn't have to be a competition, bruv, does it? Shake hands with her, pat her on the shoulder, whatever. Job done."

Jack stopped walking and stared at Eggsy, as if trying to determine whether the British agent was messing with him or not. Eggsy continued walking for several paces before stopping and turning back around to face him.

"The hand is not a mucous membrane, Eggsy. Nor is

the shoulder. They teach you *anything* at Kingsman?"

Eggsy frowned in confusion. "What are you talking about?"

"Our trackers are designed to enter the bloodstream. They circulate harmlessly, providing full audio and GPS."

Jack started walking again, and Eggsy followed.

"But… mucous membrane is like… inside your nose, innit? How am I supposed to put my finger up her…" Realization struck him then. "It ain't just your nose, is it?"

"No, Eggsy," Jack said, sounding amused now. "It ain't. They train you in seduction?"

"Yeah. Rule one: be attractive. Rule two: don't be *un*attractive."

Jack sighed. "Great. I'll take first crack. Only fair, since I'm the one whose balls ain't been milked yet today. Watch and learn, buddy."

Despite being located in the middle of a field, the bar resembled a proper pub, Eggsy thought. Except for the grass on the ground. *And* the fact that everyone here had money and were trying awfully hard to look like they didn't. After all, VIP didn't stand for Vastly and Irrevocably Poor. The men and women in the tent were young, and while most of them dressed down in grubby shirts and (deliberately) torn jeans, many wore clothes inspired by the fashions of the sixties and seventies. A number of the festivalgoers in the tent had patches of weird blue blotches on their skin. Eggsy had never seen anything like it before. He took a couple pictures with his eyeglasses to send to Merlin. An attractive blond woman wearing a short, tight dress with a riotous blend of color that could only be described as psychedelic sat at the far end of the bar: Countess Clara Von Glucksberg. She had a mostly empty wine glass in front of her, and she was bent over her phone, thumbs flying across the screen as she texted or posted on Instagram. Eggsy hung back while Jack made a beeline for her. The American agent took the stool next to her and lost no time in getting down to business.

"Miss?" he said. "Forgive me for troubling you, but what time are you playing?"

Clara turned to him with a laugh. "I'm not in a *band*! Oh god! Who did you think I was? Oh please say it's not someone ghastly!"

"Well, now I feel like a fool! Truth be told, I just assumed that a woman with your charisma just *had* to be *somebody*."

She laughed again, louder this time. "Right! Thank you."

Jack smiled. "It's okay. I know you didn't mean to make me feel like a dumbass. How about you make it up to me by letting me buy you a drink?"

Her eyes narrowed, and she tilted her head to the side. "Are you hitting on me?"

Jack's smile became a grin. "Well, ma'am, I believe I am."

She paused to finish the last of her wine. She put the empty glass on the counter and returned her attention to Jack. She then swiped her finger to the left. Jack looked at her, confused, so she did it again. When he didn't respond, she said, "I'm swiping left? Don't you have Tinder in America?"

Jack frowned. "Tinder what?"

Eggsy was close enough to hear their conversation, and he winced inwardly at Clara's savage takedown of Jack. But he knew a cue when he heard one. He headed over to the two of them and slid next to Clara.

"I think it's a generational thing," he said to her. He turned to Jack and spoke loudly and slowly, as if to an old person. "She's saying she ain't interested, mate."

Jack was only in his forties, but Clara was in her early twenties, and if she thought Jack was too old for her, then—for the time being, at least—Eggsy did too. Jack locked eyes with Eggsy for a moment. Eggsy grinned and Jack gave him a glare before turning back to Clara. He touched the brim of his hat in farewell. "Be good and be cool," he said, and moved off. Eggsy quickly slid onto the stool Jack had vacated.

"Thanks for that." She looked Eggsy up and down, and evidently she liked what she saw, for she smiled and held out her hand. "I'm Clara. Hi."

Eggsy shook her hand. "River." When they were finished shaking, he took a quick look at his phone. "Bloody hell, is it only four o'clock? I'm so jet-lagged, I don't know whether I'm coming or going."

"Where've you been? Anywhere nice?"

"South America. I'm sort of living there for a bit? Training with a shaman, connecting with my spirit animal, you know." He tapped his chest. "Crow. And something tells me yours is a... jaguar?"

Her eyes widened in delighted surprise. "Oh my god, seriously? That's amazing! It totally is! How did you even know that?" She turned and tugged her dress off her shoulder to reveal a tattoo of a black jaguar.

How did I know? Eggsy thought. *You post enough bloody selfies on Instagram.*

"*Ino Moxo,*" he said. "The black jaguar. Nice."

"You read Manuel Córdova-Rios? You know what, I'm going to buy you a proper drink."

Eggsy smiled. *Score: Britain 1, USA 0.*

Merlin and Ginger stood side by side in a dark room. They both wore night-vision goggles, and, to them, the room appeared bathed in a strange greenish light.

"I thought *our* tests were eccentric," Merlin said.

A huge bull lay on the floor, sleeping. And sitting on the animal's back—still wearing his gray tracksuit—was Harry, head down, eye closed. A rope lashed Harry in a seated position to the bull's middle.

"Oh man, seriously," Ginger said. "You should see this when we do it with a full class of candidates."

"Not sure I even want to see it now," Merlin muttered.

Ginger smiled and stepped toward the bull. She drew a pair of hypodermic needles from her pocket. Shifting one to her left hand, she deftly lifted the fabric of Harry's tracksuit and injected into his hip. The effect was instantaneous. He raised his head and opened his eye. Unfortunately, he wasn't wearing night-vision goggles, which meant that to him, he'd awakened to total darkness.

"Oh god. Now what?" he said. He pulled against the rope tying him to the bull, then reached down with his free hand to pat the animal's hide. "What *is* this?"

Ginger switched hypodermics and plunged the fresh one into the bull's flank. She then pulled it free and quickly stepped back. Merlin decided that gaining a bit of distance from the animal might not be a bad thing, and he retreated until he was pressed against the wall. The bull began to stir, groggily at first, but then its head seemed to clear and it rose to its feet.

"Oh no," Harry said, almost pleading. "No..."

Ginger stepped to a door and shoved it open, flooding the room with light. The bull—fully awake now and mad as hell—charged forward, carrying Harry with it. Merlin and Ginger quickly removed their goggles and stepped through another doorway that led to a safety barrier where they could watch the action from ringside.

The bull ran into the middle of a rodeo arena—Statesman-owned, of course. The seats were empty, so there was no audience to watch as the bull bucked and twisted, trying to throw Harry off. *At least he's spared the indignity of being other people's entertainment*, Merlin thought.

Harry screamed and held on for dear life as the bull's exertions became increasingly vigorous. Finally, and unsurprisingly, the bull won. Harry slipped free of the rope, and he went flying through the air. *Tuck and roll,*

Harry! Merlin thought. *Tuck and roll!*

Harry tumbled as he came down and landed hard. But he didn't stay down long. He scrambled to his feet and faced Merlin and Ginger.

"You bastards!" he shouted at them, his face purple with anger. "For god's sake, is this a joke? What is *wrong* with you people?"

The bull had trotted off after ridding itself of Harry, but now it turned and started coming back toward him, picking up speed as it went.

"Harry, watch out!" Merlin shouted.

But his warning came too late. The bull smashed into Harry from behind, hurling him into the air like a rag doll. He hit the ground even harder when he came down this time, the impact sending up a cloud of dust. But the bull hadn't finished playing with its toy yet. It angrily pawed the ground, ready to go at Harry again, and Merlin doubted Harry could survive another of the animal's attacks.

"I've got to help him," Merlin said.

"Wait, wait…" Ginger said.

But Merlin couldn't stand by and watch his friend suffer any longer. He vaulted over the barrier and into the arena. He waved his arms, trying to get the bull's attention.

"Hey, hey! Over this way!" he shouted.

The bull looked at him, cocked its head to the side for a second as if considering, and then it charged.

"Oh shit," Merlin said.

Just as the bull was about to hit Merlin, Ginger fired a

tranquilizer dart at the animal, and the beast went down with a heavy thud.

"Good shot," Merlin said.

"Thanks. You've got three minutes until the bull wakes up."

"Right." Merlin walked over to Harry. The man still lay on his back, but his eye was open.

"Harry, I think you and I deserve a drink. Don't you? Come on."

He helped Harry to stand and together they walked out of the paddock.

Merlin and Harry sat at a small table on the covered porch outside the distillery's gift shop. Merlin smoked a pipe while Harry sipped a cup of warm tea. It had started to rain, and they watched riders leading their horses to the stables. After a time, Harry spoke.

"Merlin, you say you were my friend, but a true friend wouldn't put anyone through this torture. Whatever your dream is for me, it's proving to be my nightmare. Please, *please*... end this. I beg you."

It tore at Merlin's heart to see his old friend like this. He wanted to tell Harry that yes, it was over, and that he wouldn't have to endure any further sadistic tests. As he looked into Harry's one eye, he thought of how Galahad—*this* Galahad—had given his life in the fight against Richmond Valentine. Or nearly so. Maybe Harry would be happier this way, without any memories of the battles he'd fought in the service of Kingsman, the lives he'd been forced to take in the performance of his duties. Especially all those people in the South Glade Mission Church. Who would want to live with the memory of what it was like to be turned into a homicidal lunatic, trapped in your own body, aware of your actions but unable to stop yourself? It sounded like a living hell to Merlin. Maybe Harry deserved to retire from Kingsman without such a mental burden. And he *had* wanted to be a lepidopterist once. Now he could have a chance to live a life he'd originally turned away from, explore a road not taken. He could literally start anew, and how many people ever got that chance?

But Merlin knew that personal feelings—no matter how strong—were unimportant when stacked against the fate of the world. Kingsman was gone, save for Harry, Eggsy, and him. Yes, there were their new allies, the agents of Statesman, but the world was always hovering on the brink of disaster, and it needed all the help it could get. Besides, the Harry Hart who'd been Agent Galahad would never want anyone to give up on him, not as long as there was the merest chance of helping him return.

Merlin put his hand on Harry's shoulder. "I'm doing this because I *am* your friend, Harry. And because Kingsman needs its greatest spy back. Don't you want to be yourself again?"

Harry looked at him for a moment, and when he replied, his tone was bitter.

"I'd rather smash this cup, and slash my wrists. If

Chapter Seven

———— ✖ ————

Clara ushered Eggsy into her personal safari tent. The outside had large peace signs emblazoned on it, and the inside smelled like incense and was decorated with Indian rugs, Chinese lanterns, strings of fairy lights, and—smack dab in the center—a king-sized bed with tie-dyed sheets. It looked to Eggsy like a hippie's idea of the afterlife.

"Sorry we never found your friends," Clara said.

Of course, he'd had no friends at the festival to find. The ruse had served two purposes: one, it made it seem like he hadn't come to the festival alone in search of someone to shag, and two, it gave them time to talk and get to know one another. He was glad the faux friend quest was finished, though. He was tired of the crowds and the noise—although he *had* gotten to hear some decent live music while they'd walked—and he was especially tired of coming up with bullshit New Age dialogue that "River" would speak. Unfortunately, it looked like he was going to have to keep up the patter for a bit longer.

"We all go on our separate journeys," he said, "but we

will all arrive at the same destination—"

Before he could finish, Clara grabbed him, pushed him onto the bed, and flopped down next to him. She put her arms around his neck and moved in for a kiss. Eggsy pushed her arms off him, sat up, and scooted several inches away from her.

"Know what?" he said. "I'm busting for a pee."

She giggled. "You can do it on me if you want."

Eggsy fought to keep his smile from looking too strained. "Maybe in a bit."

"Okay, but hurry up, River! I've been waiting all night for you to at least *kiss* me." She giggled again and gestured to the back of the tent. "The loo's that way."

Eggsy had intended to leave the tent—he had a very important call he needed to make before this went any further—but Clara had indicated an arched doorway in the back of the tent, leading to a tented tunnel. *Naturally, she has her own bathroom*, he thought. No woman with the title "Countess" in front of her name would ever use a smelly *public* toilet to relieve herself. His excuse for leaving gone, Eggsy had no choice but to walk through the doorway, down the tunnel, and into another tent. He was expecting something the size of a phone booth with a small chemical toilet inside. But this was another full-size safari tent, done up as a luxury ensuite bathroom with a porcelain toilet, glass-enclosed shower stall, claw-foot bathtub—the works. If they ever managed to put Kingsman back together, he'd have to talk to Merlin about getting some of these fancy shitters. It would make field work a hell of a lot more comfortable.

There was no flap to zip closed on this tent's entrance, just a cloth curtain—tie-dyed, of course—that could be drawn over the entrance for privacy. The curtain wouldn't provide much sound insulation, but he was far enough away from Clara that she probably wouldn't hear him if he spoke quietly. Plus, the noise outside the tents would help drown out his voice. He removed his phone from his pocket and face-timed Tilde. She answered right away. He could tell from the background that she was still in the hotel room where they'd met earlier. God, it was so good to see her. He wanted to ask her how she was, what she'd been up to since they'd parted, if she'd had dinner, and if so, what was it and had it been any good? But he didn't have time for that, so he got right to the point.

"Babe? Bit of a nightmare. I need to sleep with a target. But I won't do it unless you agree it's all right."

She frowned. "The old guy you were with?"

"A girl," he said.

Tilde's face clouded with anger. "You've got to be fucking kidding. So what was *I*? Target practice?"

Eggsy hurried to explain. "Babe, surely it's better that I'm honest with you? Than me just doing it and not telling you."

She gave him a skeptical look. "I don't get how screwing someone is gonna save the world."

"It's complicated. But please trust me. I wouldn't if I didn't have to."

And it was true. The instant Clara had shoved him onto the bed and practically attacked him, he knew he couldn't go through with the mission. Not without speaking to Tilde first. He loved her so much, and the idea of betraying her made him feel ill. But if she *understood*, if she gave him *permission*, then he thought he could do it.

Tilde considered for several moments before finally asking, "What does she look like?"

Eggsy was quick to answer. "Nowhere near as pretty as you."

She gave him a look that said flattery wasn't going to work, not in this situation.

"Send me a picture."

He'd downloaded several photos of Clara onto his phone to show Jack so he could help spot her. He selected the worst of the lot—which wasn't saying much because Clara took *great* photos—and texted it to Tilde. She received the text almost immediately, and examined it.

She shook her head. "No fucking way. What is it with the whole cliché of spies only sleeping with gorgeous women? Forget it. This is bullshit." The angrier she got, the more pronounced her Swedish accent became.

Eggsy was beginning to fear that he'd made a serious mistake by calling Tilde, but he'd had no choice. He simply couldn't complete the mission without her approval. He wished Jack hadn't been so lousy at seduction. If the American agent had managed to entice Clara into bed, he and Tilde wouldn't be having this conversation right now.

"It's not like it's for *fun,* Tilde," he said, sounding desperate but unable to help it. "I love you. I only want *you*. You know that."

Clara called out from the other tent. "Hurry up! If you make me wait any longer, I'm gonna get my vibrator!"

"What the fuck? Who even *is* this slut?" Tilde was practically shouting now, and Eggsy quickly lowered the volume on his phone.

He shouted back to Clara. "Yeah! Sorry! Nearly done!" Then he spoke quietly once more to Tilde. "Babe... Please. Believe me. I *love* you. You're the person I want to spend the rest of my life with."

Some of Tilde's anger drained away, and a thoughtful look came into her eyes.

"Is that a proposal?"

Too late, Eggsy realized he'd managed to corner himself. It wasn't that he was averse to the idea of marrying Tilde. Not at all. But marrying her would mean becoming part of her family—the *royal* family. More than that, Sweden was the only monarchy in the world where the firstborn, regardless of gender, inherited the throne. Tilde was her parents' first child, which meant that someday she would be the ruler of her country. How could he—a kid who'd grown up rough on the dodgier streets of London—possibly be good enough to be the consort of a queen?

Eggsy struggled to find the right words to reply to Tilde and failed miserably. "Um... Well, I... not—"

Tilde went on as if she hadn't heard him. "Because I think... You know, I think I'd say yes. Having that security, knowing that we were... committed. I think in that context... Yeah. I'd feel different."

Eggsy wanted to tell Tilde about his self-doubts, but he couldn't bring himself to. He knew he shouldn't be ashamed of his background—and he *wasn't*. The lessons he'd learned on the streets had served him just as well in Kingsman as anything Harry had taught him. But there was no denying that the idea of becoming royalty made him feel extremely uncomfortable.

"Babe, I'm... I wanna be with you. But suddenly being a prince? A public figure? That's a bit of a... factor. With my job. And..."

He trailed off when he saw Tilde's face fall and her eyes brim with tears. He realized he would only make the situation worse by continuing this conversation.

"Darling, we need to talk. Properly. Y'know? I'll come to the hotel. Call you back in five minutes, okay?"

Tears began to flow down Tilde's cheeks, and her tone became hard and bitter.

"Don't put yourself down, Eggsy. I'm sure you can last longer than that."

The screen went dark and the words CALL ENDED appeared. Eggsy stared at the words, feeling as if he'd been punched in the gut. *No, no, no!* He started to call her back, but then he thought better of it. The way he was going tonight, he'd only hurt her worse.

He slipped the phone into his pocket and made his way back to Clara's main tent. He found her waiting for him on the bed, wearing a red silk robe.

"What's the matter?" she asked.

He was sad, confused, and angry—mostly at himself—

and he wasn't up to pretending otherwise.

"Nothing, I just feel… our spirit animals need more time to get in synch. Find a… harmonious bond on the… spiritual plane and—"

"Totally," she said. "Or… we could just fuck."

She smiled as she rose from the bed and allowed her robe to slide off her. Underneath, she wore only a crimson bra and panties. She had an absolutely *stunning* body, and the Eggsy he'd been before meeting Tilde would've shucked off his own clothes quick as lightning and hopped into bed with her. But the man he was now only admired her body in the abstract. He felt no desire stir within him.

"Clara, I… don't think I can."

She looked at him for a long moment, as if gauging his sincerity. Then, looking disappointed and more than a little embarrassed, she turned around to pick up her robe, revealing a golden circle at the base of her spine.

Eggsy swallowed. He had no choice now. He had to go through with it.

"Maybe I *could* stay for a bit," he said.

Clara turned, grinning, and came toward him, arms outstretched. Eggsy smiled as he reached into his pocket and slipped Statesman's tracking deployment device— aka the micro-condom—onto his index finger.

Jack sat alone in the VIP bar, drinking the watered-down piss that passed for whiskey in this country and brooding over Clara's rejection of him. He knew it was unprofessional—not to mention childish—but he couldn't help it. But that's the way it went when you were an agent. A lot of times you were forced to sit around and wait until it was time to act. All that sitting led to thinking, thinking led to brooding, and brooding could lead you down some truly dark paths if you weren't careful.

Lela...

One of the things he hated about sitting here was watching so many rich brats having something a little extra along with their drinks. No one smoked pot in here. That would be way too obvious, even for an outdoor music festival. But he saw plenty of pills being passed from one person to another, pills that were quickly swallowed before anyone could notice. Anyone but him, that is. He saw small packets of powder being passed around as well. Not everyone in the tent was selling, buying, or doing drugs, of course. Less than a quarter, Jack guessed. But as far as he was concerned, that was a quarter too many. Nothing he could do about it right now, though. He was on a different mission tonight.

He wore a small earpiece, and up to this point it had remained silent. Now it came alive, and he heard the rapid breathing of a woman on the verge of reaching orgasm. He grinned and raised his glass in a toast to Eggsy.

He tapped the earpiece to turn it off. He'd turn it back on when Eggsy was done plowing Countess Clara's field. He downed the rest of his whiskey and then, to give his British cousin some time to finish his work properly, he stood and ambled over to the bar to order another.

* * *

Merlin and Ginger sat next to each other at a workstation, monitoring Eggsy's progress from the lab at Statesman headquarters. Merlin was doing his best to remain clinical and detached, but he couldn't help feeling uncomfortable around Ginger given the particular, ah, *parameters* of Eggsy's mission. She was an extremely attractive woman, both mentally and physically, and although it was sometimes a necessity for agents to engage in close contact with a surveillance target—sometimes *extremely* close— he was all too aware of the amazing woman sitting at his side, and he found himself feeling more than a bit embarrassed. Not so much by what Eggsy was doing but because it was making him have thoughts about Ginger that were less than professional.

When the GPS came online, Merlin told Eggsy that he'd succeeded. He glanced at Ginger and was surprised to find her looking at him and smiling.

"Don't worry," she said, as if sensing how he felt. "I've been through this with Whiskey before." She paused, and then added, "Nice to be working with an agent who knows what he's doing."

Merlin's throat was suddenly dry. "Indeed," he said.

Eggsy and Clara lay on her bed. She was still in her bra and panties, and Eggsy was fully clothed. Eggsy withdrew his hand from her panties, and Clara shuddered one last time then drew in a deep breath and let it out slowly.

He heard Merlin's voice in his ear. *Device delivered*, he said.

No shit, Eggsy thought.

A light sheen of sweat covered Clara's body, and she gave Eggsy a *very* relaxed smile.

"*Wow.*" Her smile turned naughty. "My turn, Mr Crow…"

She reached down and began undoing his belt. Eggsy, nearly panicking, pulled away from her.

"I'm sorry, but… I should go. I'm in a relationship."

"That's adorable. Listen, so am I. Don't worry about it. What happens at Glasto stays in Glasto."

Eggsy took hold of her wrists and moved her hands away from his belt. His index finger was now bare. Statesman's mini-condom was designed to dissolve after it had done its work, so a target would have no idea it had been used.

"I'm sorry," he said. "I just… can't."

Then he turned away from her, got off the bed, and practically fled the tent.

He knew he should go find Jack, but he was too upset. It was dark outside now, but he made sure to move a good distance away from Clara's tent anyway. He didn't want her coming after him, angry because he'd left so abruptly. When he thought he'd gone far enough, he took out his phone and called Tilde. She didn't answer, so he called again, with the same result. *This is Princess T. Please leave a message.* He tried the hotel's front desk, and this time someone picked up. He started speaking before the clerk could say hello.

"Hi, could you get a message to room seventeen, please? My girlfriend's not picking up, and…" Eggsy paused as the desk clerk spoke. "Checked out? When? Maybe she's still outside; can you go and look?" Another pause as he listened. "Yeah. I understand… Okay."

He ended the call. He stared at his phone for a moment, not knowing what to do, desperate to speak with Tilde. If he could get to the rental car fast enough… No, she'd hired a driver to take her from Heathrow to the hotel, and by now, she was no doubt making the return trip. It was possible that he could catch up to them—Christ, was he tempted to try—but if she wouldn't take his calls, why would she speak to him in person? Especially if he came racing up on her car like some kind of crazed stalker.

Without any other course of action open to him, he headed for the VIP bar, the sounds of music and partying, of people laughing and enjoying themselves, seeming to mock him as he walked. He figured the bar was the most likely place he'd find Jack, and after he'd rejoined the American agent… well, he supposed he'd do his best to continue trying to discover what the Golden Circle was up to. It was, after all, his duty. But he knew his heart wouldn't be in it.

* * *

A dozen men and women in business attire sat at tables in Poppy's diner, eating pancakes. Despite their food—which Poppy knew was absolutely yummy since she'd made it herself—her guests looked unhappy, if not downright miserable. She told herself their sour mood had nothing to do with the food or this meeting—at least, not directly. Reaching her compound was not easy, which was exactly the way it was designed to be. It wouldn't be much of a *hidden* compound otherwise, would it? So the trip through the jungle had been long, hot, and uncomfortable for her guests, and although they'd been given time to freshen up after they'd arrived, they still tugged at their collars or fanned themselves with their hands. The diner's air conditioning was going full blast, but there was only so much it could do to counteract the jungle's humid air. She didn't take her guests' grumpiness personally. She'd lived in Poppyland for close to ten years, and she still hadn't fully acclimated to the surrounding environment—*and* she was a natural redhead with fair skin. She was lucky she didn't burst into flame every time she stepped out into the jungle sunshine. She could've conducted this meeting virtually, she supposed, but she preferred face-to-face contact when it came to working out delicate business matters. It made everything so much more… intimate.

Poppy, as always, had dressed for the occasion. She wore her best pearls and an expensive—but tasteful—cream-colored dress with a pattern of red orchids and a *darling* pair of ankle-strap heels. She also wore an apron. These clothes were far too nice to risk getting any stains on them. Charlie sat at the counter, wearing a navy pinstripe suit, white shirt, and a gold tie. She thought the latter was an especially nice touch. He looked every inch the successful young businessman, if you overlooked the fact that one of his suit sleeves had been removed to make room for his robotic arm. She'd decided to call his look *Corporate Terminator*, and she thought it quite suited him.

Suited... get it? She almost laughed aloud at her own joke, but she knew it wouldn't be appropriate.

To get the meeting started on the right note, she'd decided to serve her guests breakfast. After all, who didn't love pancakes? She'd just finished the last batch and set the plate on the counter. She picked up a sugar shaker, sprinkled some on the pancakes, and then looked at the shaker with a grin.

"Didja see that study that came out?" she asked her guests. "Sugar's eight times more addictive than cocaine. In the US, sugared drinks cause twice as many deaths as cocaine every year. And *this* stuff's legal! Crazy, right?"

Time to get started, she thought. She removed her apron, draped it over a stool, and began speaking.

"I want to thank you all for joining me. I assure you that your long journeys from all 'corners' of the Circle have been worthwhile. Because tonight marks the beginning of a new age. For us all. As my global heads of sales, the Golden Circle has brought you untold wealth and power. And yet I suspect each of you feels as I do: imprisoned in a gilded cage. I can buy anything. And yet I have... nothing."

Her guests exchanged looks of uncertainty, but Poppy

continued, walking slowly behind the representatives as she spoke.

"You think I *want* to live out here under twenty-four hour guard? No. I'll tell you what I want: I wanna be a law-abiding taxpayer. I wanna see a Broadway show. Shop on Rodeo Drive."

She stopped behind the British representative, a handsome man in his fifties wearing a light blue suit and tie, dark blue socks, and shoes with a Union Jack design on them. She gripped his shoulders and started massaging them.

"Take a cute guy to a hot restaurant and screw his brains out in a nice hotel suite."

Everyone laughed, the British rep most of all. Poppy smiled and gave the man's shoulders a final squeeze before moving on.

"I wanna go to the Met Gala. The Oscars. Dinner at the White House. I wanna host *The Apprentice*. I want a *normal* life! I'm talking *freedom*, people. I'm talking *legitimacy*. I look around this room, and I see the most successful businesspeople in the world. And I want to see each of us get the kudos that we deserve!"

The representatives burst into applause, and Poppy smiled. She'd thought they might clap after that line. By this point, she'd made a complete circuit of the table, and was once more standing at its head.

"So say goodbye to the shadows, my friends. Because we're about to step proudly into the spotlight." She leaned forward and placed her palms on the table, her eyes shining with excitement. "And here's how… Let's go to the videotape."

She directed everyone's attention to the TV screen above the counter.

Eggsy sat slumped in one of the leather seats on Statesman's private jet, scrolling through a text message conversation with Tilde on his phone, although *conversation* was stretching it a bit since most of the texts were from him.

EGGSY, PLEASE STOP TEXTING ME. I NEED SOME TIME TO THINK.

CALLING U NOW.

WHY AREN'T YOU PICKING UP?

BBY, I NEED TO TALK TO U

LEFT VOICEMAIL.

TRYING U AGAIN NOW.

Jack—back in his usual outfit—stood at the pool table, taking a few shots.

"You *sure* the Wi-Fi's working?" Eggsy asked without looking up from his phone.

"Yup." Jack sank the four ball in a side pocket before turning to look at Eggsy. "Only thing that *ain't* working is your relationship. How about you put the damn cellphone down and clear your head for five minutes?"

Jack went to the rack, selected another cue stick, and held it out to Eggsy. He reluctantly put his phone in his trouser pocket and stood up to take it. Jack racked the balls, and they began to play. This time they decided to play rotation, and Jack let Eggsy take the first shot. Eggsy's concentration was off, and he didn't run the table like he had on the trip over, so the two of them took turns shooting as they spoke.

"She never ignored my texts before," Eggsy said.

"You never told her before that you guys didn't have a future," Jack countered.

"But we would have! I mean… if I didn't have to be a fucking *prince*. I love her." He paused and then asked, "Haven't you ever been in love?"

Jack had leaned over the table, ready to shoot, but he froze. For several seconds he remained motionless, not even breathing, but then he spoke. "Yeah. Once, a few years back. Didn't work out." He hit the cue ball and sent it rolling straight for the five ball. There was a loud *clack* as the balls bounced off one another, and the five rolled toward a corner pocket and sank in smoothly. Jack smiled, satisfied with the shot, and turned to Eggsy.

"Look, your girl's doing you a solid. You're only seeing the hole and not the donut, kid. Our line of work, we get to travel the *world*. Bang the hottest girls and blow straight outta town. Brand-new day, brand-new pussy. Wash, rinse, and repeat." He turned back to the table and began looking for his next shot.

"To the old me, that would've sounded pretty damn good," Eggsy said.

Jack didn't have a good shot at the six ball. He gave it a try, but all he managed to accomplish was to rearrange the pattern of balls on the table. It was Eggsy's turn, so Jack stepped back and continued talking while Eggsy contemplated how he was going to sink the ball.

"No fights, no meet-the-folks, no trying your best to change. No Achilles heel threatening your security as a spy. Just a whole lotta action. If it don't sound good to you *now*, you ain't thinking about it hard enough." He paused, and then added, "If Harry was here, he'd be giving you the exact same advice."

Eggsy had no more luck sinking the six ball than Jack did. He stepped back from the table and turned toward his fellow spy.

"Maybe," he allowed.

"'Hop on the bus, Gus,'" Jack said.

Eggsy frowned. "What?"

"It's a song," Jack said. "I used to play it a lot back when Champ helped me through some tough times a while ago. It's 'Fifty Ways to Leave Your Lover' by Paul Simon."

"I don't think I know it," Eggsy said.

Jack took out his phone, called up his music app, and selected the song. His phone was tied into the plane's sound system, and when music began issuing from the cabin's speakers, Jack sang along.

Eggsy found this impromptu performance more than a little weird, but it was nice to see Jack let go and not be so serious for a change, and he smiled at the absurdity of it all.

"Yeah. No. I... don't know it," he said awkwardly.

When the song ended, Jack looked at Eggsy with an expectant grin.

"I promise you'll feel better once I get you some southern comfort. And I ain't talking about liquor."

Eggsy smiled, caught up in Jack's enthusiasm.

"Lick her? I'd love to. Long as she licks me back afterward."

They laughed.

When the video ended, Poppy looked at the sales reps gathered around the table, and tried to gauge their reactions. After a moment, they broke into anxious, muted applause. A less enthusiastic response than she'd hoped for, but not bad. She smiled as if they'd given her a standing ovation.

"Any questions?" she asked.

Silence. Some of the reps exchanged glances, but no one spoke. Then finally, the British man with the Union Jack shoes stood.

"Uh... I'm sorry to say this—" he began.

"Hi, 'Sorry to Say This.' I'm Poppy!"

A smattering of nervous laughter came from the group. Not from the British man, though. He looked as if he might be ill.

"Just messing with you," Poppy said to him. Then to the others, "Team, this is Boris Batko, Southeast Asia."

She turned to Boris and nodded. "Go ahead, Boris."

"Madam Poppy… You say that where America leads, other nations follow. But what if they don't? How are we protected?"

Poppy pursed her lips in irritation, but before she could respond to Boris, a second man stood. He was shorter than the Brit and dressed more conservatively in a black suit, white shirt, and black tie. He was balding, which was probably why he'd grown his goatee and mustache, Poppy thought. She didn't think black was a good choice for the man. Made him look too much like a mortician.

"Madam Poppy? Boris is right. And already this plan of yours is underway! What if we did not wish to be involved?"

Poppy had to fight to keep from gritting her teeth as she spoke next. "For those who don't know, this is Grigor. Eastern Europe." She faced the man and spoke to him gently. "You can still opt out, Grigor. Would you like to opt out?"

Grigor looked to his fellow sales reps for support, but none would meet his gaze. He turned back to Poppy and swallowed nervously. "I… I think yes."

Poppy nodded, smiled, and then she placed two fingers in her mouth and whistled.

Bennie and Jet burst out of their kennels and came racing across the diner toward Grigor. The man shrieked in terror and ran for the exit. Poppy didn't think he would make it, but he was a lot faster than he looked, and he managed to get outside before the robot dogs caught up to him. He didn't get much farther, though. Bennie and

Jet raced after him, and a few seconds later, everyone heard screaming combined with the tearing of flesh. The screaming didn't last long, but the dogs continued ripping Grigor's corpse apart. Bennie and Jet might be artificial constructs, but her babies needed regular exercise just like real animals (which Poppy thought of as *meatimals*) in order to keep their programming sharp.

"Ooh!" she said. "They've made a real dog's dinner of him."

The dogs—and what little remained of Grigor—could be seen clearly through one of the diner's windows. Copious amounts of blood were splashed all over the ground, and Bennie and Jet had gotten quite a bit of the red stuff on them as well. She'd have to have Charlie give them a clean later.

She looked at her sales representatives. They were all gazing upon the carnage outside the window, eyes wide, faces pale, bodies trembling. Poppy smiled. This was more like it.

"Anyone else?" she said. "How about you, Boris? Any more questions?"

Boris had remained standing throughout as Grigor suffered his grisly demise, but he quickly shook his head and practically flung himself back into his chair. The other reps turned to look at her and slowly, fearfully, shook their heads.

Poppy clapped her hands together, and the sudden noise made the reps jump.

"Great!" she said. "Then we're ready to go public!"

She turned to Charlie, who was still sitting at the counter, now looking a little queasy. Funny, he could kill without so much as batting an eye—witness how easily he'd snapped Angel's neck—but when it came to spilling a little blood, okay, a *lot* of blood, he became downright squeamish. People could be so inconsistent. That was one of the reasons she preferred machines. As long as they were well maintained, they did exactly what they were designed to do. You could always depend on them. People? Not so much.

But machines had limitations, and Bennie and Jet were no exception. They could kill as savagely as any animal on earth, but they had no need to consume their prey. Because of this, they tended to leave some nasty messes lying around.

Before Poppy could say anything to Charlie, he sighed deeply, as though reading her mind, hopped off his stool and headed out to find a body bag.

Good boy.

Eggsy ran down the hall toward Harry's cell. When he'd returned to the distillery, Merlin had filled him in on Harry's progress regaining his memory. Or, rather, lack thereof. Everyone—Champ, Ginger, even Merlin—had decided Harry was a lost cause. But Eggsy wasn't ready to give up on Harry yet.

The door was open, and as Eggsy entered the room, he saw Harry standing next to his bed, packing his meager belongings into a small bag. Eggsy watched him for several seconds. He didn't even *move* like Harry Hart. Harry had moved with a calm, almost zen-like assurance. He'd been a man completely at home in his own skin, who knew who he was and what he had to do at all times. This Harry didn't behave anything like that. His movements were tentative, hesitant, as if he wasn't quite sure of anything. It broke Eggsy's heart to see him like this.

Eggsy leaned back and knocked on the open door to announce his presence. Harry looked up, wary at first, as if he thought someone had come to perform another awful test on him. Eggsy had heard about those tests and how they'd turned out. But since Eggsy wasn't Merlin or Ginger, Harry smiled and gestured for him to enter.

Eggsy walked over to Harry and extended his hand. "Harry."

They shook hands, and Harry looked at Eggsy, frowning slightly. Eggsy felt a stab of sorrow when he realized Harry was struggling to recall his name.

"It's Eggsy," he supplied.

Harry frowned. "Eggy? I should have remembered. Most unusual name."

Eggsy didn't bother to correct him. Harry released his hand and returned to his bed.

"What's going on?" Eggsy asked.

"Just packing." He removed a couple of bottles from his bag and held them up for Eggsy to examine. "Look at these lovely toiletries Merlin very kindly gave me as a leaving present. Try this Kingsman aftershave." He unscrewed the top of the aftershave bottle and sniffed. "Kingsman. Wonderful!" He held it out for Eggsy to try.

Eggsy managed a faint smile. "I know. It's my brand too." He paused, trying to find the words to express what he wanted to say. "Harry... you can't give up *now*."

"Give up? *Au contraire*." Harry put the top back on the aftershave and returned the bottle to his bag. "I'm about to achieve my dream. Researching rare butterflies alongside some of the finest minds in entomology."

"You won't find a more interesting butterfly than me, Harry."

Harry gave Eggsy a quizzical look. "Sorry?"

"When we first met... I was just a maggot."

"Maggots turn into flies," Harry said, not unkindly. "Perhaps you mean 'larva?'"

"Larva. Whatever. Point is, everyone wanted to crush me underfoot. But not you. You helped me grow into a caterpillar. Now I have wings. I'm flying higher than I ever dreamed. And it's all thanks to you."

This seemed to take Harry aback somewhat. "I'm... pleased to have been part of your transformation. Honored."

"You *can't* just walk away," Eggsy said. "Kingsman needs you. And... so do I."

Harry looked at Eggsy and smiled sadly. "Eggy, whoever the Harry was that you knew... he's gone, I'm afraid. And I... need to finish packing and get some sleep."

What else was there to say? People had the right to choose their own paths in life, didn't they? Who was he to stand in Harry's way? Even if this Harry wasn't *his* Harry. They couldn't keep holding the man against his will in hope that one day the real Harry Hart would wake up inside. And how long might that take? Weeks? Months? Years? Forever? This Harry could spend his whole life in captivity, and die here, without ever knowing freedom, without being allowed to live. Eggsy couldn't do that to him.

Depressed after his talk with Harry, Eggsy decided he needed to get out for a while. He drove into the nearest town and stopped at the first bar he came to, a local dive called, appropriately enough, Shitkickers. He sat at the bar and ordered a martini. A few moments later, the bartender sat a shot of whiskey in front of him.

"That ain't a martini," Eggsy said.

"It is in Kentucky," the bartender replied, then stepped away to tend to another customer. Eggsy stared at the drink miserably, remembering the time Harry had taught him how to mix the perfect martini.

A dry vermouth is essential, and despite what Mr Bond says in the movies, stirring is always preferable to shaking. It allows one more control over the final product. When he finished, he raised his glass. *Here's to you, Eggsy. You're exactly what Kingsman needs.*

But that Harry was gone for good. His body might be alive, but the person inhabiting it wasn't him. Or at least, not *all* of him.

He decided to check his voicemail in the hope that Tilde had finally called him back. He took out his phone, and paused for a moment to gaze sadly at the picture of Tilde and JB that served as the device's wallpaper. Calling his voicemail, he listened to a recorded voice say, "You have NO new messages." He sighed heavily.

He pulled Tilde's name up from his contacts list, and wrote her a text.

BABE I'VE NEVER NEEDED U MORE THAN NOW. I LOVE U. HOPE UR OK.

He hit SEND and then sat staring at the screen, whiskey untouched.

Stockholm, Sweden

———————⊘———————

Tilde lay on her bed, the nameless little pug curled up beside her. The puppy wasn't sleeping, though. Its eyes were wide open and watching her intently, as if it knew she was upset but didn't know what to do about it. Her face was wet with tears, and she was fighting to keep from crying again. It seems that's all she did now: cry. She wasn't upset because Eggsy might've slept with that slut whose picture he'd sent her. She hoped he hadn't, of course. What really hurt was that she'd thought Eggsy loved her enough to commit to their relationship. But he obviously didn't. And part of it—so he claimed—was because she was a princess, destined one day to be queen of her country. But she couldn't help that! She'd been born into the royal family. She'd spent her whole life trying to live in two worlds: one, the world of a princess, with all of its duties and responsibilities, and the other, the world of a regular girl. Someone who wasn't special because of who her mother and father were, but because of who *she* was.

Someone who had her own thoughts and ideas, her own *dreams*, who didn't have to worry about protocol or the potential national and international repercussions of her actions. That was why she had this apartment in the city. It was a place where she could go and be just plain Tilde, princess be damned. It was a small place—a living area, kitchenette, bathroom, and bedroom—but it was *hers*.

The pug whined softly, as if sensing her emotional turmoil, and she smiled and scratched its head. What she needed was something to help her calm down, to take the edge off. She reached into her nightstand drawer and took out a joint and a lighter. She lit up, took her first toke, held the smoke in her lungs for several seconds, and then let it out slowly.

God, that was good. She felt better already.

This was *definitely* something she couldn't do in the palace. Marijuana was illegal in Sweden, and most Swedes viewed it as no different from harder drugs such as heroin or cocaine. Alcohol was legal—although Swedes weren't generally big drinkers—and Tilde saw little difference between it and cannabis. As long as one was careful not to overindulge, she saw no harm in it. She knew her parents wouldn't see it the same way, though. The princess smoking an illegal drug? What a scandal! Even so, she smoked rarely, and now was a special occasion. The man she loved may have loved her back, but he didn't love her enough to truly *be* with her, not in the way that mattered most, and this had shattered her heart.

She took another toke as her phone buzzed. She picked

it up, read Eggsy's latest message, and then deleted it. She tossed the phone onto the bed, lay down, exhaled a cloud of smoke, and despite her intention not to cry anymore today, new tears began to flow.

Chapter Eight

———————◆———————

Eggsy paid for the drink he hadn't touched and left the bar. But instead of getting back in the car and returning to the distillery, he decided to go for a walk. Maybe the night air would help clear his mind. Or maybe he'd get lucky and some drunk sod in a car would lose control of his vehicle, jump the curb, plow into him, and put him out of his misery. He'd lost Harry. He'd lost Tilde. Roxy, Brandon, and JB were dead, as were the other Kingsman agents, most of whom he'd gotten to know to one degree or another. It sucked righteously, as a matter of fact, and there wasn't a damn thing he could do about any of it. What was the point of being a highly trained secret agent with access to some of the most sophisticated technology on the planet if you couldn't fix the things that mattered most?

He walked past darkened storefronts, the sidewalk dimly lit by evenly spaced pools of fluorescent light, the headlights from approaching vehicles momentarily blinding him as they rolled past. He walked with his hands in his pockets, head hanging low, sinking deeper into depression with every step. Because of this, he almost missed it. But something caught his attention. Maybe it was the neon glow from the sign over the door. Maybe he saw the store's name out of the corner of his eye and it registered on his subconscious. Or maybe it was just sheer dumb luck. Whatever the reason, he raised his head and turned to look across the street. And there it was: Furry Friends Pet Store.

The letters were blue against white, and although the store was closed, the sign still blazed in the night. He looked at it for a moment, frowning. His brain was trying to tell him something, he knew that, but what—

And then it hit him.

A wide grin came onto his face. He ran across the street, earning several angry honks from drivers who just barely missed running him over. When he reached the store entrance, he withdrew from his pocket a small gadget resembling a tin of breath mints, one of the pieces of equipment he'd gotten from the Statesman's jet. He touched it to the lock, activated it, and an instant later there came a satisfying *snick!* He opened the door and slipped inside the darkened store, swift and silent as a shadow.

The meeting was over, and Poppy had dismissed the sales reps. Some had accepted her offer to stay overnight in the guest quarters she provided, which were as luxurious as any five-star hotel. But most had opted to leave as swiftly as they could, ostensibly to return to their individual territories and get back to work, but she knew the real reason: none of them wanted to end up as playthings for Bennie and Jet, like the dear departed Grigor. She had to admit that she was a little stung by their lack of trust in her, but, all in all, the sooner the Golden Circle resumed normal operations, the better. If her plan worked—which it would, because *she'd* designed it and it was *brilliant*—there was going to be a lot of work to do.

She sat in one of the diner's booths, laptop open on the table in front of her, watching the video she'd made. She'd watched it maybe a dozen times now, and she was certain it would accomplish what she needed it to do. She wasn't reviewing it because she was nervous. She just liked watching herself. After all, she *was* damn impressive on screen.

Charlie entered the diner and trudged over to her. He was soaked from head to foot, and he looked monumentally irritated.

"The dogs are clean," he announced. "You didn't tell me they liked to… *frolic* in water."

Bennie and Jet's central processing units incorporated brain tissue from actual dogs. This meant that from time to time they exhibited a certain playfulness that she found charming. It seemed Charlie, however, had a different opinion on the matter. She smiled.

"Must've slipped my mind."

"Of course it did. If there's nothing else you need me for, I'd like to go dry off."

He turned and started to walk away.

"Charlie…" she said.

He stopped but didn't turn back around to face her.

"Sit down for a minute."

He hesitated, but then he returned to the booth and slid into the seat across the table from her. She closed the laptop and looked at him for a moment before speaking.

"Why drugs, Charlie?" she asked.

He looked at her, uncomprehending.

"I mean, why would someone like me, with both military and business training, decide to go into the drug trade?"

He shrugged. "I hadn't really thought about it. I guess I assumed it's because you like to make money. A lot of it."

"Well, of *course* I like making money! That's the whole point of business, right? The acquisition of profit. But there are far easier ways to make money, Charlie. Safer ways. Ways that don't require a person to live like a hermit in the middle of a bug-infested jungle."

"Maybe you're a user, and after being an amateur for a while, you decided to go pro," he ventured. "Good way to ensure you have a never-ending supply of drugs on hand."

Poppy laughed. "Goodness, no! I *never* touch my product, Charlie. I don't take drugs. I prefer to be in complete control of my mind and body at all times."

"All right then," he said. "Then why drugs?"

"When I was a kid, do you know what I wanted to be when I grew up? I wanted to have my own ice cream truck. Do they have those in England? I wanted to drive around neighborhoods in summer, music blaring from the loudspeaker, and sell ice cream bars and popsicles to all the excited children." She paused, smiling as she pictured the scene in her mind. "To be honest, the frozen treats from those trucks weren't very good, but it wasn't really about them. It was about hearing the truck coming down the street, grabbing a handful of change, running outside and down to the sidewalk and hoping you got there before the ice cream truck passed your house. It was the *experience*, Charlie, don't you see? And for a lot of those children—ones who didn't have picture-perfect families and happy home lives—that short time in their day was a break from their miserable little existences. A respite. A fucking *oasis*. Do you understand?"

Poppy realized that her voice had grown steadily louder as she spoke until she was practically yelling. She pictured other things in her mind, now... things she didn't want to remember, that she'd worked goddamn hard her entire life to forget, as a matter of fact. When both your mom and dad were in the military, and you were an only child, *and* nothing you did was ever good enough for them, they made sure to let you know it— with their words, their fists, whatever object happened to be within reach at the time...

"Poppy? Are you all right?"

"Hmm?" She realized then that Charlie was staring at her. "Of course I am! Never better!" She smiled, and the memories that had come close to surfacing sank back down into the forgotten depths of her mind where they belonged. "Life is hard, Charlie, and people need to do whatever it takes to make it through. Unfortunately, something as simple as ice cream won't do the trick, not with the kind of world we live in. But drugs... well, they help make life bearable for millions of people. Some of those drugs society approves of. Others, it doesn't. Caffeine, nicotine, sugar... But in the end, they're all the same. They're medicine for the *soul*, Charlie. And that's why I went into this business. Because the world needs someone like me. Every now and then, the world needs a break so it can keep going."

She looked into Charlie's eyes to see if he'd gotten what she was trying to say. But then she decided she really didn't care if he'd understood or not. She had a sudden craving for ice cream.

"Go dry yourself off," she said, then slid out of the booth and headed for the kitchen. She hoped there was some Rocky Road left in the freezer.

Harry sat at the desk in his study, sipping a lovely cup of tea and reading the newspaper—or, at least, *trying* to. It was a most peculiar thing; the harder he focused on the words, the more difficult they became to make out, as if the ink was in a constant state of flux, perpetually sliding from one configuration to another, unrecognizable as part of the English language. He supposed it was due to some sort of printing error, and he was considering calling *The Times* and lodging a formal complaint when he heard a thumping noise from downstairs.

He lay the paper down and listened. An intruder, perhaps? To a Kingsman, a garden-variety burglar wouldn't prove to be any real threat, so he felt no fear at the thought. Then again, if someone could get past *his* security measures, then he or she could hardly be called "garden variety" now, could they?

He continued listening for several moments, but he heard nothing more. He might've thought he'd imagined the thump, but as a highly trained agent, he wasn't given to flights of fancy. If he'd heard a thump, then most likely it was real and something or someone had caused it. He slid his chair back from the desk slowly, to make as little noise as possible, and stood.

He then walked, silent as a cat, out of the study and toward the stairs. In the hall, he passed a grandfather clock, one that had been in his family for generations. Instead of numbers, tiny heads poked through holes in the clock's face, all male, all wearing Kingsman eyeglasses. Harry recognized them as fellow agents, but when he looked more closely, he saw they were all the *same* agent. Him, as a matter of fact. The hands of the clock were two-headed axes, and the hour-hand axe was pressed against the neck of the miniature Harry whose head was in the ten position, while the minute-hand axe had already begun to cut into the neck of the Harry in the seven position. Blood trickled from the wound, and Harry Seven's tiny features were contorted with pain and fear.

How very odd, Harry thought and continued to the stairs.

He listened as he descended, the wood absolutely silent beneath his feet. He kept his home in tip-top condition for occasions such as this. No creaking stairs or squeaking door hinges in the Hart residence, thank you very much. He would be absolutely mortified if he gave himself away to an intruder in such an amateurish fashion, and he'd deserve whatever fate befell him.

For an instant he saw an African-American man standing grim-faced before him, a Heckler & Koch P30 gripped in his right hand. The man raised the weapon, aimed, and fired. A bullet discharged from the muzzle, but instead of flashing instantaneously across the space between them, the round traveled slowly, so much so that it barely seemed to be moving at all. Harry couldn't move, couldn't so much as breathe. All he could do was stand frozen in place and watch the bullet make its tortuous way toward him, one millimeter at a time. And then, when the tip of the round had almost made contact with the left lens of his eyeglasses, it accelerated to normal speed. The lens shattered, the bullet plunged into his eye, and everything went dark.

Harry staggered on the steps, grabbing hold of the railing to keep himself from falling. He had no idea what that horribly disquieting vision was, or what had inspired it, but it was gone now, leaving him with only a dull pain in his left eye to remind him it had happened at all. He pushed all thoughts of the vision aside. He was a Kingsman, and he had a mission—investigate the mysterious thump—and he had to remain focused. He continued downward.

When he reached the bottom of the stairs, he saw the door to the first-floor bathroom was open. He didn't remember leaving it that way, but he didn't remember *not* leaving it that way either. He didn't seem to recall much, actually, including how he came to be sitting in his study having tea in the first place. He stepped into the bathroom, and at first everything seemed normal. No one else was in the room. The butterfly displays still hung on the walls, and Mr Pickle's taxidermied body rested on the shelf above the toilet. The reason he'd put Mr Pickle in here was because Kingsman trainees had to take their pups with them wherever they went and whatever they did—which included answering nature's call. When the training period was over, and Harry took Mr Pickle home, there was no longer a need for the Yorkie to accompany him to the loo. But Mr Pickle would sit outside the closed door, whining and scratching at it until Harry relented and allowed him in. Thus, the bathroom became a symbol to Harry of Mr Pickle's loyalty, of how the little dog wouldn't allow any barrier to separate them. So after Mr Pickle died, Harry had his body preserved and placed it in the bathroom as a way of showing that not even death could separate the two of them. Sentimental tosh, perhaps, but there it was.

He was about to leave the bathroom and check the rest of the downstairs, when he noticed that a square space on the wall was empty. Strange that he'd missed that. He looked down at the floor and saw one of his displays— this one featuring brushfoots such as the monarch, the painted lady, and the mourning cloak—had fallen to the floor. Well, now he knew what had caused the thump

he'd heard. Fearing the specimens had been damaged—
for no matter how carefully one prepared and mounted
butterflies, their bodies were still quite fragile—he knelt
down to look closer at the display. He didn't pick it up
right away, out of concern he might cause further damage.
Instead, he leaned closer and examined it. Upon first
glance, everything appeared to be in order. Some of the
butterflies' positions had shifted slightly, but he thought
he'd be able to set them right without too much—

The painted lady's left wing moved.

Not much, just a little, as if stirred by a breath of air.
Only one problem: he was holding his breath.

The painted lady burst into sudden life, flapping her
wings furiously. She pulled herself free of the mounting
pin and took to the air, flashing past Harry's face in a blur
of orange, black, and white. He felt a sharp sting on his
right cheek, and when he reached up to touch his face,
his fingers came away with dots of blood on them. The
painted lady had cut him as she'd flown by. He knew it
was a ridiculous thought. Butterfly wings were far too
soft to cause any sort of injury simply by brushing against
human skin. But then again, a dead butterfly suddenly
returning to life and flying around your bathroom was
ridiculous too, but that's exactly what had happened.

Harry, struggling to understand this tiny miracle,
stood and watched the painted lady circle lazily around
him. She was beautiful—mesmerizing, actually—and he
couldn't take his eyes off her. She darted down toward his
hand, then dipped her right wing to his skin and sliced

another quick cut before pulling upward. Harry hissed in pain and drew his hand back. Blood welled from the wound, quite a bit this time. She'd cut him deep. He clapped his other hand on top of the cut to staunch the blood, and looked this way and that, trying to spot the painted lady before she could strike again.

That's when he heard the fluttering of wings—dozens upon dozens of them—and he saw that all the butterflies in the displays were alive and fighting to free themselves from their mounting-board prisons. One by one they succeeded and took to the air, and a riot of color swirled around Harry, as if he were caught in a brilliant multicolored storm. Butterflies dipped toward him, wings sharp as shattered glass, slicing the exposed skin of his face, neck, and hands just as the painted lady had. He swung his arms wildly in an attempt to fight them off, but they easily avoided being struck and continued attacking.

A blue morpho nearly severed his left earlobe, and a peacock sliced into the skin just below his Adam's apple and blood ran down to soak his shirt. A red admiral cut the skin above his left eye, causing blood to flow downward and obscure his vision, and a meadow brown cut across the tender flesh of his upper lip and blood filled his mouth.

Mr Pickle raised his head then, and his glass eyes gazed into Harry's. A voice issued from the dead dog, although his stitched-together mouth never moved.

Best get a move on if you don't want to be sliced into confetti, Harry.

Harry thought that was a capital idea, just ace. Leave it to good old Mr Pickle to cut to the heart of the matter with canine good sense.

He turned and fled. But when he stepped across the bathroom's threshold, he didn't return to the first-floor hallway of his home. Instead, he found himself standing in the aisle of the South Glade Mission Church.

Bodies of men and women were strewn everywhere, lying on the floor, draped across overturned pews, hanging halfway out of broken stained-glass windows. They had been shot, stabbed, bludgeoned, burnt, or simply had their necks broken. The harsh tang of gunpowder hung heavy in the air, along with the coppery smell of blood, and the stink of released bowels and bladders. A few of these people had killed each other, but Harry knew he was responsible for the majority of deaths that had occurred here.

This church had been a haven for a bigoted hate group whose members saw everyone who wasn't white, straight, and their version of godly as less than human and worthy only of contempt. Nevertheless, they had been human beings—massively flawed, perhaps even in their own way evil—but they had done nothing to deserve the savage deaths he'd visited upon them. He felt an overwhelming sense of guilt, so strong it nearly drove him to his knees.

"I'm sorry," he said softly into the church's quiet. "I... had no control."

He heard a woman speak. "He says he's *sorry!*"

The first victim of his madness, a blond woman in

a pink blouse and gray skirt whose face he'd destroyed with a bullet, rose from the floor. She moved with awkward, stiff motions, as if her body was having trouble remembering how to function. Her face was a ravaged, crimson ruin with gobbets of shredded flesh clinging to blood-slick bone, but her eyes were intact, and they glared at him with pure hatred.

"Well, sorry don't feed the bulldog, mister!" she said. Her lips were gone, as were most of her front teeth, but she still somehow managed to speak clearly.

Others began rising, one by one, moving with the same jerking motions as the faceless woman, until the entire congregation was on its feet and staring at him with absolute loathing.

The faceless woman was incapable of smiling, but Harry heard the grim satisfaction in her voice when she next spoke.

"Time to pay for your sins, you jew-nigger-fag lover!"

The congregation surged forward, and before Harry could do anything, blood-smeared hands took hold of him and lifted him off his feet. He was carried to the front of the church, the rest of the worshipers parting to make way for the procession. Two of the larger men grabbed hold of his wrists and pushed him against the wall. Harry struggled to free himself, but the dead men were inhumanly strong, and there was nothing he could do. The faceless woman walked up to him, accompanied by the church's minister, a man in a blue jacket, a mustard-yellow shirt, and a truly hideous tie. He held three long metal rods with sharpened ends and grinned with blood-coated teeth.

"Let's see how you look once *you've* been mounted, Butterfly Man," the faceless woman said.

She held out her right hand, and the minister gave her one of the rods. She gripped it tight, and then she rushed forward and thrust the pointed end through the palm of Harry's left hand and into the wall behind. Harry screamed as blood gushed from the wound. The minister gave the woman a second rod, and she stabbed this one through his right palm. Harry screamed again. The men holding his wrists let go then, for they were no longer needed to hold him in place.

The pain from his wounds was so intense that Harry felt on the verge of blacking out. His head drooped, but the minister handed the last rod to the faceless woman who stepped forward, took a handful of his hair, and lifted his head so he could see her.

"If thine eye offend thee…" she said, and thrust the rod into his left eye.

He screamed one final time as darkness rushed in to claim him.

Harry was sleeping when Eggsy stepped into his room. *Probably dreaming of butterflies*, Eggsy thought. He stepped quietly to the side of the cot and gently placed a Yorkie puppy next to Harry. The puppy padded over to Harry's face and began licking his cheek. Harry woke with a start, eyes filled with fright, as if he'd been having a bad dream. But then he realized that an adorable little dog was licking his face, and he smiled in confusion and reached out to pet the Yorkie.

"Got you a leaving present," Eggsy said. "He's lovely, isn't he?"

Harry realized that Eggsy was in the room, and he turned to look at him, confused. He sat up, picked up the puppy, and held it in his lap. Before he could ask any questions, Eggsy raised his Kingsman pistol and aimed it at the Yorkie.

"Think I should shoot it?" he asked.

Harry gaped at him in horror. He snatched the puppy up in his arms, and twisted his torso away from Eggsy, attempting to shield the Yorkie with his body.

"Are you quite mad?" he demanded. "You'll have to shoot me! No one's sick enough to shoot a puppy!"

"You were, Harry," Eggsy said. "Do you remember?"

Harry's expression changed. His features went slack, and a faraway look came into his eye, as if he was remembering something. Eggsy had a good idea what that something was. He imagined a younger version of Harry standing in Arthur's office, looking at Mr Pickle, gun pointed at the animal as Arthur said, "Shoot the dog." He pictured Harry's hand trembling, his lips pressed into a tight line as he forced himself to squeeze the trigger…

"It was a blank!" Harry shouted. "It was a fucking blank! I would *never* hurt Mr Pickle! He lived to a ripe old age. He died of *pancreatitis*, he…" Harry broke off, confused. He looked down at the puppy he was holding, and the Yorkie licked his nose.

Eggsy lowered his gun, ecstatic. "Yes! Yes, Harry!"

Harry turned away from the dog to look at him. His eye narrowed and he said, tentatively, "Eggsy?"

The two men stared at each other for a moment, and then Eggsy couldn't restrain himself any longer. He rushed forward and gave his mentor a hug.

Harry pushed Eggsy away. "Eggsy! Valentine has to be stopped. He has a device…"

"It's okay. It's been sorted." Eggsy grinned. "We have a lot of catching up to do."

"So, Galahad… I suppose I should cancel your taxi."

They turned to see Merlin had walked into the room. Harry smiled. "Yes. If you don't mind—Merlin."

Merlin grinned. "Welcome back."

Elton John strolled down Poppyland's main street, bored out of his fucking mind. He told himself to look on the bright side: at least Poppy hadn't locked him up again. *Since keeping you in a cage didn't keep you out of trouble, you might as well have the run of the place*, she had said. He didn't quite understand why she'd been so upset that he'd accepted Angel's offer to party a bit. After all, she *was* a drug lord, wasn't she? Not exactly the type of person you'd think would object to some mild recreational use. And speaking of Angel, where *was* he? Elton hadn't seen the man anywhere. He hoped he hadn't gotten into *too* much trouble for trying to make his stay chez Poppy a bit more tolerable. Maybe Poppy would dock his pay or something.

He honestly had no idea how Poppy had managed to abduct him. One moment he'd been sipping champagne at a benefit to raise funds to combat climate change— sponsored by Richmond fucking Valentine of all people—and the next thing he knew, he found himself waking on a bed inside a cell somewhere in Cambodia, the pet musician of the absolutely barmy Poppy Adams. He assumed she—or more likely, one of her people—had slipped a sedative of some kind in his drink. He sighed. Why couldn't she have been a Keith Richards fan?

So far, being free to wander around this lunatic asylum wasn't much better than being a prisoner. He was still in a cage, only this one was a lot larger. He'd considered trying to escape, but where would he go? Without a guide and supplies, he'd get lost in the jungle and likely die there. He'd stopped in at the bowling alley, but he'd never been all that fond of the game, and he'd gone to the beauty parlor and attempted to have a conversation with the robot stylist who worked there, thinking that— as an artificial life form—she might have an interesting perspective on the human race. But she kept trying to get him to put his feet in a tank of *Garra rufa* fish. He might have gone for it if he hadn't spotted bloodstains on the edges of the tank.

He was considering returning to his cell and taking a nap, when he spotted the diner up ahead. Angel had told him something about a hamburger he'd eaten there.

Elton couldn't remember what precisely, as neither of them had been especially clear-headed at the time, but a burger sounded good. Maybe with a root beer float.

When Elton reached the diner, he looked through the main window and saw that Poppy and Charlie were inside, talking. He didn't want to see Poppy right now, not after that humiliating duet she'd forced him to sing with her. And while Charlie was handsome enough to look at, he was—not to mince words—an utter prat. Elton decided to move along, but before he could step away from the window, he heard a sound behind him, a soft whirring, like a computer's cooling fan. He spun around to see Poppy's robot dogs Bennie and Jet—god, how he *loathed* those names—standing in the street, looking at him, their optical units glowing an angry red.

Elton was scared shitless. He'd never seen the beasts in action, thank god, but Angel had told him about them and about what they would do if they caught any intruders. Poppy had said it was all right if he roamed the compound, but what if she hadn't informed the dogs of that? Or worse, what if she'd planned it this way, tricked him into leaving his cell so these two metal monsters could tear him to shreds? It would be just like her.

One of the dogs walked up to him. Elton tried to pull back, but there was nowhere to go, and he only succeeded in bumping into the window. The dog didn't lunge at him right away. Instead, it pressed its face against his leg and held it there. Words scrolled across the creature's optical scanner: SNIFFING... IDENTIFYING... ELTON JOHN.

The dog's scanner switched from red to green, as did its companion's. Then the creature turned and the pair scampered off down the street, presumably in search of someone else to terrify.

Elton let out a ragged gasp of relief. *That was too fucking close!*

He nearly had a heart attack when Poppy's voice issued from a speaker hidden somewhere on the diner's exterior.

"Sit!"

The dogs obeyed her command.

"Curiosity killed the cat, Elton! And you *really* don't wanna be a cat with my dogs around. So skedaddle."

"I'm sorry, I'm sorry!" Elton said.

"I know you are, sweetheart. Hurry up."

"Fucking bitch," Elton muttered beneath his breath and started walking.

Eggsy, Harry, Merlin, and Jack sat at a booth in Shitkickers. Harry still wore the gray tracksuit the Statesman agents had given him, but his bearing had changed completely. He sat straight and projected a combination of relaxed calm and keen alertness. His eyepatch had gotten him some looks when they'd first entered, but people soon ignored it. They'd ordered drinks—whiskey for Jack, scotch for Merlin, and a draft beer for Eggsy. Harry had opted for a glass of water. He'd only just gotten his senses back, and he wasn't ready to take leave of them again just yet. When Eggsy tasted his beer, he found it weak as

Harry's water. He wished they stocked bitter here.

"Any questions, Agent Galahad?" Jack asked. The American agent had just finished filling Harry in on everything that had happened since Valentine had shot him. Jack was decked out in his usual black outfit and cowboy hat, but tonight he'd added a new accessory to his look: a leather handle he wore attached to his belt. It resembled the handle of a whip but with nothing attached to it. Eggsy had asked Jack about it, and the American agent had smiled and said simply, *This old thing? I never leave home without it*.

At first, Eggsy thought Jack had been speaking to him when he'd said Agent Galahad. But of course he'd been addressing Harry. *Looks like I'll need to get myself a new code name*, Eggsy thought. *Maybe Lancelot, to honor Roxy*.

Harry took a small sip of his water before answering. "Well, I'm still a bit foggy, but... I do want to thank you for agreeing to hold this debrief off-property. I really needed to get out." He smiled. "I've been stuck in your HQ a long time."

Jack acknowledged Harry's gratitude with a nod.

Eggsy was beyond thrilled to have Harry—the old Harry—back again. It was as if, after the deaths of Roxy, Brandon, and the others, the Grim Reaper decided he'd gone a step too far and had sent Harry back by way of apology. He only wished they could've found a more... genial location to hold their celebration of Harry's return. This place was more than a bit on the rough side. The men wore John Deere caps, flannel shirts, grimy jeans, and heavy work boots. The women wore tight low-cut shirts, tighter jeans, and far too much makeup. The concrete floor was covered with stains whose chemical composition Eggsy preferred to remain ignorant of, and the phlegm-yellow paint on the walls was coming off in scale-like flakes. Numerous holes and gashes in the plaster spoke of the many fights that had broken out in here over the years, and the tables were covered with poorly spelled and mostly obscene graffiti cut into the surfaces by generations of knives. The people were loud, and there was an undercurrent of hostility in their voices, an anger simmering just beneath the surface that threatened to erupt at any moment. It all made for an atmosphere of roiling tension, and Eggsy felt constantly on guard, unable to relax and simply enjoy having his friend back. All in all, it seemed like exactly the sort of place where Jack belonged, and Eggsy wasn't surprised the American agent had brought them here.

Eggsy told himself to forget about where they were and focus on the reason they were here. He smiled at Harry. "If we're done with the debrief, we've got some welcome-back gifts for you." He'd brought them with him in a large shopping bag that he'd placed on the floor next to his seat. He reached into the bag now, drew out a Kingsman watch and umbrella, and handed them to Harry, who accepted them with a grateful smile. He lay the umbrella across his lap and put the watch on his left wrist.

Eggsy then brought out a small box and slid it across the table to Harry.

"And *these*," Eggsy said. "Merlin made them just for you."

Harry opened the box to find a pair of AR glasses with a black left lens. He looked at them a moment, before lowering his face, slipping off his eyepatch, and donning the glasses. He then raised his head and tucked the eyepatch away in his trouser pocket.

"Thank you, Eggsy, Merlin." He nodded to each in turn and then smiled happily. "How do I look?"

Before either of them could answer, a man sitting at the table next to them—a very large, very *drunk* man—spoke.

"Like a faggot looking for an eye-fucking," he growled. "Why don't you get out of our bar before I take out your other one?" His head was shaved, and he had a brown mustache and goatee with hints of gray in the latter. He wore jeans and a black T-shirt that had an image of a coiled rattlesnake on the chest above the words DON'T TREAD ON ME, MOTHERFUCKER!

Three other men sat at the table with him, all of a type: beards, tats, with mean eyes and meaner mouths. They laughed at their friend's words, but Rattlesnake didn't join in. Instead he kept his hate-filled gaze fixed on Harry.

Jack scowled, and when he spoke, his voice was tight with anger. "That how you welcome a visitor from out of town, Moonshine? I suggest you apologize. *Right now*."

"Yeah," Eggsy said, turning to face the man. "Don't fuck with the Brits. Ever hear about what happened to all them rednecks at that church down the road?"

Rattlesnake glared at him. "Aw, suck my southern dick, bitch!"

The man's friends weren't laughing any longer. Now the four rednecks were glaring at the four of them, and Eggsy knew it was only a matter of seconds before a fight broke out.

"I don't think *that* will be necessary," Harry said.

He picked up his umbrella and stood, winking at Eggsy before turning to face the table of rednecks.

"I think discretion is the better part of valor," he said evenly. "Good day, gentlemen."

The men guffawed, and Rattlesnake said, "Yeah, you *git*, boy!"

Harry walked to the door and began locking it. The rest of the bar had gone quiet and everyone was watching.

"Manners maketh man," Harry said slowly. "Do you know what that means?" The men said nothing, and Harry turned and gave them a small smile. "Then let me teach you a lesson."

Jack started to rise from the table, but Eggsy put a hand on his shoulder to stop him.

"It's okay," he said, settling back to enjoy the show. "Just watch."

Jack looked doubtful, but he sat. Merlin looked concerned as well, but he didn't say anything. He didn't look at the rednecks, either. Instead, he watched Harry, eyes narrowed, observing him intensely.

Harry flipped his umbrella into the air, caught it by the end, and swept the handle toward Eggsy's beer mug. He caught hold of it, and in a single smooth motion, hurled it at Rattlesnake. Eggsy expected the mug to strike the loudmouthed bastard on the forehead, but instead it sailed past him, missing him by almost a foot. The mug kept going until Jack caught it.

The four rednecks stared at the mug in Jack's hand, as if they weren't sure what had just happened.

Harry stood there, confused, his eye darting back and forth as if he were looking at something that wasn't there. *Butterflies?* Eggsy wondered.

"Are we going to stand around all day?" Harry said, his eye still tracking the invisible somethings. "Or are we going to—"

The rednecks bellowed in rage, flew out of their seats, and attacked Harry. They started swinging punches, and while Harry managed to block some of the blows with his umbrella, more than a few got past his defenses. At one point, Harry opened his umbrella and held it out before him, but before he could activate any of its weapons, one of the rednecks punched him through the umbrella's fabric. Within seconds, Harry was down on the floor, dazed.

"Well, pick him up," Jack said.

Eggsy and Merlin quickly rose from the booth to tend to their friend, and Jack stood and walked over to the rednecks. Eggsy and Merlin helped Harry back to the booth while Jack regarded the four men who'd attacked Harry.

"That's not what *I* call a Kentucky welcome," Jack said, eyes narrowed and voice tight. "'Manners maketh man.' Let me translate that for you."

Jack pulled the leather handle from his belt and thumbed a switch on the side. A length of rope emerged from the handle, the tip coiling around and tying itself into a lasso. He swung the rope, caught hold of a chair, and flung it into one of the rednecks. The chair broke apart with a crack of splintering wood, and the man went down. Jack retracted the lasso into the handle, and then extended it toward a second man. The rope encircled him, and Jack spun him toward the bar. The man's head collided with the bar with a sickening thump, and he collapsed to the floor.

Rattlesnake drew a knife and rushed toward Jack. Jack flung the rope toward the man, jumping through the loop as he did so. The lasso caught hold of the man's knife hand and drew tight around his wrist. Jack yanked, and the knife flew out of the man's hand. He pulled the man toward him, caught the knife, and stabbed the bastard in the shoulder with it. The man screamed, and Jack loosened the lasso to release him, and then threw him against the bar. The man bounced off and went down to lie next to his companion.

The last redneck attacked, and Jack caught him with the lasso and hurled him onto a table. The impact caused the table to collapse beneath him, and he lay there, stunned.

By this point, the other three rednecks had gotten to their feet. They might have been a bit the worse for wear, but they were mad as hell now and ready to get back into the fight. Jack pressed a control on the handle, and the lasso untied itself and became a whip. He spun it around and cracked it against the floor, as if daring the rednecks to come at him. They took the bait and charged.

Jack lashed the whip toward one, catching him around the neck and flipping him onto a pool table. He caught a second man's wrist, yanked him in, and punched him in the face. He threw a third man onto the concrete floor, and he slid a dozen feet before coming to a stop. The fourth redneck—Rattlesnake—came stumbling toward him. He caught hold of a chair, swung it into the fucker, and the impact sent him crashing through a window.

Eggsy looked at Jack, impressed as hell. He'd taken out those four bastards in seconds without breaking a sweat. Jack smiled at Eggsy, tipped his hat. He thumbed a switch on the handle, and the whip retracted. He then replaced the handle on his belt and walked back to the booth.

The other bar patrons had watched the fight in silence up to this point, but now that it was over, they burst into wild applause, whistling and cheering. Jack acknowledged their reaction with a nod of his head, and several other men took it upon themselves to collect the unconscious rednecks and begin dragging them outside.

Harry, a bit roughed up but essentially unharmed, turned to Jack as he approached.

"Thank you," he said. "Impressive work with that lassoo."

"It's pronounced *lasso*," Jack said, scowling. "Rhymes with asshole."

Harry turned away from Jack, no longer able to meet his gaze.

"I… I don't know what happened. I… saw butterflies. They were all around me. I…"

Eggsy and Merlin exchanged glances, and then Merlin put a hand on Harry's shoulder. "We rebuilt your neural pathways. It'll take time to get coordination back. Time and retraining. And you may experience... episodes. Lapses of clarity. I'm sorry."

Harry nodded his understanding, but Eggsy could see that Merlin's words deeply troubled him.

Just then, a loud burst of static noise blasted from the TV mounted in the corner behind the bar, and everyone in the place turned to look at the screen, Eggsy, Harry, Merlin, and Jack included.

A golden circle appeared briefly on the screen, and faded to reveal a red-headed woman, wearing glasses and a yellow jacket, seated in a black leather chair. On the wall behind her was a sign that read POPPY'S PHARMACEUTICALS. Her expression was serious, and her green eyes shone with intensity.

"Mr President. My name is Poppy Adams. I am a proud American, a military veteran, and CEO of the Golden Circle, worldwide distributor and manufacturer of non-regulated pharmaceuticals. I believe that the UN has no teeth, so I have selected you, as the leader of the free world, to receive this communication. And I am inviting you to begin negotiations in the largest scale hostage situation in history."

She rose from her chair and began walking across the stage, still facing the camera.

"Over the past week an engineered virus has been released, contained in all varieties of my product: cannabis, cocaine, heroin, opium, ecstasy, and crystal meth. Alas, it's already too late for the early birds. But here's what the rest of the world can expect in the coming days."

She stopped before a row of opaque isolation cells, four in all. She snapped her fingers and one of the cells became transparent, revealing a man dressed in a tracksuit, his skin covered with a blue rash.

"After a brief incubation period, victims will begin to show first-stage symptoms: a blue rash."

She stepped to the second cell, snapped her fingers again, and a woman in a tracksuit with the same rash was revealed. But unlike the man, who seemed calm, she was clearly distraught, almost frenzied, pounding on the glass and yelling, although no sound was emitted from within the cell.

"Next, victims begin to present with stage two symptoms as the virus invades the brain: disinhibition, delusion, dementia... *Very* distressing for the victim and those around them."

A third cell, a third snap of the fingers, another rash sufferer revealed. Unlike the previous two, this man lay on a bed, unmoving, his body rigid.

"Stage three: paralysis. Muscles enter a state of catastrophic seizure. And once the muscles of the thorax are affected, breathing becomes impossible."

As if on cue, the man's eyes bugged out, projecting absolute terror. After several long moments of suffering, his gaze dulled, and it was clear that he was gone.

"Leading to a very nasty death. But I have good news

for the millions already infected: it doesn't have to end this way."

Her grave expression brightened as she went to the last cell. A snap of her fingers revealed Elton John, also wearing a tracksuit. He was covered with the blue rash, standing rigid, eyes desperate and pleading. Inside the cell, a male nurse stood next to Elton, holding a small vial of liquid.

"I have an antidote," Poppy said, smiling.

The nurse held up the vial for the camera to see, then put it to Elton's lips and gently poured the contents into his mouth. Within seconds, the rash began to fade, and Elton's body relaxed. Able to move again, he rushed toward the glass and started pounding on it, yelling at the nurse.

"Get out! Get out! Get out of my fucking room!"

Poppy ignored Elton's outburst.

"One hundred percent effective, and ready to ship out worldwide at a moment's notice. You have my word that I'll make that happen. If the following conditions are met. First: you agree to end the war on drugs once and for all. All classes of substance are legalized, paving the way for a new marketplace in which sales are regulated and taxed, as per alcohol. Next: my associates and I receive full legal immunity. And finally: the Golden Circle becomes a registered corporation, with an IPO in twelve months. Meet my terms, and I look forward to helping you keep our beloved country great—boosting our ailing economy and relieving spending on law enforcement. Or continue this blinkered, outmoded, and frankly *disastrous* exercise in prohibition, and live with blood on your hands."

A slogan appeared on the screen beneath her image: SAVE LIVES—LEGALIZE.

The camera remained focused on her face for a few seconds longer, and then the screen went dark.

The bar's patrons remained absolutely silent for several moments, stunned by what they had just seen and heard, then everyone began talking at once in loud, fearful voices. Jack's watch buzzed. He glanced at the dial and then looked up at the others.

"Champ wants to see us. Now."

Poppy may have addressed her message to the American president, but it was broadcast worldwide, and people across the planet reacted with shock and dismay.

The trading floor at the New York Stock Exchange was in total chaos as terrified Wall Street traders panicked.

At Glastonbury, festivalgoers swarmed the medical tent.

There was panic in Magaluf as partygoers freaked out.

The streets in Compton erupted in mayhem.

In an assembly at a posh British school, uniformed students tried to hide their alarm from the concerned headmaster on stage.

In overrun hospitals around the world, medical staff relying on "alternative medications" to help them combat the effects of sleep deprivation felt the same terror as their virus-infected patients.

In the American states where marijuana remained

praying she'd see some movement in it. And then, there it was! Faint, but unmistakable—a pulse. But one so weak, she knew it wouldn't hold. Tequila was going to die, and there was nothing she could do about it. At least, there was nothing she could do about it *now*. But if she put him in cryogenic suspension, he'd remain as he was, hovering between life and death, until she could discover a cure. Assuming, of course, she succeeded. If she didn't, Tequila would remain frozen forever. It wasn't much of a chance, but it was the only one the man had.

Working swiftly, Ginger prepped a cryo tube, slid Tequila into it, sealed it, and turned it on. She watched as the tube's plastic window became covered with frost, hiding Tequila from her view. She let out a long, shuddering sigh. She'd done all she could. She hoped it was enough.

She wondered where Merlin was right now. She could use someone to talk to, someone who understood what it was like to wear so many hats and carry so much responsibility. More than that—she needed *him*. But first, she had to tell Champ what had happened to Tequila.

She pulled her phone from her slacks pocket and made the call.

The Oval Office, Washington, D.C.

Fox Nouvelle sat across the *Resolute* desk from the president. Queen Victoria had given this desk as a gift to Rutherford B. Hayes in 1880. It was made from the wood of the British Arctic exploration ship *Resolute*— hence the name—and had been used by many presidents in the years since. The desk had a long and distinguished history, something Fox wasn't certain she would be able to say about her tenure at the White House. Being the president's chief of staff was a high-stress job in any administration, but working with *this* president—with his hair-trigger temper, mercurial whims, and tendency to seek vengeance for any slight, large or small, real or imagined—was nothing *but* stress twenty-four seven. She felt as if she were always on the verge of being fired, or worse: summoned by Congress to testify about one scandal or another that the president was embroiled in. Fox's job was a combination of personal secretary, sounding board, babysitter, and ego-booster, and she never knew which role the president expected her to play at any given moment.

So things were bad enough around here on a regular day. But this had ceased being anything *close* to a regular day the moment Poppy Adams had broadcast her video message for the entire world to see. Before the video had finished playing, world leaders began calling the president to urge him to comply with Poppy's demands. So many had phoned that the president had been forced to have staffers speak to them. Except the Russian president, of course. They were old friends, and the president *always* took his calls.

The president was standing, hands on his desk,

leaning forward as if he might leap over it and attack Fox at any moment. The president was a tall man, over six feet, and although he was in his early seventies, he possessed the presence and energy of a much younger man. He was wealthy enough to afford the finest tailored suits, but despite this, his clothes were always rumpled and ill-fitting, and his hair—what there was of it—was an unruly, untamable tangle, as if it were a reflection of the brain beneath.

Another of the president's trusted advisors, General Bannon McCoy, stood nearby, hands behind his back, expression stern. He always looked like that. Fox thought the man's face would probably shatter into a thousand pieces if he ever tried to smile.

"Prepare the bill for legislation," the president said. "And tell intelligence and law enforcement to stand down. We're going to dance to this lady's tune."

Fox felt a wave of relief at the president's words. "Good. We can make this work. Spin it that it's not a matter of negotiating with terrorists, it's—"

"No. I'm proposing that we *appear* to agree to her demands to prevent global panic. Then we let the junkie scum go down in flames and take Poppy Adams and her so-called Golden Circle down with them. No users, no drug trade. We're in a win-win situation here."

There was no way to predict what might come out of the president's mouth at any given moment, and because of this, Fox was used to maintaining a noncommittal expression whenever the president spoke to her. But now her mouth fell open in shock.

"Mr President, sir, we're not talking about a handful of hostages. We could be looking at the deaths of hundreds of millions, worldwide!"

The president plopped back down in his chair and folded his hands across his paunch. "Hundreds of millions of criminals and burdens to society," he said.

Fox knew the president hated to be challenged, but she felt in this case she needed to push the matter a little harder.

"Sir, that's not... What about people who were just experimenting? Folks who self-medicate? Functioning professionals? Kids?"

"Ugh, spare me your crap, Fox." The president grinned. "Fact is, this presidency just won the war on drugs. No drug users, no drug trade." He turned to the general. "Am I right, McCoy?"

The general, still grim-faced, nodded, but Fox thought she could see a gleam of satisfaction in his eyes.

She did her best to smile, because it was expected of her. But inside, she was thinking, *This is going to be a disaster.* She looked longingly at the Oval Office's liquor cabinet. The president didn't drink, but Fox sure could use a belt right now. And that bottle of Statesman whiskey sitting on the shelf at the back of the cabinet looked mighty tempting...

Eggsy, Harry, and Jack had gathered in Champ's office at his request. Harry had donned a Kingsman suit, and—except for the one black lens of his glasses—he finally looked like his old self. Champ sat behind his desk, the other men sat in front of it, and resting on the surface of the desk was a belt buckle in the shape of the Statesman logo. In reality, the buckle was a powerful audio receiver, one that picked up transmissions from agency listening devices. And right now, it was tuned in to one device in particular: the one hidden within the Oval Office's liquor cabinet. They'd just finished listening to the conversation between the president, Fox, and General McCoy, and none of them had liked what they'd heard.

Champ had been tasting a new batch of whiskey for quality control while they'd listened. He spit a mouthful into a spittoon on the floor next to his chair, then capped the bottle and set it on his desk.

"Whether they broke the law or not, those victims are human beings," Champ said. "Tequila's a great guy and a great agent. And right now, he's lying in a deep-freeze, waiting on our help."

Eggsy noticed that Jack didn't look at Champ as he spoke. He looked *past* Champ at the stock ticker screen on the wall behind him. Eggsy was no expert, but if he was reading the bloody thing right, Statesman's share prices were plummeting. It made sense. Poppy had said nothing about her virus being spread through alcohol, but alcohol was a drug too, and it looked like people didn't intend to take any chances.

"We can't make this personal, sir," Jack said.

"Personal?" Champ practically roared the word. "Agent, we can't stand by and allow folks like Tequila to die. We're

217

these people's only hope. We have to find that antidote."

If Jack felt stung by his boss's rebuke, he didn't show it. "Poppy's stockpiles could be anywhere," he said.

"She must have *some* at hand, though," Harry said. "Locate Poppy and we could obtain a sample for analysis. Then maybe it could be replicated."

The receiver on Champ's desk beeped. Champ touched the buckle, and a new voice issued from the device. It was Ginger.

"Gotta cut in, guys. Countess Clara is on with Charlie. Looping you in now."

Countess Clara's voice cut in, and she sounded desperate.

"Why didn't you just *tell* me? All you said was, 'Don't take any drugs!' It was a music festival, for fuck's sake!"

Eggsy understood what had happened. Clara had the blue rash. The next voice they heard belonged to Charlie.

"Shit. Shit! Okay... Listen. You need to get to the lab in Italy. Remember where we went skiing? I'll meet you there and give you the antidote."

They both fell silent, and the transmission ended.

"Jet's ready. Whiskey, Galahad—good luck."

Eggsy, Harry, and Jack all stood.

"You guys really need to fix this code-name thing," Jack said before turning to Champ. "And with all due respect, sir, I don't think Galahad senior is ready to return to field work."

Champ looked suddenly uncomfortable. "Yeah. I, uh, did actually mean—"

"Of course," Harry said. And then, more softly, "Of course."

He sat back down quickly, obviously humiliated. Eggsy couldn't stand to see him like that. He glared at Champ.

"And with all *dis*respect, I'm not going anywhere without him." He pointed to Harry, "Brains," then himself, "skills," then Jack, "skipping rope."

Champ laughed.

"It's a lasso," Jack said in a toneless voice.

"Whatever," Eggsy said.

Finding out where Clara was going was simple: she'd posted pictures of her skiing trip to Italy on her Instagram. As the Statesman jet flew once more across the Atlantic, Harry, with Eggsy's help, spent the time working through a series of physical and cognitive exercises designed by Merlin and Ginger to speed his recovery. Some of the exercises were simple: playing games like chess and poker, which required strategy and a certain amount of hand-eye coordination. Some were more complex, such as working through logic puzzles or decrypting coded messages. Some were entirely physical: maintaining a handstand for as long as possible or going through a series of tai chi routines. And some were geared more specifically to being an agent, like Harry using his non-dominant hand to hurl daggers at a target or defending himself against an attacker while wearing a blindfold. Eggsy got to play the role of attacker in the latter exercise, and he earned more than a few bruises for his trouble.

Jack made it clear that he thought the exercises were a waste of time. One day Harry might get back to being the agent he was before he'd been shot, but no way was he going to do it in a handful of hours. Eggsy did his best to encourage Harry, but inwardly, he feared Jack was right. Harry was the most amazing person Eggsy had ever met, but he was still human, and he could only heal so fast.

He supposed they'd find out if the exercises did Harry any good when they reached their destination. But he hoped he hadn't made a mistake when he'd pressed Champ to let Harry come along on this mission. He'd just gotten his friend back. He didn't want to lose him again so soon.

Courmayeur, Italy

The three agents stood in the cable car depot at the foot of Mont Blanc in the Graian Alps. The peak rose into the air and loomed over the region like an ancient god. Despite its intimidating presence—or perhaps because of it—people were drawn here from all over the world to experience some of the best skiing Europe had to offer. But Eggsy, Harry, and Jack weren't interested in outdoor sport. They'd come here to hunt.

The agents were waiting for the cable car to descend and return to the depot. Eggsy and Jack were decked out in ski gear and each carried skis and poles, while Harry wore Tequila's cowboy hat, tan shearling jacket and carried an overnight bag.

Harry glared at Jack. "Shame you only had *two* ski suits."

"We need you down here anyway, Galahad," Jack said. "Secure the control room."

Harry gave the man a grudging nod.

Eggsy shot Harry an apologetic look and Harry smiled in response.

The cable car made its appearance, and Jack and Eggsy got on. The car was empty, and Eggsy thought that was one good thing about this being the off-season: they weren't going to have to worry about crowds. Unfortunately, that also meant the three of them stuck out like a trio of sore thumbs. Made the *covert* part of covert operations a bit harder to manage.

Eggsy waved farewell to Harry, and the cable car began its return trip to the mountain. The car was round, and it revolved slowly to treat passengers to a three-hundred-and-sixty degree view during their ascent. Eggsy found the outlook stunning, and he remembered what Jack had said during the flight back from England, about how one of the perks for spies like them was getting to see the world. The man was definitely right on that score. Still, he wished Tilde were here with him. The view would mean so much more if he could share it with her.

As the car drew near the summit, they saw a visitor center, and Eggsy and Jack exchanged bemused looks. Merlin had continued tracking Clara since they'd listened in on her panicked call to Charlie, and according to the Scotsman, her GPS signal said she was presently located right where the center was. But a visitor center wasn't exactly the first thing that came to mind when one thought of "Insane Drug Lord's Secret Lair." *Not much secret about* that *place*, Eggsy thought.

When the cable car reached the summit, Eggsy and Jack disembarked. There was a ski rack close by, and they left their skis and poles there and continued on to the center.

Back at the cable car depot, Harry—irritated at having been left behind to do a junior agent's job—found the control room. He knocked on the door, and a moment later a man in his sixties with thick white hair and a matching beard opened the door a crack and peered out. Harry spoke to the attendant in Italian.

"I'm here to inspect the system."

"May I see your ID, please?" The man seemed friendly enough, but he didn't open the door any further.

Harry nodded politely and then raised his watch and fired a tranquilizer dart at the man's neck. The dart missed by a fraction of an inch and *thunked* into the door frame. The man looked at the dart, eyes wide, and then he turned to face Harry.

"Terribly sorry," Harry said.

Moving swiftly, he stepped forward, snatched a fire extinguisher off the wall, and slammed it against the man's head hard enough to knock him unconscious. He caught the man as he fell, and he stepped inside and closed the door behind him, removing the dart from the jamb first, of course. He tossed the dart to the ground and then gently lowered the attendant to the floor. The man might be one of Poppy's employees, but he might be a civilian who'd simply been in the wrong place at the wrong time. In that case, there was no need to injure him any further.

Harry cursed his bad aim, but it was comforting to know that he could still get the job done, even if he was forced to resort to less elegant methods. Maybe it was a matter of depth perception. He did, after all, have only one eye now. He made a mental note to speak to Merlin about it, and then he stepped over to the depot's control panel and put the extinguisher down. As he stood there, he began doing the one thing he hated most about spy work: waiting.

Eggsy and Jack stood in an open area outside the visitor center. Clara was nowhere to be seen, and neither was anyone else for that matter. The place appeared deserted. Eggsy remembered when he and Merlin had first discovered Statesman's hidden headquarters.

"I reckon she is…" Eggsy pointed to the ground. "We just need to find the way down."

He set off toward the visitor center. After a moment, Jack followed.

Aside from a clerk sitting at an information desk, the place was empty. Eggsy and Jack walked around, pretending to browse pamphlets detailing local attractions and perusing an historical exhibit about the mountain. But in reality they were using the sensors in their watches to scan for hidden entrances. Eventually they found themselves in a quiet corridor, and Eggsy's watch indicated one section of the wall that appeared to be what they were searching for.

"Looks like a door about... here." He stopped in front of a wall and pointed.

Jack stepped forward and held his watch close to the wall. He was wearing his Statesman eyeglasses, and he reached up with his other hand and gently tapped an earpiece to activate them.

"Ginger? You see anything?" he asked.

Eggsy pictured Ginger in her lab at Statesman HQ, looking over the data Jack's watch was transmitting to one of her computers. He wondered if Merlin was sitting by her side. Probably. Ever since they met those two had been joined at the hip. *Peas in a pod*, he thought, and smiled.

"Yep. Concealed door. Some pretty complex electronics... Looks like it needs a smart key. Gonna take me about an hour to crack, unless you can send me higher-res data."

When Eggsy heard Ginger's assessment over his own comms, he stepped forward and scanned the wall with his watch. Nothing against Statesman gear, but Merlin had made this watch, and Eggsy knew the quality of the man's work was second to none. He wasn't surprised to hear Merlin's voice next.

"That's better. Galahad's is crystal clear. Mind if I have a go?"

This was followed by the sound of someone typing swiftly on a keyboard.

Several moments later, a hidden door slid open, revealing a stone staircase leading downward.

He gave Jack a grin, as if to say, *One more point for Kingsman.*

"Go," Jack said. "I'll cover the door."

Eggsy nodded and started down the steps. A second later, the door slid shut and lights built into the ceiling activated. The steps descended for quite a way into the mountain, but eventually Eggsy reached the bottom and found himself standing in a cavernous laboratory. Several dozen people wearing lab coats, safety goggles, respirator masks, and rubber gloves were working at long tables filled with chemistry equipment. On one side of the lab were huge steel vats, along with complex control stations; on the other a warehouse space, with forklifts, packing material, and stacks of cardboard boxes. And there were guards of course—a *lot* of them—stationed all about the place, wearing black uniforms and caps with the Golden Circle logo on them, and armed with Heckler & Koch submachine guns.

And as Eggsy stepped into the lab, every single person stopped what they were doing and turned to look at him. Including, naturally, the guards. For an awkward moment, no one spoke or moved, and then one of the guards walked over to Eggsy.

"Who are you?" the man asked. He didn't seem as if he were challenging Eggsy, exactly. He sounded more confused than anything.

Eggsy smiled. "You guys did *not* make this place easy to find."

Eggsy knew he had to think fast before the guards came to their senses and unleashed a hellstorm of machine-gun fire. He looked around and saw a pile of cardboard boxes that had been left near the lab entrance. On the top box was a sticky note with FOR COLLECTION written on it.

"I'm... here to collect these," Eggsy said as casually as he could manage under the circumstances.

The guard frowned. "For Boris Batko? Singapore?"

Eggsy didn't bat an eye. "Yeah."

The guard checked a clipboard. "You're... Wu Ting Feng?"

Eggsy smiled. "Yup."

The guard took a step closer to Eggsy. The man's eyes narrowed and he raised his gun barrel a couple of inches. Eggsy's smile didn't falter.

Finally, the guard shrugged and gestured to the box. The deep breath that Eggsy wasn't aware he had been holding rushed out of him. He gave the man a nod of thanks, and reached for the box. But before he could take hold of it, an electronically synthesized voice shouted from the other side of the lab.

"How are you still alive?"

Charlie was coming toward them, and Clara was with

him. When they reached Eggsy and Jack, they stopped and stared in shock.

"River?" Clara said. "What are you doing here?"

There were no blue splotches on Clara's skin. Obviously, she'd been given the antidote.

Charlie looked at Clara, then at Eggsy, his face darkening with dawning fury.

Eggsy smiled. "What happens at Glasto stays at Glasto." He winked at Charlie, grabbed the box on top of the stack, and turned and ran like hell.

"Motherfucker!" Charlie shouted.

Angry voices echoed in the tunnel as Eggsy raced up the stairs, and he could hear the footfalls of his pursuers. With each passing second, it sounded as if they were closer. Eggsy assumed Charlie was one of those on his tail, along with a number of guards, but he didn't turn back to look. He was just grateful they couldn't fire their weapons and run up the stairs at the same time, or else he would've been done for.

When he reached the top of the stairs, the secret door slid open, and he jumped through into the corridor, surprising Jack.

"Jam it, Ginger!" Jack shouted, and the door instantly slid closed.

A second later, they heard shouts and pounding from the other side.

Eggsy and Jack ran through the visitor center, passed the shocked woman at the information desk, and plunged outside into the cold mountain air. They ran for the ski rack, grabbed their skis and poles, and flew into the cable car, which Harry—as per their plan—had returned to the summit and made sure remained there until they needed it. The car immediately began to descend, but as it did, Eggsy saw Charlie and a group of guards come racing toward the cable car stop.

Too late, mate! Eggsy thought.

Jack shouted to Harry over his comms, "Galahad! We're coming! All clear at the bottom?"

Eggsy couldn't wait any longer. He tore the box open and saw a number of vials that looked exactly like the antidote on Poppy's video. He removed one and examined it more closely to make sure, and a huge grin split his face. Fuck, *yeah*! They'd done it!

He flipped Charlie the bird and held up the vial so he could see it.

Harry replied to Jack. "All clear, but—"

Harry's words cut out, and the cable car lurched to a halt.

Eggsy looked through the car's window and saw Charlie holding a computer tablet and grinning. The bastard had shut the cable car system down by remote control. He heard Charlie's voice over his glasses' comms.

"Hello, Eggy. Enjoy the ride, bruv."

Charlie's fingers flew across the computer screen, and his face took on an expression of cruel delight. Eggsy understood why when the cable car began to rotate. Eggsy and Jack grabbed hanging straps and held tight. Their feet lifted off the floor as the speed of the car's rotation increased rapidly, and soon they could no longer maintain hold of the straps. Their hands slipped away and they slammed into the wall, pinned there by centrifugal force.

Eggsy heard Harry's voice come over the comms.

"Controls are gone. The thing's out of control. You're on your own, Eggsy."

The cable car spun faster and faster, and Eggsy felt as if a giant hand were pushing him against its wall, increasing its pressure with each passing second. A dark grayness nibbled at the edges of his vision, and he knew he was on the verge of losing consciousness. He almost blacked out, but when the box of antidote was torn from his fingers, a jolt of adrenaline shot through him, and his mind cleared. He watched in dismay as the vials spilled from the box, flew around the cable car, struck metal surfaces, and shattered. *Wait!* What about the one he'd been holding? He couldn't turn his head to look, but he could feel the vial in his hand. His fingers must've reflexively closed around it when the cable car began to spin. *Thank god!*

And then he felt the vial begin to slip from his hand. He fought to hold onto it, knowing it was their last chance to cure Poppy's virus and save millions of lives, but the force of the spinning car had grown too strong. The vial left his hand in a sudden rush, and he expected to hear it shatter like the others, but he only heard it *clink-clink-clink* as it rolled around on the wall, held there by the same centrifugal forces that trapped them. He tried to reach for the vial, but his arms were pinned to the wall so strongly, it was as if his body was becoming part of the metal.

The car continued to spin faster, ever faster.

Eggsy's surge of adrenaline was subsiding, and the blackness was back, sliding across his vision like a dark cloth. *Like an eyepatch*, he thought. He'd been experiencing vertigo since the car had begun its mad spinning, but now it seemed to increase a thousand-fold, and he felt a punch of nausea in his gut.

Now Harry had returned from the dead, it was his time to die. *Irony's a bitch*, he thought.

Eggsy saw Jack reach for his lasso handle. Or, more precisely, the *button* on the end of the handle. Like Eggsy, Jack couldn't pull his arm away from the wall, but he was just barely able to stretch his fingers enough to brush the button. That was all it took, though. The rope unfurled as if it had a life of its own, and an aura of crackling energy surrounded it, transforming it into a curling, whipping length of light. Eggsy realized he was looking at an honest-to-Christ electro-lasso.

That. Is. Fucking. AWESOME! he thought.

Jack wasn't able to take hold of the lasso's handle, so the coiling energy flailed wildly around the cable car's interior, lashing the walls and floor, burning through metal and leaving blackened scorch marks. The rope almost struck Eggsy's left hand, missing it by inches, only to shear off the tip of Jack's right boot. The electrified rope then curved upward, struck the car's ceiling, penetrated the metal, and sliced through the cable above.

Eggsy's stomach catapulted up into his throat as the car

became a giant pendulum and began to swing downward. With the centrifugal force diminished, the remaining vial of antidote fell toward the floor. But Eggsy was no longer pinned to the wall, and he dropped to the floor in time for his hand to shoot out and catch the vial before it shattered. His relief was short-lived, however, for the car swung downward in a wide arc and hit snow-covered ground. It detached from the remains of the cable, and began sliding down the slope. As soon as he'd been able to move, Jack had deactivated the lasso's electric energy setting—which kept them both from being sliced and diced—but the impact of striking the snow knocked them both off their feet, and the vial flew once more from Eggsy's hands.

For fuck's sake! He tried to grab hold of the vial again, but he was sliding around the car, as was the vial, and it continued to elude his grasp. It didn't help that their skis and ski poles were bouncing around the car's interior as well. But then the vial went flying through the air past Eggsy's face. His hand flashed outward and he caught hold of it once more.

Yes!

The car picked up speed as it careened downhill, and Eggsy and Jack managed to brace themselves and get a good look through a window at where they were headed. Neither of them liked what they saw. The car was sliding straight toward a building where a number of people— old folks, it looked like—sat outside, watching. *Some kind of retirement home?* Eggsy wondered. Whatever it was there was nothing they could do now but hold tight and hope for the best. The car slammed into a signal tower of some kind, bounced off, slid some more, struck a tree, and finally came to a stop less than a dozen yards from the building. Many of the old people looked terrified, but a number clapped, as if they'd just witnessed a particularly impressive magic trick.

For several moments Eggsy and Jack sat in the cable car—windows smashed, ceiling half gone, walls bent inward—stunned to still be alive. Eggsy glanced at his hand to reassure himself he still had hold of the vial and it was intact. He did and it was. He started to let out a relieved breath, but then he detected a rumbling sound, quiet at first, but quickly growing louder.

The two spies looked behind them, and through one of the cable car's broken windows they saw a white tank hurtling down the mountainside toward them, tracks churning snow, the machine sliding back and forth as it plunged recklessly onward.

Jack and Eggsy glanced at each other for a second with the same thought in mind: *Who the hell has a snow tank?*

The tank's turret swiveled to bring its barrel into position, and a blast of flame erupted from the muzzle, sending a high-explosive round soaring toward them. The tank was too far away for the crew to get a good shot, and the round missed the cable car by a wide margin. It did, however, manage to obliterate several innocent trees. As fast as the tank was moving, Eggsy knew it would be in range quickly, and if he and Jack didn't get out of here ASA fucking P, they were dead—and so were millions of people around the world infected with Poppy's deadly virus.

Jack grabbed his skis and poles, scrambled through one of the car's broken windows, and began to put his skis on with swift, deft motions. Eggsy followed after Jack, but he didn't bring his skis, and he merely stood and watched.

"Get your skis on!" Jack shouted.

Eggsy's face burned with embarrassment. "I… can't ski."

"You… you're fucking kidding? What kind of agent can't ski?"

Eggsy shrugged. "The kind whose only childhood holiday was to a caravan park in Skegness?"

Jack got to his feet, a ski pole in each hand. The two men glanced backward and saw the tank bearing down on them. It would overrun their position within seconds.

"All right," Jack said, "here's what we're gonna do."

Chapter Nine

J ack slalomed between trees in an effort to put some cover between them and the tank, but it was fruitless. The tank simply mowed down the trees and made its own path as it charged onward, unimpeded, closing the distance between them with every passing second.

Eggsy had been telling the truth; he couldn't ski. He could, however, hold onto Jack as *he* skied, and he did so now, clinging to the American agent like a small child. *I hope to god Harry never finds out about this,* he thought. He'd never live it down—provided he lived at all, of course. His current position might be somewhat lacking in dignity, but it had one advantage: he could look over Jack's shoulder and tell him what their pursuers were doing.

Jack was only using one pole to help him ski. That, plus Eggsy's added weight, slowed them down and made it more difficult for Jack to maneuver. Jack had insisted Eggsy keep hold of the second pole, which he was doing. The tank turret swiveled again, bringing its barrel to bear on them. The machine was so close now it was practically on top of them, and it would be a race to see how they died: blown to charred bits by an explosion, or ground into crimson paste beneath its tracks.

"Left! Go left!" Eggsy shouted.

Jack veered just as the tank fired another round. The sound of the blast echoed through the forest, and the round shot past them. Trees exploded in a ball of flame and smoke, and broken branches and splintered wood rained down around them.

The tank swerved and got them in its sights once more.

"Right!" Eggsy shouted.

Another shot, another miss, more trees blown to hell.

Eggsy and Jack reached an open space, and now that there weren't any trees in the way, Eggsy raised his ski pole, braced it on Jack's shoulder—the sharp end pointing toward the tank—and flicked a button on the shaft. A gunsight popped up, and Eggsy peered through it. He took a second to aim, then flicked the button again. The point of the shaft blasted outward, and a miniature missile streaked toward the tank's barrel. It slid into the muzzle as if slathered in lubricant, and an instant later, the barrel exploded in a spectacular blast. As devastating as the impact appeared, a missile that size could only do so much damage. The barrel now looked something like the blackened, curled strip that formed the remnants of a villain's guns that had exploded in his face in old cartoons. But the tank's engine and its tracks were still fully operational. The vehicle's driver gunned the engine, and the tank jumped forward. With no other weapons left to them, the crew was going to try to run them down.

Eggsy shouted for Jack to go faster, and immediately ate his words. They were heading straight for a ravine.

"What are you doing?" Eggsy shouted, but Jack didn't answer.

They shot over the edge of the ravine, and Eggsy cried out in fear. If he had to choose between falling to his death and being flattened by a tank, he'd take the tank. At least it would be over faster.

Jack let his pole drop and then yanked a toggle on his ski suit. With a loud rushing sound, a parachute deployed from the back of the suit, caught the air, and snapped all the way open. Eggsy instantly noticed the design; the two of them hung beneath an enormous Stars and Stripes. Their descent immediately slowed, and Jack let out a cowboy whoop.

"America!" he shouted. "Fuck yeah!"

Eggsy, holding onto Jack even tighter than before, watched over the man's shoulder as the tank reached the edge of the ravine, flew off the cliff, and dropped like a stone. When the vehicle hit the ground, the crash was spectacular.

Eggsy contacted Harry over his eyeglasses' comm.

"On our way down, Harry," he said.

Harry's image appeared.

"Roger that. I've got you on GPS."

"Meet us there."

Harry nodded and his image faded.

"You always this happy after you just pulled off mission impossible?" Jack said.

"Nah. This just… reminds me of a jump I made with someone else. Roxy. Kingsman agent, good friend." He paused, and then added, "Charlie killed her."

Jack took a moment before responding. "And now you're one step ahead of him. Your time will come, trust me."

It can't come soon enough, Eggsy thought.

They descended toward a wooden mountaineering hut recessed in the side of the mountain's face. They glided to a landing near the hut, and Eggsy was finally able to let go of Jack. While the American agent gathered his chute, Eggsy opened the hut's door and peered in.

"No one here," he called out to Jack. "Let's wait inside."

Once they were both in the hut, and Eggsy had bolted the door, Jack quickly got a fire going in the grate. As Eggsy warmed himself, he removed the antidote vial from his pocket and marveled at it.

"So weird to think this little thing could save the world," he said.

Jack reached out his hand. "Let me see that?"

He was about to hand the vial to Jack when there was a knock at the door.

"It's me!" Harry said. "Open up!"

Eggsy stood, unbolted the door, and opened it.

Harry, overnight bag in hand, broke into an excited grin when he saw Eggsy holding the vial.

"You got the antidote," he said, pleased. He stepped inside, closed the door behind him, and deposited his overnight bag on the floor.

Before Eggsy could respond, the hut was peppered

with gunfire. The windows shattered, and Jack shouted, "Get down!"

Harry ducked his head and crossed his hands over his chest. A Kingsman suit was bulletproof, so he only needed to protect his exposed areas. Unfortunately, neither Eggsy nor Jack's ski suits could repel gunfire. Jack leaped toward Eggsy and threw himself on the younger agent, protecting him with his own body. The pair lay on the floor, while Harry remained standing in the doorway, acting as a shield. Eggsy had a horrible sinking feeling in his gut. He looked at his clenched fist, opened it, and saw the vial had shattered when Jack shoved him to the ground. Some of the shards had cut him, but he didn't care about that. He was too upset by the sight of the antidote dripping from his palm onto the floor.

"Shit," Jack said.

"You dickhead!" Eggsy roared.

"Fuck you!" Jack shouted back. "I just saved your life!"

"And cost millions of people theirs!" Eggsy countered.

Just then another volley of bullets hit the cabin, tearing through the wood and turning it into Swiss cheese. Harry was still okay thanks to his suit, but Eggsy and Jack wouldn't last long once the cabin disintegrated around them and the Golden Circle soldiers had clear shots.

Jack crawled toward one of the windows, and rose up just high enough to peer out.

"Only eight. We can take 'em." He looked at Eggsy and smiled grimly. "Let's get us some payback for your friend."

Jack stood, drew both his gun and his lasso handle,

opened the bullet-ridden door, and rushed outside.

"Cover me, boys!" he shouted.

Eggsy was still furious over the vial breaking, but he didn't have time to be angry now. He unzipped his ski suit, reached inside, drew his Kingsman pistol, and fired two rounds through the open window. He started toward the doorway, intending to go outside and help Jack, but Harry grabbed hold of him. Shocked by his mentor's behavior, Eggsy tried to pull away, but Harry held onto him.

"Eggsy, wait!" Harry said. "I think Whiskey broke the vial on purpose." He paused, and then added in a softer voice, "He could be working for the other side."

Eggsy couldn't believe what he was hearing. "The fuck is wrong with you? You're having a brain fart! Does *that* look to you like he's working with them?"

He pointed outside.

Eight guards dressed in snow-camouflage outfits stood in a semicircle in front of Jack, submachines raised and ready to fire. But Jack wasn't going to give them the chance. He activated his lasso's electricity, and using it as a whip, he flicked it toward one of the guards. It struck the guard's cap dead center in the middle of the Golden Circle logo and bored a hole through his skull, burned through his brain, and then out the other side. The man's body jerked as he fell, and the top of his head split in two as he descended past the line of the energy beam. There was no blood. The heat from the electrified lasso cauterized wounds even as it made them.

Jack didn't watch the man fall. He aimed his gun at

another guard and shot her through the circle logo on her cap as well. This time there *was* blood. It painted the snow behind her crimson, and then she fell backward, dead in an instant.

He's using the logos as targets, Eggsy thought. *How badass is that?*

Jack swiped his lasso toward another guard, this time aiming for the man's knees. The rope sliced through the man's legs as if they were no more substantial than air, and as he started to fall, Jack shot him through the head as well. He was dead before he hit the snow. The next three went down fast, each shot in the head in rapid succession. Jack swept his lasso down upon the seventh guard's head, slicing him neatly in two. As each cauterized half fell, the crackling electric aura flickered and vanished. The weapon was out of power.

The eighth guard had up to this moment been stunned by the rapid deaths of his companions. But when he realized he was the last man standing, he gathered his wits and aimed his submachine at Jack. Jack raised his gun at the man, but when he squeezed the trigger, the barrel clicked empty. He was out of ammo.

The guard grinned, thinking Jack was a dead man. But Jack threw his gun at the man and ran toward him. The gun tumbled through the air and the butt of the weapon hit the man in the head right on his cap's logo. The guard staggered under the blow but didn't fall. But he was distracted long enough for Jack to reach him, grab hold of his head and give it a savage twist. The man's neck broke with sickening *crack!* and he slumped lifelessly to the ground, a puppet whose strings had been cut.

Jack was barely breathing hard.

Eggsy, furious, finally managed to pull away from Harry.

"Lucky for you he didn't need our help," Eggsy said.

But he'd spoken too soon. A troop carrier rumbled up to the hut and disgorged more guards, twenty in all, and they were armed with what looked for all the world like mini Gatling guns.

"Shit!" Jack shouted. He ran back inside and bolted the door shut. "There's a fuck ton of 'em!" He looked at Harry and Eggsy. "How about some backup, boys? I'm out of ammo. What you got?"

Harry drew his pistol. He started to say something, but then a distant look came into his eye and he froze, as if he was uncertain what to do next. As before, his eye moved back and forth, and Eggsy knew he was seeing butterflies again.

Jack frowned. "Hey, you don't look like Ginger fixed you right."

Eggsy didn't have time to worry about Harry, and, anyway, right then he was too mad at him to care. He stepped to the window, pistol raised, as the new squad of guards attacked, the rounds from their mini-Gatlings raining hell on the cabin. Eggsy fired, ducked, then rose to fire again. Behind him, he heard Jack shout at Harry.

"I said I'm empty! Give me yours!"

Eggsy turned to see Jack try to pull Harry's pistol from his hand. Harry snapped back to reality, and resisted, refusing to let the American agent take his weapon. As they struggled, Harry's weapon suddenly discharged, and Jack went down, a bullet in his head.

The guards continued firing, but Eggsy was barely aware of them.

"Harry!" he shouted, unable to bring himself to believe what he'd just witnessed. "No! What—"

"He broke the vial on purpose," Harry said, sounding sure of himself now. "He knew I saw him."

"Fuck. Fuck! What's wrong with you?"

Harry answered coolly. "If we made it out of here, he was going to kill us both."

The sound of the guards' gunfire registered on Eggsy's consciousness once more.

"Yeah? Looks like he didn't have to."

Harry smiled. "Ye of little faith."

He walked to his overnight bag, set his gun aside, and calmly rifled through the bag's contents. He removed the bottle of Kingsman aftershave that Merlin had given him, twisted the top and hurled the bottle through the broken window. There was a flash of blue light, a loud fizzing sound, and the gunfire ceased. Quiet descended on the cabin, the absence of noise a shock after the guards' near-deafening assault.

Eggsy peered through the window and saw the guards were encased in a thick layer of strange blue foam. None of them moved, none of them so much as breathed. One threat, well and truly neutralized.

Now that they were—for the moment at least—

safe, Eggsy ran to Jack's side. He removed the man's cowboy hat and reached inside for the alpha gel sheet. He wrapped it around Jack's head, remembering Ginger saying how important it was for the gel to be applied as soon as possible after being wounded.

Harry watched Eggsy work. He made no comment, but he didn't try to interfere, either.

When Eggsy was finished tending to Jack, Harry said, "We need to go dark. We don't know who else at Statesman could be working against us."

Eggsy struggled to stay calm as he looked Harry in the eye.

"This is my fault," Eggsy said. "You weren't ready for the field, and I pushed you into it."

"He showed his hand," Harry said, insistent. "You think he'd have let us live? You should be thanking me for saving our arses."

Eggsy didn't reply. He tapped the side of his glasses to activate the comms function.

"Merlin," he said. "Can you hear me? Jack's down. He got…" He glanced at Harry. "Caught in crossfire," he finished. "We'll get him home. First, I've gotta figure out how to get back up to the lab for another sample." He tapped his glasses to break the link to Merlin, and then looked at Harry. "Stay here."

He opened the bullet-riddled door and stepped outside. He had no idea how he was going to be able to sneak back inside the laboratory, but he had to try. Too many lives depended—

His thoughts broke off as a huge explosion occurred near the summit, the vibrations from the blast shaking the ground beneath his feet, the sound echoing across the mountain like thunder. He knew the visitor center—and the lab beneath it—had just been destroyed. He was too late.

As Eggsy watched black smoke billow into the sky, a helicopter emerged from the dark cloud.

300 feet above Mont Blanc and rising

As the helicopter soared above the smoke, Charlie slipped on a pair of headphones. He gave a thumbs up to the pilot, and the man patched him into the comms system.

"Poppy? It's done. Evacuation successful, everything destroyed."

Clara sat behind Charlie, and she tugged on his elbow, biting her lower lip nervously.

"I'm sorry, Charlie! I'm sorry! Please... don't tell Poppy it was me they followed."

His message delivered, Charlie slipped off the headphones and turned to Clara. He smiled, but his eyes were cold.

"Don't worry, darling. What happens in Italy... stays in Italy."

Eggsy stood in the hut's doorway, watching as the helicopter gained altitude, frustration gnawing at his insides.

Merlin's image appeared on Eggsy's glasses. "What was *that*?"

Eggsy sighed and turned back into the hut. "The sound of plans changing. Poppy must have more antidote somewhere else. We'll follow Clara's GPS and hope that's where Charlie's headed."

The cabin's roof suddenly collapsed inward with a loud crash, and Clara hit the floor in front of Eggsy's feet with a nauseating thud. Her arms and legs were bent at unnatural angles, and her head was twisted one hundred and eighty degrees.

"Fuck," he muttered. "Merlin?"

Before Merlin could reply, Harry snatched Eggsy's glasses off his face, snapped them in half, and tossed the broken pieces to the floor. He'd already disposed of his own glasses.

He looked at Eggsy, his expression grim.

"I *said*, we're going dark."

Singapore

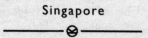

Eggsy and Harry walked down a busy sidewalk in the Central Area, which surrounded the Singapore River and Marina Bay. Harry wore his suit and carried a Kingsman suit bag while Eggsy was dressed in civilian clothes. It was nighttime, but everywhere you looked there were ultra-modern high-rises lit from inside, making it seem almost like day. The sidewalks were less crowded than during the daylight hours, or so Harry had said, but there were still plenty of people out and about. A fair amount of street traffic too: cars, taxis, buses... Seeing the cabs made him think of Pete, the Kingsman driver who'd died when Charlie had first attempted to kill Eggsy. There were times when being a spy was an adrenaline-fueled rush more intense than any drug could possibly give. And then there were times when it well and truly sucked sweaty donkey balls. This was definitely one of the latter.

He'd gone along with Harry's demand that they go dark only so he could keep watch on him. Eggsy knew Harry would do it whether he agreed to join him or not, and as angry as he had been at his mentor, he knew none of it was Harry's fault. The man had been shot in the fucking *head*, for Christ's sake, and while his recovery had been a bonafide medical miracle, it was sheer idiocy to believe his mind could return to normal functioning within the space of a few days. Eggsy now regretted talking Champ into sending Harry on the mission to Mont Blanc, and he was determined to get his friend back to Ginger's lab where she could see to his recovery properly. But that meant convincing Harry that he needed help, and so far Eggsy hadn't had any luck on that score.

Then again, Harry *had* managed to get them from Italy to Singapore without alerting Statesman, so obviously some of his skills and knowledge remained intact. The problem was the man was delusional, and nothing Eggsy said had been able to dispel his paranoid imaginings.

Harry motioned for Eggsy to stop, and he pointed

toward a balconied apartment building further down the street. Two men in dark suits and sunglasses stood outside the entrance, motionless, looking bored, but Eggsy knew that behind those glasses, their eyes were taking in everything around them, checking people out and scanning for threats.

"Only two guards," Harry said. "Good."

Eggsy decided he had to try to get through to Harry one more time before he got them in even more trouble than they already were.

"You're not listening to me, Harry. You shot an ally! You're seeing fucking invisible butterflies! You need help. And more to the point, so do we."

Harry looked at him skeptically. "Help from the people who held me prisoner? Who tried to scupper our mission?"

Eggsy was starting to feel desperate. He stopped walking. "You weren't a prisoner! They were trying to— It doesn't matter. Millions are gonna die! We've got no resources, no backup; we're down to a single shitty lead."

"It's a fine lead," Harry said. "How many people do you think there are in Singapore called Boris Batko? I found a photo of him, his address, and financial records which plainly suggest that he's Poppy's man in Southeast Asia."

"So? We might get nothing from him."

Harry smiled. "I suggest we find out."

Harry and Eggsy approached the apartment entrance. The heads of the two guards swiveled toward them as they drew near, but otherwise, neither man moved a muscle. Their expressions remained impassive, and their eyes were unreadable through their dark glasses.

"I'm from Kingsman Tailors in London," Harry said in flawless Cantonese. "I have Mr Batko's new suit." He raised the suit bag several inches as if offering the guards proof.

The guard on the left spoke in a neutral tone that still somehow managed to convey a sense of menace.

"I'll give it to him."

The guard reached for the suit bag, but Harry stepped back, moving the bag out of the man's reach.

"No, he needs to try it on," Harry said.

The guard looked at Harry for a moment before turning the spotlight of his attention on Eggsy, who did his best to look like he didn't give a fuck about what was happening. It was a look he'd perfected as a teen growing up on the streets of London, and it served him well now. The guard dismissed him. He removed a walkie-talkie from his belt and lifted it to his face.

He thumbed the talk button and spoke in English. "You expecting a tailor?"

A moment later a man appeared on a balcony high above them. He peered over, looked at them for a moment, and then shouted down in a British accent.

"No. Tell him to fuck off!"

He then went back inside.

Eggsy sighed. So much for Harry's plan. Time for plan B. He looked down the street to see what traffic was approaching. A bike, followed by a car, then a van, a truck, and lastly a bus. He did some quick mental calculations and thought to himself, *That'll work.*

When the bike was almost even with him, Eggsy ran forward, jumped, put a foot on the bike handles—to the astonishment of the man riding it—and launched himself into the air. He landed on the hood of the car, ran onto the roof and jumped again. With perfect coordination, he continued in the same way, leaping from the car to the van to the truck to the bus, gaining height each time, until he was level with the lowest balcony. He jumped off the bus and landed gracefully on the balcony with a grin. Now that was a hell of a lot more fun than standing around trying to con a couple of bone-headed guards to allow them inside.

Speaking of the guards, the two men had watched Eggsy's parkour performance with disbelief, but now they sprang to action, drew a pair of Berettas and began firing. Eggsy kept moving upward, leaping from balcony to balcony as bullets pinged off the metal railings, barely missing him. When he reached Boris's balcony, he ducked down to protect himself from the gunfire. The guards fired several more shots, but realizing they weren't able to hit Eggsy, the men ran inside the building, leaving Harry standing there, holding the suit bag, forgotten.

Eggsy poked his head over the balcony.

"Harry! Come on!" he called.

Harry smiled. "I'll take the lift, thanks, old boy."

He walked casually through the now unguarded entrance.

* * *

Ginger's lab, Statesman headquarters

———————⊗———————

Merlin stood next to Ginger as she monitored Jack. The Statesman agent rested on a gurney inside the Alpha Wave Stimulator, just as Harry had before him. From what Merlin understood, the man's prognosis was much better than Harry's. Someone—presumably one of the Kingsman agents—had applied alpha gel almost immediately after Jack had sustained his wound, and Ginger expected the man to make a full recovery. But events became much less clear after that. Instead of bringing Jack back to America, Harry and Eggsy had vanished without any word where they were going. And another mystery: when he'd examined the bullet that Ginger removed from Jack's head, he'd determined it had been fired from a Kingsman gun. But whether the round had come from Harry's weapon or Eggsy's, he couldn't say. He'd kept this tidbit of information to himself, though. He didn't want Champ and the others to think Harry and Eggsy had turned rogue, although privately that was precisely what he feared. He wanted to believe that the pair had a good reason for shooting Jack and then going dark, and normally he would've had every faith in the men. But with Harry's precarious mental condition... well, who was to say what might have happened?

"Still no word from the Galahads?" Ginger asked, speaking loudly to be heard over the machine's din. Merlin shook his head and she continued. "Something doesn't feel right. The pilot said they dropped Jack at the jet and ran. Never said their comms were down. Nothing."

Merlin had tried to contact them dozens of times, had checked various secure email accounts and message threads that he'd set up especially for agents to get in contact when they had no other means of communication. He'd tried checking numbers, stations and obscure radio frequencies… He'd even gone old school and checked newspaper personal columns. Not a single message.

"They may be under surveillance," he said. "I'm sure we'll hear something soon."

After several moments, Ginger said, "Do you ever want to do more than this?" She made a sweeping gesture to take in the entire lab.

"This?" Merlin said. "*This* is vital. Without us, they'd be lost."

"I know. But you know what I mean. Out in the field is where all the action is."

"Have you ever asked—" Merlin began.

"I have. But every time an agent position has come up, Whiskey has voted against me."

Merlin felt a surge of anger at Whiskey. Ginger was one of the most intelligent, capable people he'd ever met. How could Whiskey vote against her?

The Alpha Wave Stimulator quieted as it finished its work, and Merlin and Ginger went to Jack's side. Merlin rolled the gurney out of the machine. Jack had sensors attached to his head, and as he sat up he pulled them off. He looked at Ginger and gave her a million-dollar smile.

"Howdy, angel," he drawled, and then winked at Ginger.

She smiled with delight. She'd done it! Jack was fully recovered.

"I'm Jack," he said, his smile taking on a lascivious edge. "What's *your* name?"

Ginger's smile vanished.

Jack, dressed in a hospital gown, swung his bare legs over the gurney's side.

"How about you ditch baldy here and ride home on a real cowboy? I got a six pack of cold ones on ice, and my roomie is out all night, so you can scream my name as loud as you need to, sugar."

Jack hopped off the gurney and grabbed Ginger's waist. He started to sway his hips, as if he wanted to dance with her—or do something else. Disgusted, she pried his hands off her. Merlin frowned at Jack.

"Retrograde memory loss," Merlin said. "Regression to early life. Just like Harry."

Jack didn't appear to be discouraged by Ginger's rejection. He started humming to himself and dancing around, as if he were in a bar and listening to jukebox music that only he could hear.

Ginger made a face. "Yeah, but one collected butterflies and the other collected STDs." She shot Jack with a tranquilizer dart and he blacked out. "Harry was more my type."

Merlin was stung by Ginger's words, but he did his best to mask his reaction.

"Well, he's single," Merlin said evenly.

Ginger smiled. "I meant… before he became Galahad

again." She stepped closer to Merlin and raised her eyebrows in a suggestive manner. "I like 'em geeky."

Eggsy drew his pistol and aimed it at Boris's back, but the man spun around, Beretta in hand, and pointed his gun at Eggsy. An instant later the two guards burst in and trained their weapons on Eggsy, and they were followed by Harry, who had *his* gun out. One of the guards turned to aim his weapon at Harry, and Harry aimed his right back. The five of them stood there, gripping their weapons, tension building in the air. But none of them fired. It was a stalemate.

"Who the fuck are you?" Boris demanded.

Eggsy's gun hand didn't waver as he answered. "Let's just say I know this business. And I'm here because I think we could both benefit from having a little chat. So put the gun down. If I wanted you dead, I'd have killed you already."

Boris's eyes narrowed, and Eggsy had the sense the man was sizing him up. Finally, he sighed. "If we get blood on this carpet, my missus will kill us all." He lowered his gun. "So let's not be the last casualties of this war."

The apartment was a mix of British and Asian-inspired décor. One wall was covered with cricket bats, beneath them a leather couch with throw pillows emblazoned with the Union Jack. Another wall had framed photos of famous footballers, and beneath them was a glass-covered table displaying balls signed by players. Korean lanterns hung from the ceiling, and a third wall contained Japanese watercolor paintings of blossoms and flowing streams. Beneath them was a table displaying various-sized sculptures of Buddha. The rug Boris was so concerned about—and rightly so—was a huge antique, the design an intricately woven map of ancient China.

Eggsy gave the man a nod and lowered his gun. Boris nodded to his guards and they—very reluctantly, Eggsy thought—lowered their weapons. Harry followed suit.

"What do you want?" Boris asked, no longer demanding but sounding curious.

From Boris's accent, Eggsy could tell he wasn't a product of the upper classes, and he decided to use that.

"For us not to be the last casualties of this war," Eggsy said. "How did you get into this game in the first place? Something tells me it wasn't your sparkling résumé. I'm pretty sure that if we'd got a decent education, it ain't what we'd have picked at the job fair."

Boris frowned. "What's your point?"

"We didn't have a choice. And the day this business becomes kosher, our last option goes too."

Harry stepped over to join Eggsy.

"You know he's right," Harry said. "They'll open a Drugs-R-Us on every corner and replace people like you with smarmy suits and MBAs who'll look good in the IPO brochure."

"Exactly," Eggsy said. "There's no room for people like us in Poppy's new world. We'll be out on our arses."

Boris looked thoughtful, perhaps even a little worried,

and his guards wore similar expressions.

"Maybe," he said. "Maybe not. You don't know."

"Then let us tell you what we *do* know," Harry said. "The president is faking. He's going to let the deadline pass. Make it look like Poppy failed to deliver the antidote. Back out on the deal."

"In simple terms," Eggsy said, "all your customers are gonna die, Mr Batko."

"We share a common aim," Harry pressed. "Keeping them alive."

Boris's eyes narrowed as he considered their words. After several moments, he said, "I'm listening."

"Give us Poppy's location," Eggsy said. "We take her out and release the antidote. This whole thing's over."

"The Golden Circle loses its queen," Harry said, "and *you* step in."

Boris slowly grinned. "As king," he said.

Merlin and Ginger crouched in the dark, wearing night-vision goggles. Jack sat on the back of a bull—the same one Harry had been forced to ride several days earlier—and both of them were sleeping deeply. Like Harry, Jack was lashed to the bull.

Ginger removed two hypodermics from her pockets and gave one to Merlin.

"Merlin, you *would* tell me, wouldn't you?" she asked. "If you'd heard from them?"

He turned away, unable to meet her eyes. Which was,

of course, a more powerful response than any words he could've spoken.

"Then I pray you got a good reason," Ginger said. "Because if I've got you wrong, I want you to know… I'm gonna blame myself. Not you. *Me*. For being dumb enough to let my feelings cloud my judgment."

She plunged her hypo into Jack's thigh, and he immediately began to stir.

Merlin faced her once again. "Feeling's mutual. *Trust* me."

He jammed his hypo into the bull's haunch. The animal woke up faster than Jack. It rose to its feet, snorted, and ran toward the door of the pen. It lowered its head, crashed through the door, and charged out into the arena, carrying a suddenly awake and extremely bewildered Jack. Neither Merlin nor Ginger paid any attention to the bull or the agent.

Ginger looked into Merlin's eyes for a long moment, as if considering, and then she smiled.

"Elizabeth," she said. "My name is Elizabeth."

Merlin smiled. "Hamish."

He leaned toward her, she leaned toward him, and they met in the middle and kissed.

Meanwhile, Jack was screaming in terror as the bull bucked and kicked, flinging him about. But then his scream cut off. Merlin and Ginger broke apart and hurried to the pen's open doorway. They saw Jack— obviously himself once again—loop the rope around the bull's neck and draw it tight. The bull continued bucking for a few seconds, but his exertions lessened, and then his eyes closed and he began to topple over. As the animal fell, Jack pulled completely free of the rope and jumped off the animal's back. He landed on his feet the same instant as the unconscious bull thudded onto its side. Jack removed the rope from the bull's neck, and then he headed toward Merlin and Ginger, features contorted with anger.

"Goddamn butterfly guy shot me!" he said. "Where are they?"

"What?" Ginger said. "Merlin?" She turned to Merlin for an explanation, but he wasn't there. She quickly scanned the arena, but she saw no sign of him. Her heart sank as she faced Jack once more.

"They've gone dark," she said. She paused, then added in a softer voice, "*All* of them."

"Gone rogue, you mean," Jack snarled. "Harry's sick in the head. We can't trust them with this! People are gonna die!"

He took off running, but Ginger didn't follow him right away. She'd noticed something written in the dust on a nearby handrail. Two words: TRUST ME.

She looked at the words for several moments before wiping them away with her hand and heading after Jack.

Fox and General McCoy stood next to the president at the Oval Office window, looking down at a mass of protesters on the White House lawn. From the slogans on their signs, Fox could sort them into two basic groups:

pro-legalization and anti-legalization.

"Look at them all. Pretty soon half of 'em are gonna be happy, and the other half history." The president chortled. "Damn, politics has never been so easy."

McCoy laughed. Fox felt sick.

The president took a seat behind his desk and looked toward the wall-screen TV on which a newscast was running. Fox and General McCoy took up positions behind him on either side and watched with him. Fox had been doing her best since the crisis broke to maintain her composure, but as the news worsened, the harder it became for her to keep up a veneer of professionalism.

On the screen was a video of a huge domed stadium. Outside, uniformed soldiers escorted hundreds of people infected with the blue rash inside, while a reporter spoke about how sufferers of what was now being called the "Dancing Disease" were being taken to specially equipped field hospitals set up by the federal government in similar facilities across the country. He urged anyone who was afflicted to locate the facility closest to them and go there immediately to seek help. A 1-800 number and a website address where viewers could obtain more information crawled beneath him as he spoke.

The president was receiving good press from around the world for his "swift humanitarian response" to the crisis. But Fox knew the truth, and that knowledge turned her stomach. Inside the dome—and others like it—the infected were locked in cramped cages and stacked one on top of another like livestock. They would receive no medical treatment. Hell, there weren't even any doctors on the premises. They were to be kept away from the public eye until the disease ran its course and they died.

The president grinned. "Let the junkie scum go down in flames!"

"Congratulations, sir," General McCoy said.

"Normally, I don't indulge," the president said, "but this deserves a toast."

He rose from his desk, stepped over to the liquor cabinet, and began pouring whiskey into a trio of tumblers.

Fox couldn't take her gaze from the screen. She imagined the people inside the dome, locked away in the dark, wondering when someone was going to come help them, realizing eventually that no one was.

"This is totally unethical, sir," she said, unable to hold her tongue any longer.

The president handed the general a drink before giving one to her.

"Fox... shut up."

He returned to his desk as the words MILITARY DECLARES MARTIAL LAW appeared below the reporter's image.

Fox downed her drink in a single gulp.

The president looked over at Fox, and the man did a double-take.

"Jesus, Fox!"

He was looking at her as if she'd just climbed on top of the *Resolute* desk, hiked up her skirt, and taken a massive shit.

"What?" Fox said, and then caught sight of her hands.

The skin was dotted with patches of blue rash. Fox felt a cold, watery sensation in her guts. "Shit! Sir, like I said, this affects all people, from all backgrounds…"

The president looked at Fox, eyes flashing with anger and betrayal. The general's lips pursed in distaste.

"I'm disappointed, Fox," the president said. "Disappointed and… disgusted."

Fox's first thought was, *Dear Christ, please don't let him tweet about this!*

Her words came out in a rush. "Mr President, I routinely work twenty-hour days for you. Seven days a week. Maybe some can do that without chemical help, but— Sir, I'm a good person. Like the millions of others you're allowing to die."

The president was quiet for several seconds, and Fox hoped she'd gotten through to the man. But then he said, "Well, the good news is you'll never work a twenty-hour day again."

He walked to his desk, sat in his plush leather chair, and picked up the phone.

"Security? Escort Fox to the nearest field hospital."

Poppy's virus continued making its worldwide debut.

In the street outside a hospital ER in Chicago, a mass of people with the blue rash pushed, shoved, kicked, and punched one another in wild desperation as they fought to get inside, all in the meager hope that doctors there could do something, *anything* to save their lives. Variations on the scene were repeated outside medical facilities and physicians' offices around the world.

In London, a broadcast news reporter covered with the blue rash informed viewers of the latest developments.

"...exhibiting stage-one symptoms of the biologically engineered virus. Authorities are urging victims to remain calm." He paused, then frowned. "Excuse me." He touched his earpiece and listened for a moment as his producer spoke to him. "*What?*" He looked at his hands, which were almost entirely blue, and tears began to slide down his cheeks. He began sobbing. "Oh dear god..."

Jamal and Liam were watching the news in their flat when Jamal noticed the first patches of blue rash dotting his friend's skin. "Bruv, you got it!" Jamal said. "I told you not to do that shit!" Liam raised his hands to inspect them, and his eyes widened with horror.

Within the space of a few hours, there was almost no one on earth who either wasn't infected or who didn't know and love someone who was.

And in the Oval Office, the president sat alone at his desk and brainstormed ideas for re-election campaign slogans.

Make America... what? he mused silently.

Chapter Ten

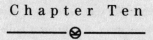

Harry and Eggsy stood in the entrance of an empty hangar at a small Singapore airport, the night sky above them cloudless, the stars bright and lovely. Eggsy had no time to appreciate such things, though. While Harry's plan to get intel from Boris Batko about Poppy's operation appeared to have been successful, Eggsy felt more tense than ever. He was achingly aware that with each passing second, more people around the planet became infected with Poppy's virus. Surely some had contracted it a while ago, which meant they were in the late stages of the infection by now, or had already died. And here they were, fucking around on an airfield in goddamned Singapore, after having allied themselves with a drug lord. He supposed it was *possible* this mission could get more batshit insane, but he honestly didn't see how. And the longer it went on, the more he feared Harry's brain was going to blow a gasket sooner or later.

He'd witnessed what Harry was capable of when he wasn't in his right mind. He'd been watching the visual feed from Harry's glasses when he'd killed all those people in the South Glade Mission Church. *That* Harry had been stripped of all empathy, inhibition, and self-control by Valentine's tech. He'd been a *monster*, pure and simple, and if he became like that once more, how could Eggsy hope to stop him short of putting a bullet through his head—again? For the first time since Harry's miraculous resurrection, Eggsy thought it might've been better if he'd died that day outside the church. It shamed him to think that way, but that didn't mean he was wrong.

"What the *fuck* are we doing here, Harry? At a fucking airfield in the middle of nowhere and there's no plane! Now what?"

They never should've contacted Batko, never should've come to Singapore in the first place. Hell, he should've forced Harry to get on the Statesman jet back in Italy. If he had, Harry would be in Ginger's lab right now being seen to, and he'd be free to search for Poppy on his own.

"Relax," Harry said calmly.

Eggsy was about to reply, but his phone pinged. He was delighted to see he'd received a text from Tilde. He needed to talk to her now more than ever. He quickly read the text, frowned, and then reread it.

HAPPY CLOUD HAT, FROG BUNS! GOT SOME NICE WATERED-DOWN DRINKS FROM AMAZON? ☺

What the fuck?

A second later his phone rang. It was Tilde.

Eggsy held up an index finger to indicate to Harry that he would just be a moment. Harry nodded, and

Eggsy walked a dozen feet away so he could speak with Tilde privately.

"Baby!" he said as he answered her call. "You okay? What's with the weird message?"

Silence for a moment, and then in a suspicious tone Tilde asked, "Who is this?"

"What? You called *me*... Tilde?"

The call abruptly ended. He felt a cold pit open in his stomach, and he quickly called her back, this time placing a video call. Even before she answered, he knew what he would see. She was covered in the blue rash.

She bared her teeth in a grotesque parody of a smile, and when she spoke, she was almost maniacally cheerful.

"Hello! Are you the banana man?"

"Oh no, no! Tilde!"

A hand snatched the phone away from her, and an instant later her father appeared on Eggsy's screen. He was angry, and his eyes were red and puffy, as if he'd been crying.

"She's in stage two," the king said. "Maybe if you hadn't broken her heart, she—"

The king abruptly stopped speaking. The image on Eggsy's phone spun wildly, and then came to a jarring stop, and Eggsy realized the king had tossed the phone onto Tilde's bed. The device had landed at just the right angle to provide Eggsy with a partial view of Tilde. She stood in her bedroom, her father and mother near. Her left arm was frozen in an awkward position, and then the paralysis spread across her body until she was completely immobile. Her eyes shone with horror as she realized she couldn't move, and the pug puppy she'd bought for Eggsy ran across the bed and in front of the screen. The dog started barking frantically. Before Eggsy had time to react, the king snatched up the phone and ended the call.

Eggsy stared at the blank phone screen for several seconds, devastated by what had happened to the woman he loved. He whirled around and sprinted back to Harry, furious and desperate.

"I'm done with this bollocks, Harry! People are gonna die! And you and me ain't gonna be able to do jack shit about it without help!" Once more, he looked across the airfield. "And still no fucking plane?"

"Patience, Eggsy," Harry said, seemingly unaffected by Eggsy's outburst. He continued looking seaward, body relaxed, manner calm.

Eggsy stood next to him, silently fretting about poor Tilde. How long did someone have left after they reached stage three? Days? Hours? However much time remained to her, he feared it wouldn't be enough for him to save her.

I'm sorry, babe, he thought. *I'm so, so sorry...*

Eggsy heard the sound of a plane engine, and as he watched, the Statesman jet rolled across the tarmac and pulled up to the hangar. He turned to Harry.

"You called Statesman?"

Harry didn't reply. The jet stopped and a moment later the cabin door opened to reveal Merlin.

Eggsy smiled at Harry, and Harry smiled back.

As Eggsy and Harry climbed aboard, Harry said,

"Merlin, you have my permission to loop Ginger in now. Whether I'm right or wrong about Statesman, we'll get there first. And if anything happens to us, the world's buggered anyway."

Merlin nodded, looking relieved.

Ginger sat in front of Champ's desk. The Statesman leader was, to put it mildly, in a mood. He downed a shot of whiskey, poured another, reconsidered, made it a double, and then downed that too.

"I trust him, Champ," she said. "Merlin wouldn't have done this without good reason. He knows there are lives at stake. And we're running out of time."

Champ slammed his empty glass down. "He took one of our planes! Weapons! And equipment! *High-end* equipment!"

Ginger shrugged. "You said they could use our resources..."

"You thinkin' straight, Ginger? Maybe you should take a nap in that brain-fixin' machine of yours. Dismissed."

Frustrated, Ginger rose and started for the door, but her phone pinged. She checked it and smiled with relief.

"It's Merlin. He's sent the coordinates for Poppy's HQ."

Champ calmed. "I apologize, Ginger. I shouldn'a doubted you. You always did have the sharpest instincts in this whole goddamn place. Send Jack to back 'em up." He frowned. "And tell him not to make this personal."

Ginger nodded, but Jack was a man of strong feelings,

to put it mildly, and Harry *had* shot him in the head. She wasn't sure Jack could *not* make it personal.

Poppy sat at a booth in her diner, Charlie next to her, across from her a balding man wearing a very expensive suit. He had a laptop open in front of him, and resting on the tabletop next to it was a thick bound document.

"So there's no way he can back out of this?" Poppy asked.

"No way," her lawyer said. "Once the president countersigns this document, it becomes an Executive Decree. Rock solid."

Poppy smiled. "Good. Get him on the line."

The lawyer tapped a few keys, then turned the computer so it was facing Poppy. A few seconds later a chat window popped up, and there he was—the man who was going to give her everything she'd ever wanted.

"Good evening, Ms Adams," the president said.

Poppy nodded to him. "Mr President. The document is signed. My lawyer will be returning it to you in person for countersignature."

As if Poppy had given him a command, the lawyer stood, gathered the bound agreement, and headed for the diner's exit. Poppy turned the computer so its camera could track the lawyer.

"Look: there he goes now." She turned the laptop to face her once again. "The moment that's done, I'll release the antidote."

The president hesitated a moment before speaking once more. "I, uh... Ms Adams, can you give me any assurance that you can get it out there in time? Where it's going to come from? How long it'll take to distribute? I'm just concerned it could come... too late."

Poppy raised an eyebrow. You didn't rise to the top of the world's drug trade without having a highly sensitive and finely tuned bullshit detector.

"If you're thinking of looking for my stockpiles, don't bother. They're hidden and secure."

The president leaned forward slightly, probably without being aware he did so, Poppy thought. Some poker face the man had! And he was always bragging about what a fantastic dealmaker he was.

"You have more than one?" he asked, a bit too eagerly.

Signing the agreement had put her in a good mood, and so she decided to toss him a bone.

"One in every major city worldwide," she said. "Unfortunately, our lab is... unable to produce more supplies. But there's plenty to go around."

"And... distribution?" he asked.

What a nervous Nellie! Poppy lifted a red briefcase off the seat next to her, put it on the table, and opened it to reveal an electronic security device.

"When I enter the access code, all stockpiles unlock remotely, and my fleet of drones will distribute the antidote automatically. So... chop chop! Time's running out."

*   *   *

Eggsy and Harry sat in the jet's passenger cabin while Merlin flew the plane. Eggsy stared straight ahead, brooding.

After a time, Harry asked, "Are you all right? What was that phone call you got?"

"Let's not, Harry. I don't think you'd sympathize. And I ain't in the mood for a lecture."

Harry walked over to the bar. "How about a martini? For old times' sake?"

Eggsy debated with himself for a moment and finally said, "Yeah, all right."

He joined Harry at the bar and watched as he mixed the drinks. When he finished, he handed Eggsy's to him, they toasted, and drank. *Perfect*, Eggsy thought. *As always*.

"I had a girlfriend," Eggsy said. "I lost her. And it broke me. And now… if this mission fails… she's gonna die. I know it's against Kingsman rules. Having a relationship."

Harry was quiet for several moments before speaking again.

"When I was shot, can you guess what the last thing was that flashed through my mind? It was… absolutely nothing. I had no ties. No bittersweet memories. I was leaving nothing behind. I've never experienced companionship. Never been in love. In that moment, all I felt was loneliness. And regret."

"I'm sorry," Eggsy said.

"Don't be. Just know that having something to lose is… what makes life worth living."

They finished their drinks, and then Harry smiled and patted Eggsy on the shoulder.

"Now… let's go save your girl."

It was at that moment that Eggsy knew his friend had truly returned, and he hugged him, grateful for his kind words.

"I missed you, Harry," he said.

Merlin stepped out of the cockpit and cleared his throat to get their attention.

"Gentlemen, I hate to break up the party, but the autopilot's activated and we're nearly there. I suggest we get ready. Follow me."

Merlin led them to the pool table and pressed the button that caused the tabletop to flip over and reveal the jet's weapons cache.

Merlin picked up a baseball and held it out for them to inspect.

"Hand grenade," he said.

He put the ball back and picked up a baseball bat, or at least what *looked* like one.

"Mine sweeper," he explained. "The perimeter of Poppy's base is the most deadly minefield I've ever seen, and the only thing Boris can't help us with. The mines are fitted with robotic roaming devices, so they're never in the same place… in case someone like Boris has ideas above his station."

He returned the bat to its place on the table.

Merlin then produced a slim, oblong velvet box from his pocket. He handed it to Eggsy.

"For the endgame," Merlin said. "Eggsy, I'm entrusting this to you."

Eggsy nodded solemnly, took the case, and slipped it inside the inner pocket of his suit jacket.

"And I'm entrusting *this* to me." Merlin lifted a huge Bowie knife off the table and held it up. One corner of his mouth ticked up in a smile, and Eggsy could swear there was a gleam in his eye.

Merlin put the knife down and led them into the plane's bedroom cabin. There was a small closet space in the cabin with a curtain across it. Merlin pulled the curtain back to reveal fresh Kingsman suits. *Three* of them. Merlin removed one of the suits and held it up to him.

"May I… ?" he asked, almost shyly.

Eggsy and Harry exchanged looks.

"Absolutely," Harry said.

When they were ready, the three of them stood in Kingsman suits, umbrellas in one hand, briefcases in the other.

Merlin spread his arms, displaying his new look. "What do you reckon?" he asked.

"That Poppy's gonna think we've come to do her tax return," Eggsy said. "Just kidding. Looking *good*, Merlin."

Merlin called up an aerial map of Poppy's compound on a wall screen, and the three agents studied it closely.

"Here it is," Merlin said. "Poppy's HQ. Very, very remote. Dense tropical forestation all the way from the coastline."

"We parachute in, let the plane ditch at sea," Harry said.

"If Whiskey ever recovers, he's gonna fucking kill us," Eggsy said.

Tilde lay on the bed in her apartment, unmoving, skin covered with blue rash, the still-unnamed pug curled up next to her, whining softly. Her mother sat on the edge of the bed, stroking Tilde's hair and crying while a group of doctors stood around, arguing with each other about the best way to treat their royal patient. Her father stood with them, listening to their useless debate and growing more frustrated with each passing moment.

Everyone thought Tilde was unconscious, or if she was aware, that she still suffered from the strange delirium that was part of stage two. Either way, none of them thought she was really present in any meaningful sense, but they couldn't have been more wrong. The true horror of stage three's paralysis was that the mind of the afflicted cleared after it struck, leaving the victim fully aware but trapped inside their prison of a body. Tilde wanted to reassure her mother that everything was going to be okay, even though she knew it probably wasn't. She wanted to tell her father to send the bickering doctors away, as they could do nothing for her. She wanted to reach over and stroke the puppy's soft fur to reassure it. But most of all, she wanted to see Eggsy's face one last time, hear his voice, and hope somehow that he would be able to look into her eyes and see how much she loved him, and how much she regretted that they were never going to have a chance to make a life together.

Don't think like that, she chided herself. *Right now, Eggsy is out there somewhere, doing everything he can to save you—to save everyone! Have some faith! He'll find the antidote, you'll be cured, and then you both will be together again—forever.*

But as hard as she tried, she couldn't make herself truly believe it. Her eyes moistened slightly, the most her body could do to produce tears in its current state. No one noticed.

Eggsy, Harry, and Merlin picked their way carefully through the jungle undergrowth, carrying their umbrellas and briefcases with one hand while holding sensor equipment in the other. Eggsy used the Statesman bat to sweep for landmines, while Harry and Merlin used handheld scanners to check for other security measures. The jungle was hot and humid but nothing the temperature-regulating properties of their suits couldn't deal with.

Eggsy had never been in a jungle before, but the place certainly lived up to its reputation. There was green everywhere he looked, and the flora was as numerous as it was varied—rubber plants, banana bushes, strangler fig trees, and many more. Colorful flowers accented the greenery that surrounded them, making this undoubtedly one of the most beautiful places on Earth. Poppy was like an infection in the heart of this paradise, Eggsy thought. Or maybe more like a venomous snake, coiled up and lying in wait for whatever prey was unfortunate enough to wander too close.

Their progress was slow, but they didn't have any other choice, not with the self-rearranging robotic mines surrounding Poppy's compound. Eggsy only saw one of them move once. At first, he thought it was some kind of giant rainforest spider. The damn thing was a foot and a half, maybe two feet in diameter, a flat black disc with thin insect-like legs. It was a dozen yards away from where they were standing at that point, and Eggsy watched it scuttle about, seemingly at random, before it stopped, and flattened itself against the ground. Then it spun around rapidly, digging its own hole. Once it was down far enough, it stopped spinning, and its legs extended upward, pulled loose soil over it, tamped the soil down, and then retracted, leaving no sign the mine was there.

That's a nasty thing, Eggsy thought, and he refocused his concentration on the mine detector.

Eventually they reached a clearing, and they saw the entrance to Poppy's stronghold. Huge metallic entrance gates stood before ancient temple structures, a neon sign proclaimed POPPYLAND to the jungle, and—no surprise here—there were ten guards armed with Heckler & Koch submachine guns. The gate was open, so that was a stroke of luck, but there was no way they could get through without making one hell of a racket.

Harry was thinking along similar lines. He motioned

for them to retreat so they'd be out of the guards' line of sight. When they'd done so, he began whispering.

"This is where we split up. Pincer movement. Merlin, you're with me. Eggsy, signal when you're in position."

Eggsy nodded and started to head off, but when he took his first step, he heard a soft *click* and felt something give slightly beneath his foot. With a sick feeling, he realized what had happened. He'd forgotten to use the mine sweeper, and now he'd stepped on one of the bloody things. Despite his suit's temperature-adjustment technology, he felt a line of sweat roll down his spine.

"Don't move," Merlin whispered urgently. "You move, we all die."

The three men stood statue-still as the full horror of what had just happened sank in. No one did anything for several moments. Eggsy—afraid to so much as twitch a muscle—breathed as shallowly as he could. He began to tremble, and although he tried to force himself to stop, it didn't work. If anything, it made him shake even harder. He knew there was no way out of this one for him, and he was about to tell Harry and Merlin to go on without him when Merlin slowly walked over to stand next to him. Merlin removed a can of Kingsman deodorant from his briefcase, and then looked at Harry.

"Get clear," he said.

Harry moved a safe distance away while Merlin sprayed the ground around Eggsy's feet. The earth turned white, crystallizing as it became icy cold.

"On three, move," Merlin said. "Ready?"

Eggsy nodded.

"One... two... three!"

Eggsy threw himself forward and landed flat on his face. He quickly stood—frankly astonished to find himself still alive—and saw that Merlin had taken his place on the mine.

Eggsy couldn't believe it. "Merlin? No... No! What did you do that for?"

"The spray only buys a split second," Merlin said. "Even if we'd all got clear, it'd detonate. Poppy's guards come running, none of us make it inside."

"Then spray it again and let me back on!" Eggsy said. "It was *my* fuck-up!"

"No," Harry said. "If it's to be any of us, it should be me."

Merlin shook the can.

"Empty. Go on, you two. Get going."

Eggsy couldn't believe what was happening. "What? No, Merlin! Why?"

Merlin smiled sadly, seeming far too calm for a man standing atop a deadly explosive device.

"Did you ever have balloon debates at school, Eggsy?" he asked.

Eggsy shook his head, unclear where Merlin was going with this.

"You pretend you're all on an overladen hot-air balloon," Merlin continued. "Everyone is doomed unless one person goes overboard. And you debate who. You argue who'd contribute most to the world if they survived.

There's... no debate to be had here, friends. The mission needs the two of you. The *world* needs the two of you."

Eggsy refused to accept this. Merlin was a fucking *genius*, practically the wizard that his code name implied. He *had* to have a way out of this. Some sort of outlandish device that he'd cobbled together in Ginger's lab, or maybe a bit of tech he'd "borrowed" from Statesman, something he'd pull out at the last minute and use to neutralize the mine. Then he'd grin, step off the inert device, and they'd continue with the mission. All three of them.

But when Eggsy looked into Merlin's eyes, he saw the truth written there. Taking his place on the mine *was* Merlin's solution to the problem. His final feat of magic.

"Besides, our journey together began many years ago," Merlin added. "When your father did the same for me."

With a shock of surprise, Eggsy realized what Merlin was saying. He'd been on the mission when Eggsy's father had sacrificed himself to save the lives of his companions, back when Eggsy was a toddler. Eggsy had known that Harry was one of those agents, and now he knew Merlin was too. Here was Merlin, doing the same fucking thing—sacrificing himself for his friends.

"Merlin, no... please." He turned to Harry, hoping his mentor would think of some miraculous last-minute method for saving Merlin's life. But the sorrow in Harry's one eye, along with the grim expression on his face, told Eggsy that Harry had no tricks left up his immaculately tailored sleeve.

Merlin didn't seem afraid. In fact, he seemed strangely at peace.

"I've lived a great and full life," he said. "But... everything Harry told you, Eggsy: he's right. Will you... give Ginger my best wishes?"

"Your best wishes?" Eggsy said.

Merlin smiled. "All right. My... love."

Eggsy nodded sorrowfully. Merlin stuck out his hand for them to shake. Eggsy first, then Harry. When they finished, Merlin gave them a warm smile.

"Go on, now," he said. "Make me proud."

"It's been an honor," Harry said solemnly. He saluted Merlin, then touched him on the shoulder before turning away. "Eggsy. With me."

Eggsy gave his friend one last nod before turning and hurrying after Harry, sweeping the Statesman bat back and forth ahead of him. He didn't bother trying to stop the tears this time.

When Harry and Eggsy were out of sight, Merlin considered his options, which, admittedly, were extremely limited. He wasn't going to live through this, that was certain. But he wasn't dead yet, and as long as he lived, he was still a Kingsman, and his fellow agents could use a distraction to help get them past Poppy's guards. An idea came to him then, and he smiled. *Why the fuck not?* he thought. *Might as well go out in style.*

He used the Bowie knife to slash the foliage around him

until he'd cleared enough to make himself visible to Poppy's guards. Then he began singing "Take Me Home, Country Roads," belting out the words at the top of his lungs.

Eggsy and Harry hugged the walls of the temple ruins as they crept toward Poppyland's main gate, each coming from a different direction. Ten guards… that was five apiece. Eggsy figured they could take them without too much trouble. Of course, it was going to be trickier without Merlin, but Eggsy couldn't let himself think about the man right now. He couldn't allow himself to be distracted, not if—

He paused as he heard Merlin's voice coming from the other side of the clearing. It sounded as if he were… singing?

Eggsy looked past the guards to Harry, who'd also stopped and was looking across the clearing, frowning in puzzlement. He turned to Eggsy and they shared a silent message. *What the fuck?*

The guards must've been thinking the same thing, for they milled around nervously, as if unsure what they should do. One of them lifted a walkie-talkie to his mouth and started speaking.

"Poppy, are you expecting a visitor?" The guard stepped forward and peered into the underbrush on the far side of the clearing. "Another lawyer or… an accountant, maybe? An accountant who might be… singing?"

Poppy's voice issued from the walkie-talkie. "Singing?" She sounded incredulous, so the guard held the walkie-talkie out toward the minefield so she could hear more clearly. After a moment, he held the device in front of his face again.

"Okay… that's weird," Poppy said. "Unless he turns out to be a threat, bring him to me alive. I'm intrigued."

The guard clipped the walkie back on his belt, raised his submachine gun, and headed in Merlin's direction. He motioned without looking behind him, and two other guards started after him.

Eggsy understood what Merlin was doing, and his respect for the man—already enormous—grew even further. What was more, he couldn't believe that such a daft plan seemed to be working!

Merlin was putting everything he had into his performance as three guards approached. As they drew close, one of the guards pointed his weapon at Merlin and shouted, "Get down!"

Merlin had been forced to discard his briefcase and umbrella when he'd shoved Eggsy, and they lay out of reach. So, without any weapons of his own, he knelt down—keeping one knee planted firmly on top of the mine—and waited. The guards moved forward and frisked him, and when they saw he was unarmed, they relaxed. Now that was over, Merlin resumed singing.

One of the guards looked at the other two. He pointed to his head and then moved his finger in circles. The message was obvious: *This guy is fucking nuts!*

Merlin launched into the chorus, and he sprang up and spun around on one foot, kicking out with the other as he went, delivering devastating strikes to each guard's face—all without ever taking his weight off the mine. The guards fell unconscious one by one, and then Merlin came round to his starting position again and put his other foot back down on the mine.

And he kept right on singing.

Eggsy heard the sound of Merlin delivering an ass-kicking, as did the remaining guards. Three of them exchanged silent nods and ran toward the minefield, leaving four behind.

Thanks to Merlin, Eggsy and Harry's odds of getting through the gate unscathed had considerably improved.

Three more guards came running up to Merlin, so intent on finding out what had happened to their comrades that they didn't actually see the men lying unconscious on the ground until it was too late. When they were in arm's reach, Merlin lashed out lightning-fast with both fists—one-two-three—and down the trio went to join their friends.

Merlin continued his song.

Seconds later, three more guards came running toward him, but they couldn't fail to see six of their group lying unconscious around Merlin's feet. They circled him, remaining just out of his reach, and raised their weapons. *Only nine*, Merlin thought. *Oh well. Every little helps.*

He delivered the last note of the song in a glorious final flourish, and stepped off the mine.

Chapter Eleven

———————— ✦ ————————

A lone guard remained, and Eggsy and Harry left their positions and sprinted toward the gate. Just as Eggsy was about to take out the guard, a huge explosion erupted in the minefield. Eggsy felt the ground shake beneath his feet, and while the guard was distracted, he ran toward him, and laid the man out with a single devastating punch.

That's for my mate, you fuck.

Eggsy and Harry locked eyes and paused a moment, honoring their comrade for all he had done to give them a fighting chance. Eggsy tossed a baseball grenade through the gate to cover their approach, and when it exploded they ran into Poppy's compound.

Unfortunately, they didn't get far before the rest of Poppy's private army—undoubtedly alerted by the explosion—came running from the various buildings that lined Main Street. Poppy's stronghold looked more like an amusement park than a drug lord's fortress, Eggsy thought, and the men and women who rushed into the street were dressed like employees of the businesses from which they'd emerged. Some were armed with conventional weapons—submachine guns, pistols, shotguns, knives—but some wielded objects that were more... unusual. The incorporation of the temple ruins into Poppy's compound blended ancient and modern in a way that made the place look even more surreal. The ground was covered by centuries-weathered stone, and thick vines snaked across brick walls that formed sections of the bowling alley and the cinema, along with other structures.

Harry unfurled his umbrella, and the AR display activated. He switched the weapon's settings to LETHAL, and began firing as he walked forward. Eggsy, briefcase in hand, followed closely behind his mentor. He pulled another baseball grenade out of his pocket and hurled it toward what looked for the all the world like a donut shop, complete with a sculpture of a giant pink-frosted donut on the roof. The grenade exploded, and the donut sculpture detached and rolled off the building and onto the ground. It kept rolling, and Harry and Eggsy used it as cover while Harry continued firing, dropping Poppy's guards one after the other.

The donut picked up speed and rolled away from the main street, exposing them once more. A man rushed forth from Poppy's cinema, shouldered a bazooka and took aim at them. Eggsy lifted his briefcase to his shoulder and tugged the handle a certain way. In response, a panel slid open and a small missile shot forth. A split second later Bazooka Guy disappeared in a spectacular explosion.

Eggsy stood next to Harry and they continued blasting

away at Poppy's army. Eggsy fired another missile, destroying a candy cart and knocking a half-dozen guards to the ground. Harry ejected the top of the umbrella, and it flew forward, a thin cable trailing behind it. It slammed into a guard and sent him flying through the air to crash into the cinema's marquee. As the man fell to the ground, Harry retracted the umbrella top, and it returned to the handle and reattached itself.

Eggsy held his briefcase out before him, and panels swung out from the top and bottom, forming a bulletproof shield. An AR display activated on the inside of the shield, and Eggsy started moving forward, Harry walking behind him now. Eggsy held the shield one-handed while firing his Kingsman pistol with his free hand. Harry aimed the handle of his umbrella at a submachine gun dropped by a dead guard. The handle shot outward, trailing a cable just as the umbrella top had. The handle hooked the weapon, and Harry retracted it. The gun flew toward him and he snatched it out of the air and began firing.

A pair of giant scissors hung over the entrance to Poppy's Salon, an oversized decoration like the one on top of the donut shop. But the scissors were made from metal, and their points looked extremely sharp. Harry decided to see for himself. A pair of guards stood beneath the scissors, and Harry fired, freeing the giant decoration from its wall mounting. The scissors descended rapidly and impaled the guards. Theory proven.

A guard approached and Eggsy slammed the shield

into him. The man staggered backward, and Eggsy dropped the shield, performed a flip, and shot the man while he was in mid-air. The next attack came from a humanoid robot styled to look like some kind of doll. She lifted a grenade launcher and fired three times: *whump, whump, whump!* The grenades landed nearby, but before they could detonate, Harry aimed his umbrella at them. A bolo shot from the tip flew toward the grenades, and wrapped around them. Harry raised his watch and pressed a button. A tiny but extremely powerful electromagnet flew toward the bolo and attached itself. Harry twisted a control on his watch face, and the magnet soared toward the robot, taking the bolo and the grenades with it. The robot exploded, and Harry lifted the umbrella over his and Eggsy's heads to protect them from falling chunks of metal and electronics.

The main street was suddenly quiet, littered with bodies from the insane massacre. Eggsy and Harry retrieved their briefcases, exchanged the weapons they'd just fired for fresh ones, and looked at each other.

"Shall we?" Harry said.

Eggsy smiled. "Let's."

They started running down the street, weaving between the bodies of Poppy's fallen army.

Poppy and Charlie were sitting in a diner booth, Poppy obsessively searching the Internet for any news about the president signing the agreement, Charlie listening to her bitch about not finding any. Four guards stood next to the dogs' kennels, looking bored. Charlie knew exactly how they felt. He was getting tired of being Poppy's errand boy. He hoped that when this was all over, he could convince her to make him one of her sales reps. After all, someone needed to fill Grigor's recently vacated position. Why not him? At this point, he'd accept a job anywhere doing just about anything, as long as it was away from her. *Far* away. He'd grown quite weary of her domineering personality, her homicidal whims, and her garish—and more than a little childish—Poppyland. And those so-called *jokes* of hers! He never wanted to be forced to endure any more of those groaners. As far as he was concerned, Poppy was only a means to an end, and that end was *money*. The rest of his family had died on V-Day, and while he didn't especially miss them, he *desperately* missed their fortune, none of which he had been able to inherit since the world believed him to be dead too. So she was his ticket back to the good life, and although he appreciated the robotic prosthesis and speech synthesizer she'd given him, he looked forward to not having to answer her bellowed summons a dozen times a day and perform whatever demeaning task she demanded of him. He looked forward to being *free*.

Poppy closed the laptop in frustration.

"I don't get it," she said. "I know the agreement was delivered. My lawyer called me as soon as he dropped it off at the White House. He even took video of secret service agents accepting it to confirm receipt. But that was *hours* ago! And not a peep from the president in the time since. I mean, how long does it take to sign your goddamned *name*?"

Charlie considered whether or not to broach a delicate subject: the notion that perhaps the president had never *intended* to sign, and that he'd lied to Poppy in order to stall for time. Maybe to see if the stockpiles of antidote could be found, maybe to send special ops teams out into the world to search for her. Frankly, who knew why that man did anything? It was no wonder Valentine had never tried to recruit the tosser to his cause. But Poppy had a *major* thing about lying. Witness what she'd ordered him to do to Angel. And while Charlie wouldn't be the one lying to her, he *would* be the only one within reach, and he doubted she had any qualms about killing the messenger. No, he decided. Best to keep quiet and let her sort out the situation on her own. It would be safer that way—for him, at least.

"I *really* don't want to make a pest of myself," Poppy said, "but maybe I should try calling." She opened the laptop again, but before she could start typing, the sound of gunfire came from outside.

"Shit!" she said. "We're under attack!"

She whistled for the dogs, but nothing happened.

One of the guards checked the monitor screens on top of the kennels.

"They're still charging, Madam Poppy," he said.

She scowled. "How much longer?"

"Five minutes for Bennie. Two for Jet."

"And you?" Poppy said, irritated. "Are *your* batteries flat? Get out there, now!"

The guards ran out of the diner, and Poppy grabbed a walkie and shouted into it.

"Code five! Code five!"

Elton was practicing piano in the auditorium under the supervision of two burly guards in usher uniforms. He hated Poppy, but he had to admit the woman knew her pianos. This Steinway was one of the finest he'd ever played.

Poppy's voice burst from the guards' walkies.

"Code five! Code five!"

"The compound's under attack," one of the guards said. "Stay here."

"Like... a rescue attempt?" Elton said hopefully. He started playing "Saturday Night's Alright for Fighting," but as he sang, he replaced "Saturday" with "Wednesday."

The first guard frowned. "Isn't it supposed to be Saturday?"

"Yeah," Elton said. "But it's Wednesday."

He stood and executed a perfect roundhouse kick, taking out the guard. The second man started to raise his gun, but another kick put him down. Elton grinned. All those years playing with one leg up on the piano had definitely paid off!

On the seat next to Poppy was the red briefcase containing the security code device. She grabbed the case and thrust it across the table toward Charlie.

"Get this somewhere safe!"

Charlie understood. If whoever was attacking—Navy SEALs, SAS, Spetsnaz, or some other special forces group—captured the briefcase and learned the location of the caches, Poppy's leverage would be gone, and her plan would fail. He couldn't very well let that happen, could he? His bank account would never forgive him.

Charlie took the case and slid out of the booth.

Eggsy and Harry burst into the diner. Harry had noticed that it was the only building from which none of Poppy's soldiers had emerged to attack. Ergo, that was where she was hiding, for she would never allow her guards to leave her side during an assault on her compound.

Poppy was sitting at a booth, and she quickly rose to her feet when they entered. Eggsy was glad to see Charlie there as well. *Two for the price of one*, he thought. Eggsy and Harry leveled their submachine guns at Poppy and Charlie.

Charlie made for the fire exit, the door closest to him. Eggsy fired a burst of ammo at him, but he managed to deflect the bullets with his robot arm before escaping. Eggsy took off in pursuit. He wasn't worried about Harry. He knew his mentor could take care of himself. Besides, how much of a threat could Poppy be all by herself?

"Tell us where to find the antidote!" Harry demanded.

A soft beep sounded from somewhere in the diner, and

Poppy smiled. She whistled, and Harry heard a scuttling on the diner's tiled floor. He turned to see a robotic dog racing toward him. He didn't waste time questioning the creature's existence. During his career as a Kingsman, he'd learned to trust his eyes—now *eye*, singular— and what he saw was a threat, pure and simple, and he responded. He fired at the dog, but the rounds pinged harmlessly off its metal hide.

Shit.

He dropped the useless weapon, turned and ran like hell for the diner's entrance, the dog almost nipping at his heels. As he burst out into the open air, he knew there was no way he could hope to outrun the beast. Even if it'd been a flesh-and-blood canine, it would've still brought him down before he made it halfway across the street, and while the thing might've had the *shape* of a dog, it was in truth a machine. He could no more hope to outpace it than he could a car. But if he could slow it down, even a little, he might have a fighting chance. He still carried the briefcase Merlin had given him, and while a few tricks remained inside, he knew he couldn't get to them before the robot dog tore him apart. But that didn't mean the briefcase itself couldn't be of assistance.

He stopped, spun around, and gave the briefcase's handle a twist. The case detached from the handle and flew toward the oncoming dog. It landed directly in front of the beast and exploded with a loud *whumpf!* It wasn't a huge blast. The self-destruct function wasn't designed to be a weapon itself, but rather to destroy the briefcase's contents to prevent them from falling into the wrong hands.

Harry threw the useless handle aside and started running again. Directly across the street from the diner was a bowling alley, and he headed for it. It might not be his first choice for refuge—a fully stocked armory would've been lovely—but needs must.

He shoved open the metal-and-glass door to the bowling alley and dashed inside. Then he turned and threw all his weight against the door just as the dog slammed into it. He'd hoped to close it, but the creature was too strong. It pressed its head to the door's outer surface, and Harry heard a deep murmuring sound. He understood what was happening: the dog's system was increasing the power output to its limbs, turning the creature into a pair of pneumatic battering rams. The increasing pressure sent cracks spiderwebbing through the glass, and the door's metal frame began to bend. Harry knew he had only seconds before the animal broke in, so he abandoned the door and ran further into the building. An instant later, he heard glass shatter and then the thudding footfalls of the beast as it came after him.

He turned to face the oncoming creature, opened his umbrella, and fired. The rounds proved no more effective against the hound than those from the submachine gun. The dog leaped forward, snarling with its synthesized voice, and began to shred the umbrella with its teeth and claws.

Harry dropped the umbrella and ran onto one of the lanes, hoping its waxed surface might prove difficult for the dog to negotiate. He was right. As the dog stepped onto the wooden lane, its metal paws had trouble finding traction, causing it to slip and slide. Unfortunately, the soles of Harry's Oxfords weren't much better. He felt as if he'd stepped onto the icy surface of a frozen lake and could barely keep his footing. When he heard a series of whirrs and clicks, he turned his head toward the dog and saw its metallic claws had lengthened, sharpened, and now curved downward, appearing more feline than canine. This adjustment allowed the dog to maneuver the waxed lane with ease, and it came rushing toward Harry, jaws open wide to reveal razor-sharp metallic teeth.

Harry ran toward the pins at the end of the alley. He managed to grab one and spin around just as the dog attacked. He jammed the pin into the creature's mouth, hoping to perhaps cause its mechanical jaws to seize up. Harry ran up the alley again as the dog shook its head back and forth, trying to dislodge the pin. There was a loud hum as it increased power to its jaws and the pin snapped apart, falling to the lane in two pieces. The dog whirled in Harry's direction and came bounding toward him. It slowed as it approached, its teeth retracted and small buzzsaws replaced them. They began to spin as the creature stepped toward him, and Harry could only stand and watch as death approached.

Charlie ran out into the street outside the diner, and Eggsy followed. He still carried both the submachine and his briefcase, but as fast as he was running, he couldn't use either. For that matter, he really didn't want to. He'd rather wrap his bare hands around Charlie's throat and squeeze until the bastard's eyes bulged, his face turned purple, and he stopped breathing. But, however satisfying that would've been, Eggsy knew there was no time for revenge. He wasn't certain what was in the red briefcase Charlie carried, but he could make a fair enough guess. There was only one thing right now that Poppy would want protected above all else: the location of the antidote caches. He needed that information. The world did. But most importantly to Eggsy right then, Tilde needed it.

He stopped running, dropped the briefcase, and raised the submachine gun.

Maybe it was the sound of the briefcase hitting the ground that alerted Charlie, maybe Poppy had implanted some kind of heightened sensory equipment in him, or maybe it was nothing more or less than pure human instinct. Whatever the reason, Charlie spun around, raised his robotic arm, and with a *fwoosh*, his hand shot forth like a missile, a metal cable playing out behind it as it went.

You gotta be shitting me, Eggsy thought.

The hand rocketed across the distance between them, fastened around one of Eggsy's legs and yanked him off his feet. Eggsy slammed into the ground hard, causing him to lose his grip on the gun. He made a grab for it, but Charlie retracted his hand a fraction and pulled Eggsy toward him until the gun was out of reach.

Just then Harry burst out of the diner and ran into the street a couple hundred feet from Eggsy and Charlie. A—

was that a *robot* dog?—a whatever it was bounded after him. Harry used his briefcase's self-destruct function to slow the dog down, and then he ran like hell for the bowling alley.

As the dog forced its way into the alley after Harry, Eggsy decided he needed to revise his estimate of Poppy's threat level.

"Looks like Jet's got himself a new chew toy," Charlie said.

He put his briefcase on the ground and walked toward Eggsy, slowly and deliberately. His hand loosened its grip on Eggsy's leg and retracted. The cable slid rapidly into the wrist aperture and the hand reattached with a *snick*.

"You're like a fucking cockroach, Eggy, you know that? No matter how many times I think I've killed you, you pop right back up again, ready for more punishment. I suppose I shouldn't be surprised, though. Your kind live like roaches and you certainly breed like them."

As Charlie drew closer, Eggsy reached over and pushed a button on the side of his watch. Charlie's eyes followed the movement, but when nothing happened, he grinned.

"Out of order? Looks like Merlin's starting to slip in his old age."

Eggsy's face darkened. "Don't you *ever* say his name."

Charlie had come within five feet of Eggsy, and he stopped now, just out of arm's reach.

"I heard him over the guard's walkie-talkie. Merlin, I mean. Although I suppose I should say the *late* Merlin, shouldn't I? Too bad he was blown to bits. Although come to think of it, it'll save on funeral costs, considering there isn't all that much left of him to bury." Charlie gave Eggsy a mocking grin. "So I guess there's a bright side after all."

White-hot rage erupted inside Eggsy, and he charged at Charlie. But just as Eggsy reached the fucker, Charlie's robot arm flashed toward him. He grabbed hold of Eggsy's collar, lifted him up as if he weighed no more than a rag doll, and slammed him to the ground. Once, twice… He lifted Eggsy again and hurled him toward the diner wall.

Eggsy hit the temple wall harder than he expected, and although he'd gotten used to rough landings during his brief career as a secret agent, this was something special. White light exploded behind his eyes, and he felt several ribs give way. His awareness cut out for a couple of seconds, and when it returned, he was lying face-down in the dirt in front of the combination of modern and ancient architecture that was Poppy's diner. There wasn't a part of him that didn't hurt like blazes, and when he tried to stand, his body refused to cooperate. It had taken enough abuse for the time being, thank you, and it intended to lie motionless until at least some of the pain subsided. A day, maybe two. Three would be grand, but it didn't want to be pushy.

So Eggsy lay there, aching all the way down to the cellular level, as Charlie walked toward him.

"Poppy calls my new toy ARMageddon," Charlie said. "At first I thought it was just another of her crap jokes, but the name's actually starting to grow on me."

One of Poppy's guards had attacked Eggsy and Harry armed with a gun in one hand and a bowling ball in the other. The man was dead, and the ball lay on the ground, only a couple feet from Charlie. He detoured toward it, picked it up with his robotic hand, and continued toward Eggsy.

"You've been a *tremendous* pain in the ass, Eggy," Charlie said. "I can't tell you how much I'm going to enjoy this."

His robot hand began to spin rapidly, and the bowling ball became a whirling weapon of destruction. Charlie stopped when he reached Eggsy. He paused as he gazed down at him, as if savoring the moment, and then he raised the spinning ball over his head.

Charlie's smile was cold as Arctic wind.

"Any last words?"

Poppy monitored the feeds from the compound's security cameras at her computer. There were two windows open on the screen, one for each of the agents—the young one and the older one—and she kept moving her gaze back and forth between them, telling herself that it was going to be okay, that she was going to *win*. So what if the agents had infiltrated her (supposedly) hidden compound and decimated her private (not worth the money) army? Charlie would handle the younger one (*hand*le, get it?), and Jet would take out the old guy. The president would sign the agreement, and she would get everything she'd ever wanted. She'd be *free*. Free to go where she wanted, when she wanted. Free to do whatever—or *who*ever— she pleased. Free to do business *her* way, without being hampered by narrow-minded politicians with outdated morals. And as her business continued to grow and expand—her power and influence increasing along with it—who could say what lofty heights her career might reach? As lovely as Poppyland was, Poppy*world* sounded ever so much more delicious.

Aren't you putting the cart before the horse here, Little Soldier?

Poppy froze. She hadn't heard that voice—the voice of the man she always thought of as The Colonel—in decades.

Your father's right, sweetie. You need to look before you leap. Otherwise, it could be a very long way down.

This voice belonged to the woman Poppy thought of as The Major.

I'm sure you think *you've planned for every contingency*, The Colonel said. *But you know the old saying: no battle plan survives first contact with the enemy.*

You're reacting, not acting, The Major said. *But we're not surprised. You've always lacked the fortitude that a* real *leader requires.*

I'm forced to agree with your mother, The Colonel said. *Running away from the world and hiding in this godforsaken jungle… working through incompetent intermediaries… Not exactly your finest hour, Little Soldier.*

"Stop calling me that," Poppy said. "I *hate* it when you call me that."

And not only is the military aspect of your operation sadly lacking, The Major said, *but your business plan leaves much to be desired as well.*

Too true, The Colonel agreed. *Even if you succeed in getting all drugs legalized, do you* really *think the world's leaders will let you go scot-free after what you've done? After all the people you murdered just so you can have your way?*

"Immunity from prosecution is part of the agreement," Poppy said.

And you believe they'll honor that? The Major said. *They'll lock you up before you have a chance to do any of the things you dream of.*

We're extremely disappointed in you, The Colonel said.

Disappointed, but not surprised, The Major added.

You've never had what it takes.

Never had the right stuff.

That's why we… disciplined you the way we did.

Wanted to toughen you up. Make you strong.

But obviously we failed you. And in turn, you've failed us.

We should've hit you harder.

And more often.

Left deeper scars. That way, you'd never have forgotten the lessons we tried to teach you.

"Shut up!" Poppy screamed and slammed her fists on her desk.

She listened, but the voices spoke no more after that.

She let out a shuddery sigh of relief. She supposed in some ways—many, actually—she had her parents to thank for the person she'd become. Oh, she had some regrets about her relationship with them, of course, but what child couldn't say that about her parents? Her only *real* regret was that she hadn't killed the two of them sooner.

Harry didn't relish the thought of being torn to pieces by a robotic dog, but he had to admit that—as deaths went—it held a certain novelty. But before the creature could fall upon him, something else did. Quite literally. A man threw himself atop Harry.

"Stay down!" he said. "It won't attack me."

The dog stepped closer and stretched its head toward Harry's rescuer. The creature's optical scanner lit up red and words scrolled across the screen. SNIFFING... IDENTIFYING... ELTON JOHN. The dog's scanner turned green, and it backed off, sat down on its metal haunches, and began wagging its tail.

Only then did the last two words that had appeared on the animal's scanner register with Harry.

Elton John?

As the man helped Harry to his feet, he saw that, yes, he was none other than Sir Elton John. After his memory had returned, Harry had done his best to catch up on important world events that had taken place since Valentine shot him. He recalled reading that Elton John had gone missing around V-Day. No one seemed to be quite clear on exactly when he'd disappeared, but the general consensus was that Elton had been recruited by Valentine—like so many other rich, famous, and well-connected people—and had died when the implants in the necks of Valentine's followers exploded. Evidently, Poppy had added kidnapper to her criminal résumé. Harry was glad to see Elton hadn't fallen in with Valentine and his gang of genocidal one-percenters, though. He'd always rather liked the man's music.

"Thank you," Harry said.

"It's fine," Elton said. "Any enemy of that woman's is a friend of mine. Just get me out of here."

"You have my word," Harry said. "But first…"

Harry quickly explained to Elton what he had in mind, and Elton agreed. Elton stepped in front of Harry to shield him from the dog, and together they slowly made their way to the closest ball return. The dog watched them, head moving to track their progress. The creature continued sitting, but Harry noted that its tail was no longer wagging.

There were three balls in the return, and when he and Elton reached it, Harry picked up two. Then, with Elton still leading the way, they walked slowly toward the dog. Its optical scanner remained green, but it tilted its head to the side, as if trying to work out precisely what was happening.

When they were close enough, Elton stepped aside. The dog saw Harry, and its optical scanner turned red. The beast lunged at him, but before it could bite him, Harry jammed one of the balls into its mouth as hard as he could. As the creature struggled to spit the ball out, he brought the other crashing down on its head. He then swung the ball upward, smashing it into the creature's lower jaw.

Harry and Elton stepped back. The dog's head was misshapen now: dented, jaws askew, optical scanner cracked. Its left ear was missing, and electricity sparked out of the circular opening. The optical sensor might have been damaged, but when Harry concealed himself behind Elton, it turned green once more. The dog didn't sit down this time, and it definitely didn't wag its tail. Given the damage to its mouth, it could no longer hold onto the bowling ball, which fell, hit the floor, and rolled away. Harry had no idea how intelligent the thing was, but it was smart enough to know he was still somewhere close by. The dog swiveled its head back and forth, as if it were an actual canine trying to catch a scent.

Elton did his best to keep himself between Harry and the dog, but it wasn't easy. Sometimes the dog would step into a position where it could sense Harry. Elton would jump in front of Harry just as the dog's scanner turned crimson, and it would quickly return to green. Their situation had become a deadly kind of dance, one that Harry knew they couldn't keep up much longer.

As Elton jumped and scurried about, Harry tried to gauge how severely the dog had been damaged. It was still functional, and its jaws—while no longer properly aligned—still looked as if they'd have no trouble tearing through flesh and muscle. But the dog listed a bit to the right when it walked, and the light from its optical scanner kept flickering. The robo-dog might have been an artificially created predator, but Harry was human, and his species were the greatest predators the world had ever seen. What other creatures were capable of killing off their entire kind as well as the planet they lived on? And as a predator, Harry understood one of the most important rules about hunting: always attack your prey's weak spot. He waited until the dog was in position for what he had in mind, and then he stepped out from behind Elton and hurled one of the bowling balls at the dog, aiming for the spot where its ear was missing. There was already damage there, and Harry hoped another good blow would finish off the damn thing. The ball struck the dog's head with a loud clang, sending forth a fresh shower of sparks. The dog took a step back and shook its head, sending sparks flying everywhere, but it didn't go down.

"Fuck you, Poppy!" Elton shouted. "Fuck you!"

Poppy's voice came over the bowling alley's sound system.

"You're breaking my heart. Jet, kill Elton! Kill them both!"

Harry understood what was happening. He'd taken note of the security cameras in here, as well as those in the diner. Poppy had her eyes on every part of her dominion, and when she realized that Harry had been using Elton's invulnerability to the robot dog against it, she'd revoked the privilege.

The dog's flickering optical scanner turned red, and the beast—listing rightward—charged them. Harry and Elton each grabbed a ball from the return, and the two men stood their ground. When Jet was almost upon them, they brought their bowling balls down on the creature, striking it over and over. The balls hit like pile drivers, and Jet's metal skull split open like an egg. The dog went down and stayed down. The two men stepped back, and what Harry saw inside the creature's head—attached to wires and various electronic bits—made his gut twist with nausea. It was a living brain, or at least part of one. A dog's brain, no doubt.

You poor creature, Harry thought. He had a quick flash of pointing a pistol at Mr Pickle in Arthur's office, but he banished it from his mind. This wasn't some mindfuck of a test to prove his worth to a stodgy old spymaster, and he wouldn't be killing this dog any more than he had killed Mr Pickle. This was a mercy.

Without hesitation, Harry raised the ball and brought it down on the robo-dog's head. Once, twice, a third time. More sparks flew, and the dog's limbs flailed as its system crashed, and then it slumped to the ground and lay still.

Harry lowered the blood-smeared ball and gulped air.

Elton looked at the red, wet ruin that had been the robo-dog's brain, and whispered, "Holy shit."

The men put their gore-slick balls back in the return, and then Harry turned to Elton.

"Thank you."

"Thank *you*," Elton said. "Now, go save the world."

"If I save the world, can I have a ticket to your next concert?" Harry asked.

"Darling, if you save the world, you can have a

backstage pass." He blew Harry an air kiss.

There was a large hole in the bowling alley wall, and Elton ran for it, plunging through and out into the jungle. Harry ran toward the bowling alley's entrance, but before he could reach it, he heard Poppy's voice once more.

"Bennie! He killed Jet! Get him!"

Harry groaned. There were *two* of the damn things?

He burst out onto the street in time to see Bennie come hurtling out of the diner toward him. He also saw Eggsy fighting Charlie not far from the diner, and it looked like Eggsy was getting the worst of it. He wanted to go to Eggsy's aid, but he knew there was no way he could reach Eggsy before Bennie got him, so he turned around and headed for the closest building, the one next to the bowling alley, an establishment called Poppy's Salon.

Seems safe enough, Harry thought, and dashed inside, the robo-dog close behind.

Chapter Twelve

For once, Eggsy's mind was blank. *Fan-fucking-tastic,* he thought. *Here I am, about to go to my grave, and instead of making a witty remark or a profound statement about the true meaning of life, I'm staring at Charlie with my mouth hanging open like a git.* He was about to tell Charlie to just get on with it and kill him, when his watch beeped. Eggsy looked at the device's face and saw a readout displaying the words CIRCUITS INTEGRATED. Now he knew *exactly* what to say. He looked up at Charlie and smiled.

"Here's my last words, arsehole: Merlin says hi."

Charlie sneered and… did nothing. He didn't bring the ball down on Eggsy's head. He continued holding it up, the ball spinning madly. Charlie's brow furrowed in concentration and he gritted his teeth, as if he were putting forth extreme effort, straining every muscle, but without any result.

Eggsy stood and brushed dirt off the front of his suit.

"Like my new watch? Merlin made it especially for me. Or rather, for *you.*"

Charlie's eyes widened, first in surprise, then in horror

as he understood what was happening. Eggsy tapped a touchpad on the watch face, and Charlie's arm brought the spinning bowling ball down and slammed it into his crotch. His face contorted in agony and he doubled over, tears of pain streaming from his eyes.

Eggsy tapped his watch, and Charlie dropped the bowling ball. His metallic fingers curled into a fist and smashed into his very *non*-metallic nose. Blood spurted, Charlie cried out in pain, and Eggsy tapped the touchpad once more. Charlie's arm pulled the fist back, paused, and then pistoned forward again, this time striking him in the mouth. There was more blood, accompanied by the sound of teeth breaking. Eggsy made the fist hit Charlie again. And again.

"Why're you hitting yourself, Charlie?" Eggsy said. "Why would you do that? Right in the *eye*? That's mental!"

Eggsy forced Charlie to hit himself a few more times, and then he made the arm freeze in place.

"Lucky for you, one of us understands what it means to be a gentleman," Eggsy said. "Let's make this fair."

He tapped the watch's touchpad once more, and Charlie's robotic hand shot up toward a tree. It grabbed hold of a branch, and Eggsy caused the cable to retract, lifting Charlie off the ground. He flew toward his hand, and when he reconnected with it, he hung from the branch, unable to free himself. Eggsy let him hang there for a moment, then he tapped his watch a final time. The arm detached from Charlie's shoulder, and he fell a dozen feet to the ground.

Charlie rose to his feet. "How's that fair?" he said through bloody, swollen lips.

"Like this." Eggsy put his right hand behind his back, stepped forward, and with his left hand cracked Charlie across the jaw.

Harry ran into the salon. It had the usual trappings for its type of establishment, except for a large metallic structure next to one of the salon chairs that looked like a fountain of running liquid gold, with a thin hose attached to it terminating in what appeared to be a needle. A *tattoo* needle, he realized. Obviously, this contraption was the origin of the gold body implants found on Poppy's people.

Too bad Merlin couldn't have seen these machines, Harry thought. *He'd have found them fascinating.*

Bennie crashed into the salon and headed straight for Harry, its optical scanner blazing red. Harry ran to the counter behind the salon chairs and began grabbing whatever products he could get hold of—hair gel, mousse, nail polish, acrylic nail powder (assorted colors), shampoo, conditioner, facial cleanser—and yanked off their lids before hurling the contents at the dog. Or more specifically, at its optical scanner. Within seconds, a mass of thick goo covered the scanner, and Bennie stopped chasing Harry. It turned its head right and left, as if trying to locate him, and then it sat down and tried to scrape the viscous mess off its scanner with a rear leg, looking for all the world like a real dog scratching an itch. But all it succeeded in doing was smearing the goo around.

"Can't get me if you can't see me!" Harry said.

While the dog was occupied, Harry ran to one of the hairdryer stations and tore a dryer hood from the wall. He returned to Bennie and smashed the hood down on its head. He and Elton had stopped Jet by destroying its brain, and he intended to do the same to this creature. Unfortunately, a dryer hood wasn't as effective a tool for the job as a pair of bowling balls. Harry bludgeoned Bennie again and again, but aside from a few scuff marks on the metal, he didn't seem to be doing any real damage to the creature. Frustrated, he hit Bennie with all the strength he could muster, and the creature slid backwards several feet.

Unfortunately, the last blow had knocked most of the gooey mess off the dog's optical scanner.

"No!" Harry said. "No! No!"

The instant Bennie's scanner was clear, the dog bounded toward Harry, jaws stretched wide, razor-sharp teeth glinting in the salon's bright lights. Harry lifted a table to use as a shield, but the beast quickly tore it apart. A scented candle burned on the counter—Poppy likely used it to create a relaxing ambiance, he guessed—and he took hold of it, grabbed a nearby aerosol can, and turned toward Bennie. He used the candle flame and the aerosol to create a makeshift blowtorch, but the flame had no effect on the creature. Harry threw the candle and aerosol can at the dog, and backed away, unable to think of anything more he could do to stop the beast... until he bumped into the chair next to the gold fountain. He fell into the chair, and as Bennie rushed toward him, he reached up, grabbed hold of the fountain, and yanked it forward.

Molten gold poured all over the robo-dog, slowing—but not halting—its advance. It continued struggling to get to Harry, its entire body juddering with the effort. There was a hairdressing sink close by, and Harry ran to it, turned on the water, grabbed the shower hose, and aimed it at Bennie. The cold water began cooling the gold immediately, causing it to harden around the dog. Its movements slowed even further, and then it ground to a halt, motionless.

Who says you can't teach a gold dog new tricks? he thought.

Harry tossed the shower hose back into the sink and leaned against it, taking advantage of the moment to finally catch his breath.

Eggsy continued holding his right arm behind his back while he fought Charlie. Charlie got in a couple of good licks, but he'd had nowhere near the amount of experience in hand-to-hand combat that Eggsy had by this point. Charlie attempted to strike Eggsy with a martial arts kick, but Eggsy easily avoided the blow. He stomped down hard on Charlie's outstretched leg and felt as much as heard the bone snap. Charlie howled in pain and fell. Almost immediately, he pushed himself up and hopped on his good leg. Despite himself, Eggsy was rather impressed by the bastard's tenacity. Charlie swung a wild punch at Eggsy, and Eggsy stepped forward, hooked his arm around Charlie's, and flipped him onto the ground. He quickly crouched down and put Charlie in a one-armed chokehold, still keeping his other arm around his back.

Charlie laughed weakly. "Stupid fucking chav. The briefcase is useless to you without the access code."

"So give me the code," Eggsy said.

Charlie fixed Eggsy with a hateful glare and spit blood at him.

"Only Poppy knows it."

"Then you're no use to me, are you?" Eggsy paused for a moment, his features hardening. "For the record, Charlie, I'm more of a gentleman than you'll ever be. But right now, it's time to drop the 'gentle' bit. This is for Roxy, and Merlin, and Brandon… and JB. Night, bruv."

He gave Charlie's head a fast, hard twist, breaking the man's neck with a sound loud as a gunshot. Eggsy released Charlie's head, stood, and walked over to retrieve the briefcase, his injured ribs protesting as he bent over. He gazed upon Charlie's lifeless body for a moment. He expected to feel something—joy, relief, triumph, *something*—but he felt nothing. Charlie's death wouldn't bring his friends back. The man had just been another problem to be dealt with, and he had. The world was better off without him in it.

Eggsy and Harry reunited outside Poppy's diner, Eggsy clutching the red briefcase to his chest. Both agents looked the worse for wear, but they were still standing, and that's what mattered.

"Charlie's dead." Eggsy patted the briefcase. "And this sets everything in motion to release the antidote. We get the access code, we can save the world."

"Not trying to top you or anything," Harry said, "but I just met Elton John."

Eggsy picked up a discarded pistol off the ground, while Harry chose a submachine gun. The two men exchanged nods and walked into the diner.

Poppy had set up an office space for herself in the diner, and she sat calmly behind her desk, watching as Eggsy and Harry approached. Eggsy noted the huge metal machine behind the diner's counter, but he had no idea what it was for.

"You might as well come in, boys," Poppy said. "Just the three of us left now."

They trained their weapons on her.

"Give us the code," Harry demanded.

"Or what?" Poppy said. "Surely you're not the kind of gentlemen who'd hurt a lady?"

Harry arched an eyebrow. "Call me old-fashioned, but I don't see genocide as terribly ladylike."

Still, both he and Eggsy placed their guns on the counter. Eggsy set the briefcase on the desk in front of Poppy and opened it, revealing a keyboard.

"Don't bother trying to crack it," Poppy said. "It'd take

over seventy-two days. I had my security experts try it."

"Enough small talk," Eggsy said. "Just give us the code."

Poppy smiled, got up from her desk, and sauntered over behind the counter.

"I don't think so," she said in a sing-song voice. "I've been trained in interrogation resistance. For example, you could try this…"

She placed the palm of her right hand on the grill. There was a loud sizzle and wisps of rising steam, but her face showed no sign of pain. She smiled serenely.

Eggsy and Harry exchanged looks. Poppy was even crazier than they'd thought.

"There's really no point," she smiled. She paused to sniff the air. "Is it just me or does that smell kinda delicious?"

She tried to pull her hand from the grill, but it was stuck. She grabbed a spatula, slid it under her hand, jiggled it around, and finally freed her half-cooked hand.

"Or you could try this."

She flipped on the industrial-sized mincer, and as the blades began to whirl, she moved her burnt hand toward it.

"Don't bother," Eggsy said. "We read your file."

"We came prepared for even this scenario," Harry said.

For a moment, it looked like Poppy was going to shove her hand inside the mincer anyway. But then, seeming somewhat disappointed, she switched off the machine and came out from behind the counter.

"Oh really? What do you suggest we do?"

Harry rushed forward and pressed Poppy down on

the counter. Eggsy reached into his inner jacket pocket and removed the velvet box Merlin had given him. He opened it to reveal a syringe filled with amber liquid. He took the syringe from the box, plunged the needle into Poppy's neck, and injected the contents. He then tossed the empty syringe onto the counter.

"Heroin," Eggsy said grimly. "Where I come from, this shit you've been peddling has ruined a lot of lives. But yours is even more deadly."

"Our colleague Merlin, may he rest in peace, managed to synthesize your horrible little formula and speed up its effects."

Patches of blue rash immediately erupted all over Poppy's body.

Harry released his hold on Poppy and allowed her to stand.

"I'd say you have a little under eight minutes before paralysis sets in and you stop breathing. But of course you know all about that."

"So here's the deal: *you* release the antidote worldwide, *we* make sure you get a dose too."

Poppy smiled sleepily as the heroin began taking effect, and she slurred her words as she spoke.

"Ooh, clever... *veeery* clever. I have to give you the code to live. So smart! *I love it.* Darling, you should work for *me*."

"Just give us the code," Eggsy said.

Poppy's eyes were half closed, as if she were on the verge of drifting off to sleep.

"Ah, why not?" she said. "Decree's getting signed soon

317

anyhoo… It's 'Viva Las Vegan'. Get it? Viva Las Veg…"
She smiled at Eggsy, and rose unsteadily from her chair.
"Mmm, come snuggle with me. C'mon."

She reached out to Eggsy with both arms, as if she
wanted to embrace him, but then her eyes rolled back
in her head, and she collapsed to the floor. Her body
twitched a couple times, and then fell still.

The sensors in their eyeglasses read Poppy's vital signs,
or rather, the lack thereof. "She's OD'd!" Harry said.
"You gave her too much!"

Eggsy gazed down at Poppy, surprised. He wasn't
particularly sorry she was dead—after all, she'd been
responsible for the deaths of who knew how many
people—but he hadn't intended to kill her.

"Did I?" he said. "I really don't have as much experience
with all this drug stuff as everyone thinks. That better be
the right code." He stepped over to the briefcase to enter
the code, doing a passable Elvis Presley imitation as he
sang, "Viva Las—"

He broke off as a loop of rope dropped over Harry's
head and tightened around his neck. Harry immediately
reached up to try and free himself, but the rope was too
tight. He could still breathe, but only just.

"Viva… Lasso?" Jack said.

Eggsy turned to see Jack Daniels aka Agent Whiskey
standing there, gripping the lasso's handle, thumb resting
lightly on its button. In his other hand, he held a six-
shooter, and he had it aimed at Eggsy.

"Don't move, kid," Jack said. "You go near that case, I

turn this thing electric. You saw me cut that cable car line. Give up your guns, fellas. Slide 'em on over."

Eggsy picked up their weapons by the barrels, knelt, and slid them across the floor toward Jack.

He straightened. "Whiskey, listen to me. We're all on the same side. You had a head injury. This is exactly what happened to Harry. You're having some kind of... brain glitch."

Jack gave Eggsy a smug smile. "Nope. My brain's all good, kid. And I reckon the same was true for him." He nodded at Harry. "Fine instincts, I'll give him that. So stay still or I'll dice him up small enough that you can take him home in a bucket and still have room for what's left of your buddy Merlin."

"So you were—" An idea struck Eggsy. "Oh, that's just fucking great. You work for the president?"

Jack moved toward the desk, pushing Harry ahead of him, keeping close watch on Eggsy as he went.

Jack sneered. "*That* asshole? No. It's a matter of personal principle, Agent. I believe Champ backed the wrong horse. Let these people live, and the drug problem stays alive with 'em. Know what a legal drug trade would do to the Statesman share price?"

"*Those* are your principles?" Eggsy said, anger building. "Making money? Our agencies were founded to uphold peace. Protect the innocent."

"Wanna know who was innocent? My high-school sweetheart, Lela. Love of my life. Pregnant with my little boy. He'd be about your age now... if his momma hadn't got caught in the crossfire when two meth-heads decided to rob a convenience store."

Eggsy remembered what Jack had told him on the Statesman jet: how Champ had helped him through a rough time some years ago. Lela's death was what Jack had been talking about.

Jack continued. "You break the law, you pay the price. Good riddance to all of them. That's why I gotta destroy the case. Now slide it over."

Eggsy did as Jack asked.

"You know, Harry, I think he has a bright idea."

Eggsy made eye contact with Harry, and an unspoken message passed between them. Harry reached up and took hold of the rope around his neck.

Eggsy raised his watch, tapped a control, and a burst of light shot toward Jack, momentarily blinding him.

Harry pulled the loop over his head, took hold of the rope, and flung the loop toward Jack's gun hand. The loop tightened around the American agent's wrist, and Harry yanked. Jack lost his grip on his six-shooter, and it flew out of his hand. It struck the diner's tiled floor and skittered away.

Jack recovered quickly. He shook the lasso off his wrist and spun the rope over his head, allowing the loop to widen. Electric energy coruscated along the length of the rope as Jack activated its most deadly function, and then he flung the lasso toward Eggsy. Eggsy jumped through the loop without coming in contact with it, and Jack swept it to the side, slicing through the metal supports of the stools at the counter as if they were no more substantial than air.

He then swung the lasso back toward Eggsy and Harry, who had to duck quickly to avoid being decapitated in similar fashion.

Harry rushed forward and delivered a sharp punch to Jack's gut. The breath whooshed out of the American's lungs, and he lost his grip on the lasso handle. The instant it left his hand, the electric energy winked out, and the rope retracted back into the handle. Harry tried to reach for it, but Jack swung a punch at him and connected with his jaw, staggering him. Instead of following up, Jack dove to the side, not toward the lasso handle—Eggsy stood too close to it—but toward his gun. He hit the floor, grabbed hold of the gun, rolled to his feet, and started shooting.

Eggsy raised his arm in front of his head so his bulletproof suit would protect him, and ran toward Jack. He kicked the gun out of Jack's hand and tried to hit him, but Jack managed to block the blow with his left arm and strike at Eggsy with his right. Eggsy blocked that blow, and then the two agents began fighting in earnest, throwing punches and kicks, blocking as many as they landed. Jack eventually grew tired of this game, and he drew a knife and swiped it toward Eggsy's midsection. Eggsy jumped backward just in time to avoid disembowelment, the blade only slicing through his tie.

Harry stepped in and cracked Jack on the jaw, and when Jack swung the knife toward him, Eggsy moved forward and hit him from the other side. Jack turned and hurled the knife at Eggsy, but Eggsy dodged to the side and the blade whistled past him. It flew over the counter and struck the mincer, activating it.

The entire time Jack had been fighting Eggsy, he had managed to move closer to his lasso handle, and now he snatched it off the floor and activated its whip function. No electricity this time, though. Eggsy figured a device that small couldn't hold much of a charge and the battery was dead. But Jack didn't need a fancy light-saber lasso to be dangerous. He flicked the whip toward the gun Eggsy had discarded, and when the tip wrapped around it, he yanked the weapon toward him and caught it with his free hand. He then spun toward Eggsy and lashed out with the whip again. This time it coiled around Eggsy's neck, choking him. Eggsy's eyes went wide, and he clawed at his throat, trying to loosen the whip, but he couldn't get his fingers beneath it. The coils were too damn tight.

Harry started toward them but Jack aimed the gun in his direction and started firing. Harry ran toward the counter and dove over it to seek cover. He saw a meat cleaver next to the stove, and he snatched it up, spun around, and hurled it toward Jack. Jack leaned to the side, and the cleaver passed through the space where his head had been a split second before. Jack's gaze fastened on the mincer, and a dark look came into his eyes. He threw the whip handle toward the mincer, and it flew through the air and fell inside. The machine began its work, grinding and chewing, and as bits of leather began to shoot out from the front, the rest of the whip—with Eggsy attached—was pulled toward the terrible device. Eggsy grabbed hold of the whip and yanked, but it did no good. He couldn't break free from the mincer and continued to be drawn inexorably toward it.

Jack watched Eggsy's progress with a cruel smile. Harry took advantage of the man's distraction to run forward and make a grab for his gun. Jack resisted, and the two agents struggled over the weapon as the mincer drew Eggsy ever closer to its whirling blades. Soon Eggsy was behind the counter, the mincer only several feet away, and still it drew him onward toward what promised to be an agonizing, messy, and hardly dignified death.

Finally, even though Jack still had hold of the gun, Harry managed to aim it in the direction he wanted, and he placed his hand over Jack's and pressed the man's finger against the trigger. The gun fired and the bullet sliced through the whip, freeing Eggsy less than a foot away from the mincer. Without Eggsy's weight holding it back, the rest of the whip was sucked into the machine and instantly reduced to tiny shreds. Eggsy pried the coils from his neck and threw them to the floor.

"Eggsy!" Harry shouted.

Eggsy turned to see Harry grab hold of Jack and throw him into the air toward the mincer. Eggsy jumped up, and just as Jack passed overtop the mincer, he kicked the fucker into the machine.

Jack screamed as the mincer's rotating blades caught hold of his flesh and pulled him inward. The machine's inner workings whined in protest as they struggled to process the Statesman who was, after all, a muscular man, but the mincer was top of the line and in the end it got the job done. Jack's cries were silenced, and a few moments later, threads of raw meat began piling onto the metal tray.

"Put alpha gel on *that*, dickhead," Eggsy said, and then turned to Harry. "I'm so ashamed I didn't believe you," he said. "I even saved his *life*…"

"A Kingsman takes a life only when he believes it is justified," Harry said, smiling. "And you, Eggsy, are a true Kingsman."

He had retrieved the briefcase, and he now opened it, and held it out to Eggsy.

"There are several hundred million more still to be saved," he said. "I think that honor should be yours."

Eggsy nodded. He placed his fingers on the keyboard and typed VIVA LAS VEGAN. An instant later, a confirmation message appeared on the screen. INITIATING ANTIDOTE RELEASE.

Thousands of antidote-carrying drones were immediately deployed. They swarmed throughout cities and towns across America, and within less than an hour, police, paramedics, and military personnel began administering the antidote to frozen people on the street. And when those people recovered, they joined the effort to administer the antidote to others. Joyous families hugged one another in hospital ERs the world over.

In Ginger's lab, she opened the lid of a cryogenic unit and clouds of icy air billowed out. Tequila lay inside, wearing only a medical gown, his skin covered with blue rash. Ginger quickly administered the antidote, and within seconds the rash began to subside. Tequila's eyes flickered open and his gaze focused on her.

"What happened? Did I miss something?" he asked.

She smiled. "Yeah. From now on, stick to booze."

In a London flat, Jamal grinned as the blue patches on Liam's skin faded and his friend began to move again.

And in an apartment in Sweden, Tilde's parents rejoiced as their daughter unfroze and hugged the relieved pug puppy next to her.

Tilde's phone rang, and her father picked it up. The words EGGSY CALLING appeared on the screen. Tilde, moving with surprising strength and speed for someone who had only moments ago been courting death, snatched the phone out of her father's hands and answered it.

And in the White House Press Briefing Room, a fully recovered—and freed—Fox Nouvelle stood at a podium addressing reporters.

"The president actively sanctioned the deaths of hundreds of millions of civilians and lied to the public," she said. "I am proud to be responsible for his impeachment, and I promise to work toward a smooth transition of power."

Kingsman Distillery, Kentucky

———————— 👁 ————————

Inside the Statesman boardroom, Eggsy, Harry, Tequila, and Champ sat at one end of the long wooden table.

Ginger—as tech support—stood close by. Champ poured them all glasses of Scotch from a bottle labeled KINGSMAN SINGLE MALT and handed one to each of them.

Harry raised his glass. "To Merlin."

The others raised theirs, and they all drank—except Ginger. She merely held her glass with both hands and stared into its contents.

Champ gave her a sympathetic look before turning to Eggsy and Harry.

"In honor of this historic day, we've acquired a single malt brewery in Scotland. It shows the world that Kingsman has now joined the liquor business. Before, we were cousins. Now, we're brothers, working side by side. All our resources are yours. You can rebuild."

"Yup," Tequila said, grinning. "You're gonna be shittin' in high cotton."

Champ looked at Tequila—who was wearing a simple shirt—and frowned.

"Agent Tequila, this is a formal occasion. Why aren't you wearing a jacket?"

"Sorry, sir," Tequila said sheepishly.

Champ shook his head in good-natured disapproval before turning to the British agents and raising his glass.

"To our union," he said.

Eggsy and Harry raised their glasses in return, and everyone drank. The AR display on Eggsy's eyeglasses showed holographic figures sitting in the "empty" seats around the table. Statesman agents, attending the ceremony in virtual form. They raised glasses and drank as well.

Tequila frowned as he considered the taste, but then he too nodded in approval.

"Final order of business." Champ looked at Eggsy and Harry. "We'd be honored if one of you would be our new Agent Whiskey."

"Awesome!" Tequila said. "That would totally fix the whole messy 'two Galahads' thing."

Eggsy was stunned by the offer. His rebellious take-no-shit attitude *did* fit in well with the American agents, and participating in a kind of foreign exchange program *would* be a good way to cement the agencies' new relationship. And Harry was the best there'd ever been. He'd be a fantastic addition to Statesman. Eggsy exchanged glances with Harry, and he could tell by the look in his mentor's eyes that they were thinking the same thing. The offer was flattering, but they were Kingsmen to the core. They would have to politely decline Champ's offer. But before either of them could say anything, Ginger spoke up.

"Champ, I'd like to throw my hat into the ring."

Champ nodded his approval. "Let's put it to a vote. I say yes."

"Me too," Tequila said with a grin, and the other Statesman agents all agreed. It was unanimous.

Champ smiled at Ginger. "Looks like you're in. Have a seat."

Eggsy pulled an empty chair away from the table and gestured for Ginger to sit. Smiling, she did so, and everyone applauded.

Chapter Thirteen

———— ✦ ————

Stockholm, Sweden

Eggsy and Harry stood before a large ornate mirror in a small dressing room. Eggsy wore an elaborate military uniform, complete with a scabbarded sword, and Harry wore a morning suit. On a table next to them was a bottle of Kingsman single malt and two glasses. Harry poured them each a shot, and they downed it.

Eggsy handed his empty glass to Harry and gazed down at his outfit.

"Are you sure I don't look like a dick?" he said.

Harry put both glasses on the table and turned back to Eggsy. "Look in the mirror, Eggsy. What do you see?"

"A dickhead. With a fucking *sword*."

"I see a man who is honorable. Brave. Loyal. Who's fulfilled his huge potential. I see a man who has done something good with his life."

Eggsy was overwhelmed with a feeling of gratitude. "I owe you everything, Harry."

He held out his hand for Harry to shake. Harry did so, and then pulled Eggsy in for a hug.

When they broke apart, Harry said, "Ready?"

Eggsy grinned. "Not a doubt in my mind." Together they stepped out of the dressing room and into the Royal Chapel.

It was like something out of a fairy tale: everything white and gold, with a high arched ceiling, columns lining the walls alongside statues of saints, and chandeliers hanging above wooden box pews. There was a sense of deep history in the chapel, a profound stillness, as if in this place even Time got down on one knee to show respect for the royal family.

Eggsy and Harry walked down the aisle toward the altar, where a priest waited. On one side of the chapel sat Tilde's family and the king and queen's honored guests, all of them dressed in expensive finery, composed and dignified. On the other side of the chapel—Eggsy's side—sat his mum, along with Champ, Tequila, Ginger, and Eggsy's friends and relatives, all of whom wore more budget-conscious wedding attire. Jamal and Liam were there. Also in attendance—all grown now—was JB2. And sitting next to him was another guest of the canine persuasion: a grown Yorkie who Harry had named Hamish, in honor of their departed comrade.

Eggsy thought of the friends that were gone. Brandon, Roxy, Merlin… He missed them terribly, and he wished they could be here to share this day with him.

He noticed Champ look disapprovingly at Tequila, who once again was dressed casually. Champ leaned close to the agent and whispered, but he spoke loudly enough for Eggsy to catch his words.

"Agent, what did I teach you about dressing right for the occasion?"

Tequila looked down at his clothes and then back at Champ. He shrugged.

Champ sighed. "Maybe the Kingsman boys can succeed where I failed."

Eggsy smiled and continued onward. When he and Harry reached the altar, they turned and waited.

The wedding march began to play, and Eggsy looked toward the organist, a man wearing a black suit with a purple tie that matched the color of his rectangular glasses. Elton grinned and gave Eggsy a wink.

And then she entered the chapel and took Eggsy's breath away.

Tilde wore a tiara encrusted with diamonds and emeralds, a gown in not one but *three* shades of white trimmed with intricate couture lace, and a long hand-cut and hand-stitched train, the end of which was held by a royal footman. The king wore a military uniform similar to Eggsy's, only with a lot more medals, and Eggsy's little sister Daisy—looking adorable in her bridesmaid's dress—followed proudly behind.

To Eggsy, Tilde was already the most beautiful woman in the world, but in that moment, she was the very *definition* of beauty, that by which all other lovely things would be judged and found forever wanting.

As Tilde and her father reached the altar, Eggsy bowed courteously to the king, who smiled and nodded. He then looked at his daughter, happy tears brimming in his eyes, before turning and joining the queen who stood several feet away. The queen wore an embroidered chartreuse gown with a light blue sash—and her crown, of course. She *was* the queen, after all.

Eggsy and Tilde gazed into each other's eyes, bursting with happiness, madly in love.

The priest stepped forward and the ceremony began.

Eggsy didn't hear most of what the priest said. All his attention was focused on the woman he loved. But eventually—much faster than Eggsy had expected—the priest got around to the important part.

"Do you, Gary 'Eggsy' Unwin, take Tilde Ingrid Victoria to be your lawful wedded wife?" he asked.

"I do," Eggsy said.

Harry handed him the ring and Eggsy slipped it onto Tilde's finger.

The priest continued. "And do you, Tilde Ingrid Victoria, take Gary 'Eggsy' Unwin to be your lawful wedded husband?"

"I do."

With a grin a mile wide, Daisy stepped forward to give Tilde the other ring, and she slid it over Eggsy's finger.

The priest pronounced them man and wife, and they kissed.

Eggsy's side of the chapel clapped, whooped, and cheered, while Tilde's side applauded quietly with polite decorum.

Champ looked over at them.

"Hey! Lighten up, guys!" he shouted. "This ain't a

goddamn funeral! Champagne's on me! Hit it, Elton!"

Elton broke into a rousing rendition of his song "Kiss the Bride," and before long even Tilde's side of the chapel were grinning and clapping along.

Savile Row, London

The first hint of dawn colored the sky as the interior lights of Kingsman Tailors came on. A moment later, someone flipped the CLOSED sign inside the front door to OPEN. Agent Tequila opened the door and poked his head out. He quickly looked up and down the street, as if checking to see if anyone was watching, before stepping outside. He wore a Kingsman suit—a bespoke suit that not only fit him like a glove but was more comfortable than anything he'd ever worn. He still wore his cowboy boots, though. He didn't know if he would ever get used to wearing Oxfords. Damn things squeezed his feet.

In his hand he held his old cowboy hat. He started to put it on, but then he figured, what the hell? The boots were enough. He stepped inside, placed the hat atop the head of one of the window mannequins, and stepped back outside. Time to see what trouble he could get into in this country.

Grinning, he slipped on a pair of Kingsman glasses and set off down the street.

Acknowledgements

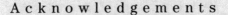

I'd like to thank my editor Ella Chappell for midwifing this book from start to finish and my agent Cherry Weiner, for both her guidance and friendship. Special thanks to Jane Goldman and Matthew Vaughn for writing such a great script in the first place, and to Matt Reilly and Royce Reeves-Darby, who made sure I had top-secret clearance at all times. Special thanks also to Steve Tzirlin and Nicole Spiegel for arranging visual reconnaissance. True Kingsmen/Kingswomen all!